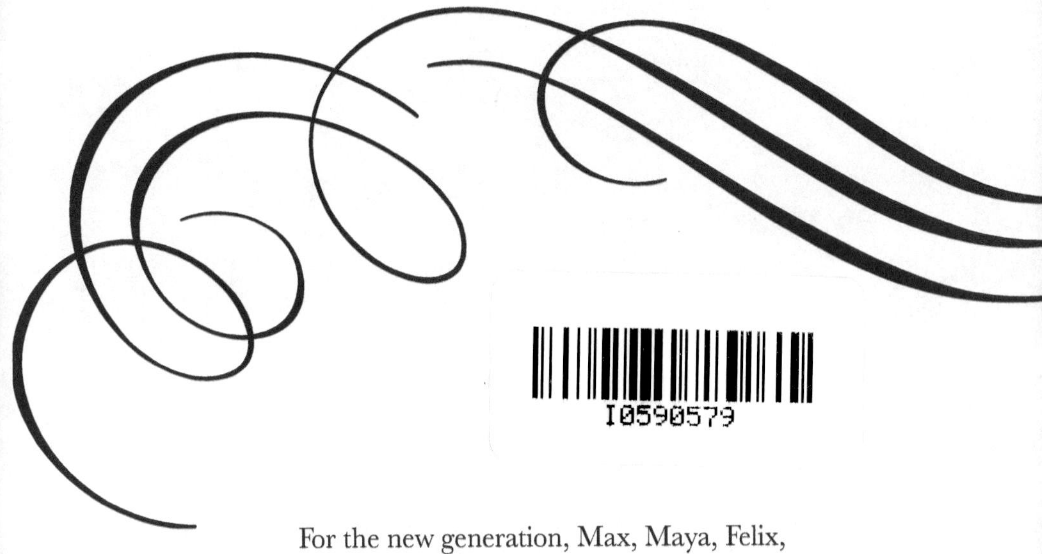

For the new generation, Max, Maya, Felix,
Ruby, Zoe, and Isabel. May each of you be
strong and may you strive to fix what's wrong.

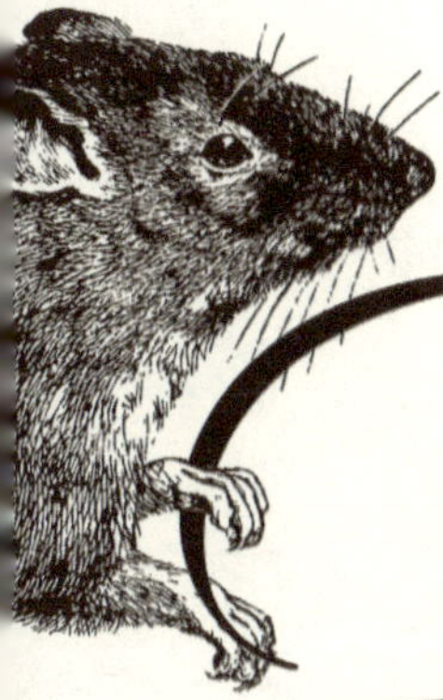

THE ACTIVISTS

RAINER LINK

This book is a work of fiction. Names, characters, businesses, organizations, places, events, and incidents are either a product of the author's imagination or are used fictitiously. Any resemblance to actual persons, living or dead, events, or locales is entirely coincidental.

Published by River Grove Books
Austin, TX
www.rivergrovebooks.com

Distributed by River Grove Books

Design and composition by Greenleaf Book Group
Cover design by Greenleaf Book Group
Cover Images: ©iStockphoto/nicoolay & ©iStockphoto/inhauscreative

Publisher's Cataloging-in-Publication data is available.

Print ISBN: 978-1-63299-301-4

eBook ISBN: 978-1-63299-302-1

First Edition

CONTENTS

PART 1

His Reign in Ruins

1

THE COSTUME BALL

Your narrator settles into his comfortable chair with the essentials nearby: the computer, cup of coffee, pencil and paper, and a morning pill. His dog lies beside his chair. Where to begin? Start with the nation's stunning election? Or give focus to our main characters, start when they first become aware of the clamor? Or should the narrative reach back into history to provide a broader context?

One thing is certain: fiction is not reportage. We must alter some particulars to conceal the identity of individuals portrayed here who remain active on our political stage. And if we are already forced to make those changes, why not add some fabulous elements to this tale? Fiction offers myriad possibilities to aim for truth.

After considerable thought . . .

Get ready, dear reader, for a costume ball in our nation's capital. It will feature our most powerful government officials along with their benefactors. Benefactors? Yes, that's right. They cling together; money is the glue. Get ready for creative costumes, French champagne, music, schmoozing, and surprises. The festivities take place in a small private ballroom in the Trump International Hotel featuring beautiful multi-layered crystal chandeliers, gold-embroidered wall decor, gorgeous ceiling-to-floor curtains, and privacy.

Get ready for an intimate event. No more than two dozen elite benefactors are invited to mingle with the aristocracy from our government.

Who doesn't like costume balls? They are colorful; they entertain; they can titillate, and in Washington they can reveal. Successful politicians craft a particular persona that functions as their emblem, their public identity. To keep the support of their voter base, they must stay resolute; their personas can't change. In addition, every politician—well, certainly most—must present an image to the public of basic decency, namely that of a hard-working, honest, determined, yet God-fearing mortal devoted to the family.

How do they do it? The pixie does it. A tiny pixie resides on the shoulder of the esteemed public servant, murmurs into the ear, mentors and guides so that the big man maintains the pretense. The pixie is usually reliable, but occasionally something goes wrong and the critter turns into a trickster. He whispers, "Do it, take the money, no one will know," or, "Go ahead, grab her pussy, you deserve it."

My reader must know that numerous formerly God-fearing pro-family types have recently been accused of various improprieties that include cheating on taxes, sexual coercion, allying with white nationalists, covertly engaging with foreign governments, and failing to pay child support. Of course, they swear innocence, repeatedly and emphatically. When finally found guilty, they become meek and blame it on the little beast who must have given bad, very bad, advice.

At the costume ball, the pixie gets a well-deserved day off; no one needs the little fellow here. The powerful are disguised; they can let loose to satisfy desires that otherwise remain tightly wrapped. Some might have been looking forward for weeks for their chance to indulge, like kids counting the days to Christmas.

Now let's place the benefactors into the ballroom. They are the ones with the ability to pay for what they want. It's not necessarily always a direct quid pro quo. Most often it's just a subtle, "Hey, can you do me a favor?" The benefactors await their counterparts, the guests of honor, who have the ability to fulfill the needs of the benefactors for the right sum.

The benefactors amble about, mixing and mingling. They introduce themselves as the character they represent: "Hello, I'm Fred Hayek," says one. "Hi there, I'm Princess Diana," says another, and she hands out little red hearts with silver sprinkles. Fred is wearing lederhosen and a Tyrolean Alpine hat. Princess Di shows off a long white embroidered dress, and wears a delicate face mask with silver and gold sparkles.

Naturally, the benefactors are curious about the identity of others.

"Oh my. Who could that be?"

"Look over there. Isn't that . . . ?"

"If that's her, then she has gained weight."

"I think I recognize . . . "

It's a guessing game in a wonderland of fantasy.

The costumed characters include some famous individuals who have molded this country into what it is today. Andrew Carnegie, the self-made billionaire before billionaires became common, stands right beside Henry Ford, who proved to be good for workers and bad for horses and Jews.

Several actors are here. You can't miss John Wayne, followed by a couple of women, one of whom is Marilyn Monroe.

Davy Crockett, the king of the wild frontier, is chatting with Oral Roberts and Jerry Falwell. All three had high moral integrity, but only Davy is the intellectual lightweight who failed to found a university.

Someone is dressed up as a generic billionaire with an outfit made entirely of $100 bills, perhaps thousands of them. The bills are only attached at one end so they flutter as he walks.

But watch out: a couple arrives dressed as Bonnie and Clyde, who, after a quick visual survey, move towards the billionaire.

That looks like Ayn Rand—is it a woman or a man?—in a short hairdo with distinctive part. Ayn fingers a vintage cigarette holder and is actually smoking, ignoring the non-smoking regulations.

A couple of intellectuals must have found something quite funny, as both Milton Friedman and William Buckley are laughing, proof that there is humor here.

Worth mentioning also are several weird outfits, two of them with slogans. A totally unconvincing costume is supposed to resemble a machine gun. The phrase "Safety Through Guns" is emblazoned on the back of the barrel.

Another poorly executed outfit has pieces of coal somehow attached to the costume. A sign on the wearer's back reads, "Coal is good for the soul."

Finally, there is a strange outfit composed only of question marks. Does anyone know what that is supposed to mean?

The costumes are limited to a certain sense of decorum. There aren't any alcoholics, homeless vets, school shooters, suicidal opioid users, or other freaks. Also, everyone is white.

An island with real palm trees in the middle of the ballroom features epicurean delights, the finest the world has to offer, including pyramids of oysters, lobster, and shrimp. It's all there: escargot, succulent sashimi and sushi, Chinese hors d'oeuvres, foie gras, crab cakes, smoked salmon, the most delectable sauces and dips, and of course, caviar from Russia, all presented in astonishing displays.

Out of the way, off in a corner, stands a New York–style gaudy food cart peddling a variety of burgers and brats with the fixings, plus fries.

A second island is loaded with beverages. It features, without question, the finest champagne, which flows endlessly into fluted glasses with golden stems, poured by elegant servers dressed not in costume but in classic attire: white shirt, dark vest, bow tie.

Excitement is building for the guests. They toast with champagne.

"To all that is good."

"To all the right values."

"To continued success."

Fanfare from a trumpet gets everyone's attention for the following announcement: "Ladies and gentlemen, you have been invited because you represent the apotheosis of the noble art of persuasion. It is time to introduce your esteemed partners who are making

America great again. Please hold your applause until the last lumi-nary is introduced."

French doors open. One at a time they enter to gasps. Some walk solemnly, looking straight ahead; some come laughing and wave.

The announcer honors each one. "The first one out is our most noble chief executive, President Reagan.

"And charging out right behind him come two of our most famous generals. Here is General George Patton himself, followed by General Robert E. Lee.

"Whoa, get a glimpse of the beautiful Cleopatra in a most stun-ning outfit.

"Oh no, watch out, Cleopatra, here comes Giacomo . . . did I get that name right? . . . Casanova, the most famous lover of all time." He is wearing a red baseball cap with the inscription, "Keg o' Beer."

"And a young Elizabeth Taylor, looking gorgeous, is right behind him.

"And all the way from Russia comes our friend, Vladimir, followed by our own Mark Twain.

"Ladies and gentlemen, don't be alarmed. More importantly, don't follow him or his advice. Here comes the Devil himself. Watch out, he may mislead you!" The Devil walks in stiffly. He looks nasty with two menacing horns and lips clenched shut.

Another figure appears from the French doors, and the announcer seems surprised. He looks at his notes and scrambles his papers as the new arrival steps through and announces himself. "I'm Tom Sawyer." He waves. "I want to recruit help in painting my fence." Ha, ha, the costumes laugh.

The trumpets sound again for another fanfare. "Ladies and gentlemen, and now for his eminence himself, General George Washington."

A figure first looks, then steps ceremoniously through the French doors with a white wig protruding stiffly below his tricorne hat. Beneath the wig is a full tanned face with, yes, excessively rouged cheeks. He wears a Revolutionary-red uniform with long coat in back, open in front. The coat covers a vest, which covers a white shirt, which covers a protruding belly. A cravat adorns his neck. Over his breeches he wears boots that reach up to his knees.

Oddly, the outfit does not fit well. It is too short and probably a couple of sizes too small for the big man. He looks constrained. Nevertheless, he shows it off, steps stiffly to the right, awkwardly to the left, and finally stands erect, popping a button. But Washington looks stern; he is fully in command as his audience claps and takes in his aura.

Everyone knows who's dressed as General Washington. He gets the microphone. "Come over here, Devil. Stand behind me, right here. You're my second in command." He waits until the Devil, looking dour, stands right behind him. "They wanted to give me a blue uniform. Can you believe that? A uniform for Democrats? How dumb can they be? I insisted on red! It's gotta be red. Anyway, last year, most of you remember, I was Caesar. But I found out he ran into a problem. He got murdered. So this year I'm Washington. He made us great, really great. The father of our fantastic country. We've had a lot of problems since then. Everybody knows I'm fixing that. I'm working really, really hard. I am making the USA great again." Even before Washington is finished, the Devil begins to clap, encouraging the crowd to applaud.

Washington gives up the mic and moves into the crowd. He grabs elbows, puts big hands on shoulders, and slaps backs. The other government luminaries follow him into the crowd of benefactors to glad-hand and flatter.

Have a look at this scene from the perspective of a drone. The room becomes a carousel of small groups of mostly threes and fours that slowly spiral and shift as new costumes join a group while others move on to a new group. They engage in spirited conversations, initially always about the incredible outfits. Costumes hold plates with tidbits of food in one hand, glasses in the other that servers with ever-new bottles of champagne keep refilling. A band starts to play, cheers pop up here and there, and the bubbly atmosphere begins to spin.

One individual—it's Casanova—isn't drinking champagne; he's got a bottle of beer in each hand, befitting of his hat. Recall, his hat says, "Keg o' Beer." He's entertaining Elizabeth Taylor. She looks to be a bit reluctant, wears a forced smile. But he is persistent, keeps proposing toasts with his beer bottle clanging on her glass of champagne.

A small group surrounds George Washington. His listeners continuously nod their heads and stay focused on him. He looks around for the Devil, finally sees him and calls him over. The Devil, now with his lips parted, is busy entertaining Cleopatra. He finishes half a glass of champagne in a single gulp, whispers something into Cleopatra's ear while he holds out his glass for a refill, then hurries over to Washington. It just so happens that the server refilling his glass overheard his sigh. He said, "You're a dream."

Surprise, that particular server has a smile as wide as the Mississippi River in St. Paul, Minnesota. She is actually one of our main characters. Three other main characters are also here, but in disguise. The rest of the costumes are frauds, every single one of them.

Tom Sawyer heads straight to the top. He pushes himself through the group surrounding George Washington and reaches out his hand. "I'm Tom Sawyer, sir. Glad to make your acquaintance."

The general stops talking, looks at Tom dressed in rags, emits a suppressed chuckle.

Tom is not shy. "Sir, you remind me of the king."

"Oh, yeah? What king?"

"Why, the king I became friends with. He and the duke were royalty from Europe."

"Oh, where was that?"

"Why, in the novel."

"Oh, ha, ha, right, you're Tom Sawyer. So, in your novel?"

"Why no, sir. In *Adventures of Huckleberry Finn*. I'm also a character there, along with the king and the duke."

"Well, that's nice. I'm a kind of king, right, Devil?"

Before the Devil can answer, Tom continues with amplified emphasis. "You and the king, you would have been great partners."

"Partners in what?"

"Why, in building shacks, of course. Shacks were the thing in the 19th century. There were swindlers all around, but you and the king would have out-swindled them. You would have built shacks all along the Mississippi. You would have become the shack king."

Washington frowns. He asks the Devil, "Hey, how about a burger?"

"Sure, good idea, king." And they both mosey over to the food cart.

The server with the big smile also overhears other nuggets of conversation. Bonnie and Clyde, now actually investing in banks, want help in eliminating certain unnecessary banking regulations. They ask if Reagan can provide a favor. "You bet," says Reagan. "I could use a nice contribution to get reelected." "You bet" is the reply. And they shake on it.

Friedman wants tariffs on certain imported products to help his domestic business. The billionaire must have a bigger tax break, and he is willing to invest to get his return. Both Falwell and Roberts represent a company that discovered new gas reserves in Yellowstone. The company is willing to generously share its profits. And so on and so forth.

Finally Washington, fingering fries, gathers the Devil, Patton, and Robert E. Lee. He might have forgotten that this is just a costume ball, it's not real, but he asks the generals if they could divert attention from some problem that might develop for him. "If those crazies come after me, can you guys get us into a little skirmish somewhere? . . . Hell no, not a war, a skirmish for peace."

Several couples are now on the dance floor. The costume getting the most stares is Casanova, now dancing wildly with Marilyn Monroe. A beer in one hand, his other hand must be heavy as it keeps sliding down from her waist. She is overheard saying, "Oooooh, not so fast, my little Casanova."

It's a party atmosphere, and the revelry intensifies as the champagne keeps flowing. The band plays music from the '60s and '70s. A performer introduces the next number. "And now here's a tune every-body remembers. The fabulous Kingsmen had a smash hit in 1963 called 'Louie Louie.' Hope you enjoy our new lyrics."

Dat, dat da da, dat da, dat da da, da da
Dat, dat da da, dat da, dat da da, da da
Blackie, blackie, oh yeah, you gotta go, go, go, go, go, go
I said blackie, blackie, oh yeah, I said you gotta go
We brought you here but now we agree
You gotta ship back across the sea
Don't stay here, you gotta go
The shithole there is your new home
Blackie, blackie, oh yeah, you gotta go.

The dancers, energized and sweaty, cheer. Washington walks over with another burger in hand. "Hey, that's great, really great. You guys are great. What's the name of your group?"

"We're the Whitemen, sir."

Washington lifts his arms and yells out to everyone, "Hey, give these guys a hand. Very fine people."

2

FRAUDS TO RATS

While the elites applaud an adulterated version of "Louie Louie" at the former post office in our nation's capital, another transformation will happen before the sun rises. But Washington, oozing with confidence, is oblivious to any threats. He asks the costumes if anyone wants to hear that song again, and, as he expects, the Trump ballroom roars a supportive cheer. The costumes crowd the dance floor once more. Any reservations some might have had before have disappeared.

> *Dat, dat da da, dat da, dat da da, da da*
> *Dat, dat da da, dat da, dat da da, da da*
> *Blackie, blackie, oh yeah, you gotta go, go, go, go, go, go*
> *I said blackie, blackie, oh yeah, I said you gotta go*
> *We brought you here, but now we agree*
> *You gotta ship back across the sea*
> *Don't stay here, you gotta go*
> *The shithole there is your new home*
> *Blackie, blackie, oh yeah, you gotta go.*

The only one not dancing is Washington. But the big man, who will be known in this tale about frauds and fools as the Big Guy, is clapping his hands to the beat, and there is some rhythmic movement of his feet: Dat, dat da da, dat da, dat da da, da da. Dat, dat da da, dat da, dat da da, da da.

It's now getting close to midnight, and the trumpets sound once more. "And now we have a little surprise for you. For your entertainment after the witching hour, here is . . . "

"Schtop. Schtop. I will introduce myself." A figure wearing a full-length flowing cloak that is ruby-red and also wearing a long-tailed hat, equally ruby-red, is already past the French doors. She walks right up to the dance floor. "Hallo. Wie gehts?"

The music stops. The dancing stops. "Sank you for inviting me. It is really gut to be mit ze most powerful people in ze vorld."

Washington beckons the Devil. He hesitates initially, then comes resolutely, or almost so, from the dance floor. "What's going on? Who is this?"

"I . . . don't know . . . sir."

"Well, quick, find out."

It just so happens that the server with the wide smile is right there refilling the Devil's champagne glass. Before he can ask, she says, "Oh, she's kind of a wizard. You've heard of Grimm's Fairy Tales, right? She's going to entertain you, do a magic show. Maybe she'll transform you."

The Devil takes a sip, peeks over at Cleopatra standing alone on the dance floor, blows her a kiss, and turns back to Washington. "Sir . . . she is . . . a famous . . . magician . . . She . . . will . . . "

"Okay, I get it. It's magic. I love magic."

The woman in ruby-red announces, "We are going to haf an enchanting night."

Someone yells, "Who are you? Introduce yourself."

"Ach, so sorry. I forgot. I'm from a small town in Tschermany. I'm Helga Trumpf."

Dead silence on the dance floor.

"Zat's what I sought."

With exaggerated flair, she takes a pin from her hair, holds it up for all to see. She bends her head down sideways, cups her ear with her hand, and drops the pin. "I heard it. Did you hear it, too?"

After straightening her head again, she continues. "No, no, it is not Trump like ze hotel, it is Trumpf with an 'f' at ze end. Ze grandfather's name of ze hotel owner was Trumpf when he came to America. Maybe I'm a distant cousin, ya?"

Washington squints his eyes. Can he see back a couple of generations?

"Ze town I'm from is unusual. Over a hundred years ago it was fairy tale poor, wis little to eat, little to do. Ze only sing men could do was dream of unavailable sings. One young man dreamt of fine food, another of fine fellowship. Both went to America, ze land for dreamers at zat time, and zey each became grandfathers to billionaires."

The costumes had previously been spread out around the ballroom. Some had been giggling under the palm trees by the food island, dipping shrimp into their glasses of champagne; others had been in the back making deals and shaking hands. Everyone has now squeezed forward to listen to the tale about billionaires.

"One of ze men found a way in America to make good food taste better. He became ze ketchup king." Helga whirls into a spinning top. When she comes to a stop, she holds up for everyone to see—a bottle of Heinz ketchup. "And zere is a happy ending for ze town. Ze Heinz family recently donated much money to renew ze old organ of ze town church. On Sunday mornings, wis church doors and windows open wide, ze beautiful sound of ze organ makes people happy." She playfully adds, "So, please, you buy ketchup from ze generous Heinz family.

"Ze destiny of ze young man wis dreams of fine fellowship is erratic. It is said he ran a bordello, zat he became a rich bordello king with fellowship galore. But—so sad—he couldn't find a proper wife. So he returned all ze way back to his town in Tschermany, found an honest woman, and brought her back to America."

Someone yells out, "Back to the bordello?"

Washington's expression shows wrath. The thick rouge on his cheeks now flashes the threatening look of war paint.

"Hold it, Mister Washington. You can take care of zat lout later. We must go on mit ze story." Helga looks over her audience and offers a wily smile. "Ze story now becomes a bit complicated, especially after all ze champagne. I will go slow so you can follow.

"Somesing happened to ze couple. Zey changed their mind, got homesick, and returned back to Tschermany. But guess what?" She spins around. "When he left as a young man, he had avoided ze draft. Now ze town shut ze door, did not want a rat back. He was forced to return back to America, where eventually his savings from ze bordello laid ze groundwork for his family's wealth. Do you want to know his name?"

Washington is ready to pounce. The costumes take a big collective breath and hold it. No one exhales. Helga mischievously waits for the faces of the costumes to turn red before she releases the pressure. "Ze town forgot his name."

Relief. The room explodes with air bursting from lungs in a group exhale.

"It is so sad. Not a single street bears his name. Zere isn't a park named after him; not even a park bench wis his name engraved on a plaque. Ze house he was born in is not a museum. Nossing is named after him, nossing at all. Not even a bratwurst or a burger."

Helga sees Washington start to twitch unrhythmically. She yells out, "We need music, we need a beat to loosen heavy feet." She lifts both arms up high, twists around and lets her cloak whirl. "Let's not get tired. Ze night is still young. I want to see you dance again." She takes off her hat and points to it. "Later I pull somesing out of my hat. It will be a rabbit or a rat. We see later, okay?"

Washington looks relieved and yells out, "Hey, let the magic begin."

"You must be patient, Mister Washington. You will see magic. You will be surprised."

Helga directs the Whitemen to perform the same song. "Ya, ya, you dance, dance. I want you to vote mit your feet. If you like ze song, you like ze beat, dance, dance wis ze white elite. If you don't like ze song, you don't sink it's right, just walk out ze door, good night.

"Play, play ze song. I want to see who dances, who sinks it's wrong."

Dat, dat da da, dat da, dat da da, da da
Dat, dat da da, dat da, dat da da, da da
Blackie, blackie, oh yeah, you gotta go, go, go, go, go, go
I said blackie, blackie, oh yeah, I said you gotta go
We brought you here, but now we agree
You gotta ship back across the sea
Don't stay here, you gotta go
The shithole there is your new home
Blackie, blackie, oh yeah, you gotta go.

Sweaty and ecstatic boppers offer champagne cheers. The reader should know, three costumes leave: the benefactor dressed as a question mark, Mark Twain, and Tom Sawyer. Everyone else stays.

"Attention, attention, to all who are still here. It's a minute before midnight, the grim fairy tale hour is near." Helga wants help to count down the seconds to midnight. She lifts an old-fashioned alarm clock out of the pocket of her cloak and holds it up for everyone to see. After a few seconds, she starts to count. "Ten, nine, eight, seven, six, five, four, sree, two, one," and the alarm from the alarm clock sounds. The crowd joins Helga in the countdown, at first just a few, then more and more, until, just like New Year's Eve, everybody cheers at exactly midnight.

Helga seems to become younger and more agile. She zips onto the dance floor twirling her ruby-red coat and comes to a standstill in front of the expectant costumes. "Now, you'll see some magic. Let's see what I haf in my long-tailed hat." She takes off her hat, holds it up for all to see, pulls the fabric inside out. "See, nossing." Then she puts her hat into a pocket of her cloak, rotates three times, whips her hat out of her pocket, lifts it up, and pulls out a rat. "Look, a rat from my hat. That means you are not cute little rabbits. You need rat costumes.

"Now we make a line behind me and we do conga dancing." The costumes seem to know just what to do, and eagerly line up behind Helga. "We go one, two, sree, kick, one, two, sree, kick, one, two, sree, kick. Keep it simple, ja?"

She nods to the band, and as they start to play the conga line begins to sway with Helga leading the way. The single line of costumes snakes around the ballroom in a circle. The movement of feet is a bit ragged at first, but becomes synchronized in a nicely coordinated one, two, three, kick, one, two, three, kick. The band has to play the song again to keep the revelers moving, then Helga leads them through the French doors, through the halls of the Trump Hotel, and out the front door into the night.

When they can no longer hear the band, Helga pulls a flute out of her deep cloak pocket. "Now we sing again, but I have new lyrics for you." She plays the introduction on her flute, dat, dat da da, dat da, dat da da, da da. "And here are ze new words: 'Big rats, small rats, oh yeah, you gotta go, go, go, go, go, go / I said big rats, small rats, oh yeah, I said you gotta go / It's very clear for all to see / your greed is causing misery / don't stay here, you gotta go / the river there is your new home / big rats, small rats, oh yeah, you gotta go.'

"It's not hard. I sing wis you, okay? Here we go. One, two, sree, kick, one, two, sree, kick, dat, dat da da, dat da, dat da da, da da. Big rats, small rats, oh yeah, you gotta go, go, go, go, go go / I said big rats, small rats, oh yeah, I said you gotta go / It's very clear for all to see / your greed is causing misery / don't stay here, you gotta go / the river there is your new home / big rats, small rats, oh yeah, you gotta go.

"Not bad. If we keep singing, we get better." Helga keeps playing her flute—dat, dat da da, dat da, dat da da, da da—and the conga dancers keep stepping, one, two, three, kick, and singing.

It's pitch-dark and the streets are nearly empty. The few guards outside the Trump Hotel and the few uniformed individuals on street corners may not have ever seen anything like this before. They shrug their shoulders and accept it as just another eccentric episode. After all, this is Washington, DC, and we are only a stone's throw from the White House.

Helga in her ruby-red cloak and her long-tailed hat lures the group in single file rhythmically, one, two, three, kick, down Pennsylvania

Avenue playing the flute, dat, dat da da. Someone should be video-taping this, but no one is. They turn down 14th Street, past the White House Visitor Center, past the US Department of Commerce. After they cross Constitution Avenue, where they get honks from a few cars, the serpentine line passes the National Museum of African American History and Culture, stepping and singing.

Helga continues to lead south towards the river. The conga dancing rats follow the sound of the flute playing dat, dat da da. Their movement has deteriorated. The rats now step haphazardly, and rather than sing, they proclaim the refrain hoarsely: "Big rats, small rats, oh yeah, you gotta go, go, go, go, go, go. I said big rats, small rats, oh yeah, I said you gotta go." With increased frequency, someone steps out to pee only to catch up again. A couple of rats help those stragglers get back into the line that keeps moving, following the lure of the flute. Helga has now charmed them to the pedestrian path along the river.

As the first faint light of dawn reaches the water of the Potomac River, Helga stops playing and steps aside. Right behind her is the Devil. She points to him, then points to an access spot to the river and says, "Zere, right zere by zat tree."

After she begins to play her flute again, dat, dat da da, dat da, dat da da, da da, the Devil, now in the lead, with lips sealed tight, as tight as a vice, starts to march without hesitation right into the river, tempting the other rats to follow.

Washington, initially right behind Helga, somehow has fallen to last in line. He looks totally disheveled. His tricorne hat is gone. His white wig is missing, revealing tousled hair. He must have been sweating, because the rouge on his checks that looked like war paint earlier has now become runny. His cravat and vest are gone and his shirt is open, revealing porcine pink flesh. He must have ditched his revolutionary uniform, which was far too tight for him, along with his boots. They are also gone. He is standing in his socks. We'll allow him to keep his breeches on.

He sees all those ahead of him follow the allure of the Devil, one at a time, into the oblivion of the river, and he can be heard saying, "Oh my God. This is terrible. This is the end of my reign. I'm fucked."

3

A PAINTING OF RATS,
A POEM ABOUT FRAUDS

Our four main characters were all at the costume ball, but they were disguised. Let's meet them now.

It's the following day, a beautiful, calm morning. The sun is bright and the ripples on the Potomac glisten. Joggers run on the path alongside the river. Walkers, single or in small groups, a few with trekking poles, enjoy the refreshing start of a new day.

Zoom stands on a stretch of grass close to the river in front of an easel holding a paintbrush. Her painting supplies are on a folding chair next to her. She wears a baseball cap with the simple inscription "I paint" in front. She stands still and looks downriver. She must see something. Is it on the river, or in her mind?

Izzy sits and leans against a tree with a notebook and pencil. She writes, erases, and writes again. Beside her rests a pile of clothes.

Roxy is on the other side of Izzy wearing an odd-looking outfit, a loose-fitting baggy blouse and pantaloon pants. What is striking about the outfit? Attached to both the blouse and the ballooning pants are question marks made of different materials, in different colors, and in different sizes. Did we not see this costume last evening at the costume ball?

What about Fritz? He's got the spectacular view of a crow, high up in the tree. He's also looking downriver, every so often yelling something to Zoom. "I see a . . . ," or "The red hat just sank." Finally, "Can't see anything anymore. It's all gone." As he climbs down from the tree, we see he's wearing a nicely tattered Tom Sawyer costume.

Helga comes ambling down the path and arrives with a smile. Her good mood matches the sunny morning. "Hallo, guten Morgen." She shakes everyone's hand. "You are up early, and I see already so busy. It turned out to be a long night."

Helga is dressed comfortably in a light-colored, loose-fitting pant-suit appropriate for the summer weather in Washington. She wears a small tan-colored hat with a feather attached. "Ja, ja, zat's my lucky feaser. As you know, my favorite hat is a beautiful ruby-red long-tailed hat, but it is much too warm for se hot day."

Helga steps closer to the edge of the river and also gazes downriver. She comes back shaking her head and goes to Zoom. "Are you painting what I commissioned? Let's haf a look."

"I'm just about done, here it is." Zoom turns her easel around so that Helga and everyone else can see. She points to a tree at the edge of the painting and says, "This is our tree right here, and that's the Potomac, of course."

She lets everyone look at her painting. A fierce wind is bending tree branches and ripping off leaves. Several figures stand at the edge of the river. Their hats, blown off by the wind, fly through the air onto the river to join other brightly painted hats already floating there. Several pieces of costume, a mask, and perhaps a couple of wigs also float in the water. Everything drifts downstream along with some other debris. The color of the standing figures, their hats gone, is gray. They have pointed noses and whiskers. In the back a thin tail protrudes.

"Zat's very gut," says Helga. "I like it. I will take it wis me and show all my friends in Europe what we accomplished in America. Zis is ze first sale of your art, yes, Zoom? I sink you will sell more."

Zoom tries to look modest, but a smile squeezes through that grows and grows until it reaches the width of the Mississippi River near her home in St. Paul.

Helga asks Roxy about her outfit. "You didn't get it from ze costume shop. Did you make it yourself?"

"Yeah, I couldn't decide who I wanted to be so I just made an outfit with question marks. Then when one of the politicians asked me who I was, my mind spit out 'an enigma.' That word suddenly came to me. Maybe it was too loud, or maybe he was hard of hearing. He kept saying 'what?,' 'what?' So I finally said, 'a puzzle,' and he said, 'Oh, great. Mario Puzo, the Godfather guy.'"

Helga turns to Izzy and wants to hear from her, but Roxy says, "Wait, there's more." Roxy is keen to continue her story. "Remember, I'm there as a benefactor, right? So the politician, he comes right out and asks me 'What do you want?' Quick as a wink, with the Godfather thing on my mind, I say I want help giving my Mafia friends a break. I admitted, okay, they're criminals, they're bad, but they're not that bad." She stops, laughs, and interjects, "I can't believe I actually said that." She continues, "And this is what he said. He said, 'You're probably right. Maybe I can help you and your friends. What can you do for me?'" Roxy has to laugh again. "He might be hard of hearing, but he gets it immediately. So I continue with my scheme, and I say, well how about a bundle of cash plus a cruise on my yacht away from snoopers. Some of my older women friends will be there."

She raises her eyebrows and says, "Get it? We kept talking, negotiating. He threw a lot of money around." Roxy gives her sign of satisfaction. She nods her head ever so slightly, and smiles. "I had such a blast."

Izzy puts her notebook down, stands up, looks at her sister with admiration. "Amazing. I don't think I can top that." Before she talks about her experience, she shows off her costume. She wears pleated, light-colored slacks, picks up a jacket of the same color from the ground and puts it on. Then she pulls a bushy mustache out of one of the jacket pockets, positions it below her nose, and finally gets a crumpled wig from the other pocket. She stretches out her arms, bows, and says, "The resurrected Mark Twain at your service to humor you."

Fritz, by now down from his tree, interjects with, "You gotta hear this. So, I'm Tom Sawyer, right? I'm chatting with Washington telling him he could have been the shack king. Mark Twain joins us and I call him 'my God' and 'my savior.' I fold my hands to pray. Washington furrows his brow. I bow to Mark Twain, and say, 'Dear God, thank you for making me in your image.' Washington, with a dumb look on his face, asks me, 'Is that some sort of Jewish belief?' I simply told him he created me. Then I left. Not sure what happened after that."

Back to Izzy. "Dressed as Mark Twain, I show up as a politician, or as I'm calling it, a taker. A benefactor comes and tells me bluntly he can bestow some gifts on me, am I interested in taking? I smile an excessive smile, and I place my finger over my lips, do 'shh,' but I don't say anything. He repeats, 'Do you want to take?' Again, I smile, and go 'shh.' He asks me if I can hear him. I say sure, but it's good to keep our mouths shut. By talking we might make fools of ourselves. He scratches his head, but I don't give him time to think. I tell him to leave. I don't deal with idiots. He goes, 'What?' I say, 'You'll drag me down to your level and beat me with your superior experience.'" That gets a chuckle out of everyone.

Helga: "Ya, ya, it was quite a night. But now I haf to tell you somesing."

Izzy, standing next to Helga, reaches out to touch her hand and says, "Wait, can I read my poem?"

"Ya, ya, of course. You haf a poem, we want to hear it."

Izzy walks up to the tree to get her writing pad. The tree stands on a small mound. She leans against the tree, looks at everyone below her, and says, "It's called, 'It's Time to Set Traps.'" She begins to read. "We have two types . . . " She stops, lowers her pad, and looks up. Is she nervous?

Izzy explains she has been thinking about Mark Twain, and how he might address our situation today. "The country could really use his wit, right? I've been wondering how he would expose today's frauds and fools." Now with emphasis, "But he didn't write my poem. I did. And I wrote it in my style, not his. I'm imagining, though, if he could hear it, he would like it."

No, she wasn't nervous. She begins to read again.

> *We have two types of frauds*
> *Frauds who take and frauds who bestow*
>
> *Of the takers there's a fraud at the top*
> *And frauds right below*
>
> *Frauds ensure their fraudulent needs*
> *By providing fraudulent deeds*
> *To takers*
> *Fraudulence guaranteed*
>
> *Frauds who bestow are rarely seen*
> *They disappear*
> *Into penthouses or yachts*
> *Or hideouts in-between*
>
> *But when suspicion begins*
> *Frauds appear with fraudulent grins*
> *And produce fraudulent spins*
> *With prayers, the fraudulent kind*
> *They stand tall, with the flag behind*
> *They declare and assert and swear*
> *They don't have a defrauding mind*
>
> *Let's tear off their costumes*
> *Let's have them stand bare*
> *It's time to set traps*
> *To catch these fraudulent rats.*

"I want everyone to know I feel gut. Izzy, your poem is gut. Zoom, your painting is gut. I sink togeser we accomplished somesing. We started a little breeze. Ze breeze must become a wind and blow the ship America back on course."

Helga invites her accomplices to lunch.

This is a good spot to stop. We will return to their lunch later. Helga has also invited some others and their discussion should prove to be most interesting. But your narrator wants to flip back the pages to a time when our main characters were kids.

PART 2

An Alternative Education for Young Minds

4

FRITZ, ROXY, ZOOM, AND IZZY

We have already met the key players as perceptive teenagers. Let's now reintroduce them as youngsters about to get a wondrous education.

Of the main characters Fritz is the youngest, but he can see the farthest. Before he ascends to the crown of the tree along the Potomac and gazes into the distance, he learns to climb onto his roof in St. Paul, Minnesota. From the upper window of their house his two oldest sisters can look to the horizon, but from the roof Fritz can see farther; he can look beyond. Fritz squints his eyes, concentrates, and he sees things that happened long ago. Because of this special ability, and of course, because he is the only boy amongst three sisters, Fritz is definitely in an enviable position.

Fritz is lean, but he can release a burst of energy like a genie escaping a bottle. He opens the window, jumps effortlessly onto the windowsill, and in a flash twists his body through the opening, feet first. He is on the second floor of an old rickety farmhouse, high enough that if he fell, he could get seriously hurt. But Fritz doesn't fall, he climbs out the window, and with his left foot finds the loop at the end of the rope attached to the very top of the roof. He swings with the rope back and forth until he can reach the roof with his other foot, climbs onto it, steps nimbly up to the ridge, and from this high point studies the horizon.

Roxy is not far behind her twin brother. She is five minutes older than Fritz, as she likes to remind everyone. Perhaps the extra five minutes gives her just a speck more experience, makes her a teeny bit wiser. She definitely looks out for her brother, likes to guide him, "Hey, because I'm older," she says. It's as simple as that.

This girl is confident and clever. At the costume ball she wears an outfit with question marks and uses it to trap a politician. Her eyes sparkle and dart around because she always has—her term—a "fantastic" idea. "Do you want to hear about my new plan? It's fantastic!" She expects others to listen quickly to what sparked her mind this time. And because her plans are usually interesting, sometimes even bold, the others definitely want to hear Roxy's new fantastic plan. We'll hear about one of her plans shortly.

She can climb well enough. She jumps onto the sill, yells to Fritz, "Hey, wait for me," squeezes out the window, and before you know it, stands on the ridge beside Fritz.

It's quite a sight, the two of them balancing themselves on the rooftop. He has uncombed blond hair; she's wearing a blue floppy hat with a decorative flower attached to the front. They stretch their necks and look over several apple trees in the yard, over the lilac hedge, past the houses of neighbors, beyond houses farther away that become smaller and smaller in the distance until their eyes reach the horizon.

Roxy asks, "Do you see anything?"

Fritz squints, continues to look, then breaks a smile.

Roxy knows what that means. She stomps her feet and shrieks with excitement.

Their sisters, Izzy and Zoom, are in the attic room below. Izzy, the oldest, lies slouched in a corner on her mattress, immersed in a book about hunter-gatherers. Zoom sits securely on her side of the room protected above by a slanted ceiling. She looks up from her drawing tablet, holds up her creation, and wants Izzy to look. "Do you like it?"

Izzy, in a trance, continues to read. She probably has not even heard what Zoom just said.

For Izzy, books are like food. They give her energy. But not energy to move, no, energy to think. Izzy wants to understand. Maybe it's because she is the oldest; maybe she feels responsible. She consumes several books a week to gain insight. It's difficult to get her attention when she reads, she is so absorbed. But Izzy also writes poetry. The reader is already aware of the poem about frauds. There will be others.

Zoom does not ask Izzy again to look at her picture. Zoom looks at it herself intensely, holds it first close, then farther away, then to the side. She is not yet totally satisfied and won't be until her creation looks just right. She knows exactly what she wants and goes back to work, adding some lines here, some details there. Now her face radiates as she smiles her broad smile, her sign that all is well in Zoomland, a smile as wide as the Mississippi River in St. Paul. It's her look of delight; she is done. Her picture is of a woman in a broad-brimmed feathered hat and a long, elegant dress. Both feathers and dress appear to flutter to the left, the result of an imaginary wind. Including the sign of wind in her creations is her mark; it signifies Zoomart. Zoom has pizazz.

Now, imagine these characters able to transpose themselves into the past, into situations that no one alive today has ever experienced. Sure, you can read books about the past, but that's not the same as actually visiting the past. You know for a fact that none of the authors of books about historical events have actually ever been there. So, how about giving these youngsters a unique education? Your narrator will place them into adventures that take place in the past.

If you, esteemed reader, should become skeptical after the first few pages or somewhere in the middle with this approach, perhaps it's best to stop. Put the book down. Recall what has been happening, check the news, flip TV channels. You live in a time when reality—what is factual, what is acceptable, what is legitimate—has lurched closer to anarchy. Given this new tilt of our world, perhaps you can accept the childhood experiences, as well as their later encounters as young adults, with an open mind.

5

THE MARVEL OF EXISTENCE

Here we go.

They've escaped into the past. Where did they go? They find themselves on a trail amongst trees they don't recognize. It's a dense, magical forest.

Fritz is in the lead walking like he's on air. He seems to glide over the uneven surface of the trail. He makes quick decisions and easily maneuvers over and under branches, fallen trees, around boulders, through thickets. The youngster is sure-footed and determined.

Roxy is right behind Fritz. Izzy and Zoom are farther behind, trying to keep up. "Hey, wait for us."

It looks like they have traveled back thousands of years. They walk along an ancient animal trail made who knows how long ago by mammoths or giant sloths, perhaps lions, now used by all the creatures in these parts. The trail is difficult. Fritz walks with self-assurance; his head moves from side to side; he looks and listens.

Roxy asks, "What do you hear?" The two others are just now catching up.

"Shhh," Fritz whispers, placing a finger over his pursed lips. He looks at them, grins, and winks an eye. "We'll find them," he says.

What are they looking for? It's mid-morning. "There, over there. Shhh." Fritz finds what he saw beyond the horizon. "Shhh. Duck down. We don't want them to see us."

Through thick brush they can make out several figures. There is chatter and laughter and movement. The figures are in a clearing; there appear to be some sort of structures. Now a dog barks, then another dog. People grasping clubs follow the medium-sized dogs through the brush.

Izzy squats down. "This doesn't look good."

In no time our Kids—we'll refer to them as Kids with a capital K—are surrounded. What to do? Roxy is sharp. Her darting eyes reveal the speed of her mind. She assesses, understands, takes action. She steps towards them, acts with utter coolness, and while they certainly cannot understand what she says, she addresses each of them, one, two, three, four, five, six, seven. "Hi, I'm Roxy. This is my brother and my two sisters. We zipped back through time to visit you, to see what you do, see how you live."

Roxy charms them. Their faces loosen and become friendly. In fact, they look surprised and inquisitive. They giggle and nod and smile. They beckon the newcomers with hand gestures to follow them.

This is the first of numerous challenging encounters where Roxy's plucky initiative will prove successful. She looks back and encourages her siblings, "I think we'll be okay."

They move into an open space surrounded by simple huts. There is a lot of activity. Fritz points. "Look, he's using a sharp stone to cut. Maybe it's an animal hide."

Izzy notices women stringing something up and hanging it over a tree branch. "Maybe they're drying meat."

People stop what they are doing and look. Others scramble out of huts, curious. They seem friendly and nod their heads to the newcomers. One of them says something, and immediately several scurry about and become active around a fire pit. He must be their leader. He wears multiple layers of beads around his neck and around his wrists. He encourages the guests to sit down near the fire. Someone else offers them drinks in containers made from some sort of plant material. The liquid is certainly different, but sort of refreshing, light colored with chopped leaves.

Zoom asks Izzy, "What does it taste like to you?"

Izzy takes another sip, smacks her lips. "It tastes like, eh, well, it's hard to say."

The people—let's call them natives—and the Kids are trying to talk, but of course, they cannot understand each other. So Roxy says she has a fantastic plan. "Let's entertain them. Let's put on a little show." Roxy suggests Zoom should draw something for them. Izzy should read a story. And Fritz can wow them with acrobatics.

Well, what a surprise. Zoom starts to sketch, and natives gather around her one by one and stare at the picture that emerges. She draws one of the women by the fire pit. The woman is just about naked, but our young artist dresses her in a full-length flower gown with a meticulous amount of detail. The natives make all sorts of delighted sounds. But Zoom says, "Wait. I'm not done yet." She includes colorful balloons, then smiles and adds, "I want them to flutter and flop in the breeze."

The natives huddle around Izzy and watch her turn the pages of her book while she reads to them, "Once upon a time . . ." For her young age, Izzy reads aloud well. She reads slowly and emphasizes key phrases. She hesitates for seconds at times to add suspense as she also looks up from her book to make eye contact with her listeners.

"Hey, look at this." That's Fritz. He elicits gasps with his incredible display of acrobatics. It looks as if he is weightless, jumping into the air and spinning his body around to land solidly on his feet.

Then it's the natives' turn. A woman with deep wrinkles on her face—is she 40 or 140?—steps out of a hut. All eyes are on her. Women on each side help her shuffle slowly towards the group near the fire. She stops to rest once, then looks around and acknowledges individual members of her clan. She finally arrives and comes to rest on a log with a cushion made of plant material.

The natives—some sitting, others standing—are rapt. The only sound comes from the movement of individuals trying to squeeze closer. From somewhere under her garments she pulls out something that turns out to be a stack of leaves stuck together by their stems with the aid of a sticky substance, perhaps pine resin. The old woman lifts her arms and shows the bundle of leaves to everyone before she begins her narration. With the bundle in her wrinkled hands she flips the leaves like pages in a book, as her voice rings out. The leaves are of different shapes, sizes, and colors. As she bends her head, looks at, and rubs individual leaves with her forefinger and thumb, her voice resonates. She sings, she chants, she speaks in a hushed voice, then with apparent urgency she becomes bold, agitated, only to become reassuring again. The natives gasp, nod their heads, make sounds of approval. They smile, frown, clap; some rise and shuffle their feet. The Kids don't understand the words, but they get it. She is reading a powerful story written in the leaves.

The ancient woman remains seated throughout her performance, but her voice, facial expressions, gestures—her occasional hesitation and one particularly long moment of silence—make this performance a stunning experience. Izzy watches intently. She frequently reads aloud to the Kids, and will later take up acting. Perhaps this magical moment will remain with her.

The leader beckons the four visitors to him. He lifts strings of beads from his neck and places a single strand around the necks of each of the Kids. Then he signals for everyone to follow him. They go to the edge of a cliff. There he takes Zoom by the hand and shows her an area with some huge boulders, and there, right there, he points to various pictographs painted on the boulders. The pictures depict human figures and some animals—a bison, perhaps also a deer. Could that be a lion? There is a figure with a spear, another figure with a hat, or is it a halo?

Someone fetches a small bowl made of bark containing a reddish-brown liquid. The leader uses a small, sharp object—is it a bone splinter?—to prick his finger, and a few drops of blood fall into the bowl. He gives the bowl and bone splinter to a woman. She also pricks her finger, and squeezes drops of blood into the bowl. Several more women do the same and then finally the last woman gives the bowl and bone splinter to Zoom. Initially flustered, she regains composure quickly, pricks her finger, and adds several drops of her blood into the bowl. The natives, all of them, express their approval with smiles and chatter. The woman now gives Zoom a brush made from what looks like animal hair and points to the boulder. Without hesitation Zoom accepts the brush, stirs the liquid, and paints a figure in the same style of the other images. She paints a second figure, then a third. But Zoom's figures are different. Their arms stretch out and touch each other. The three figures are connected. Zoom smiles her broad smile as the natives move closer to look.

Before they get back to the clearing, they hear drumming. Bump bump bah, bump bump bah, bump bump bah, bump bump bah. A group already gathered around the fire claps and stomps their feet to the beating of drums made from hollow logs. Bump bump bah, bump bump bah, bump bump bah, bump bump bah. The leader holds up his hands and the drumming stops. He guides the Kids to what appear to be special seats near the fire and gives each of them a drum. Then the drumming starts again and the Kids join in. Bump bump bah, bump bump bah, bump bump bah, bump bump bah.

What a beautiful sight seeing natives and their guests celebrate the marvel of existence. The drumming goes on and on, way into the night . . .

6

MISERY: HUMAN WORKER ANTS BUILDING EMPIRE

Time has passed since their last adventure. It is midsummer; school ended weeks ago. Each of the Kids has their own space to be still and dream. The summer is all about dreaming, trying out new things, playing with ideas, letting your mind wander. And the mind of Fritz wanders the farthest way beyond the horizon to an early civilization with formidable accomplishments. Of course, he pulls his sisters along to his adventure into the past.

It's hot, hotter, the hottest they have ever experienced. Not deep in green, cool, moist woods this time. Above them is a white-hot sky with a blazing sun, below them is hard hot ground. A few sparse plants here and there, rocks, boulders, some sand. It's desolate in all directions as far as the eye can see.

Roxy wonders, "Did we land on the hot side of the moon?"

Zoom goes, "The moon doesn't have a hot side. But if we're on the moon, where is planet earth?"

Izzy wipes the sweat from her forehead. "My mouth is parched. We need water. We've gotta find some water."

She commands Fritz to stand on her shoulders and look. Fritz can do that without anyone holding him. Which way to go? Fritz makes out something, a spot on the horizon that glistens. He points and says, "That way."

They follow Fritz and move towards the glistening whatever-it-is. As they get closer it becomes more pronounced. Zoom notices a strip of green. "Look, over there, a river. But I don't think it's the Mississippi."

They are now close to the whatever-it-is. Impossible not to look at, it draws and holds their eyes. "It's the biggest thing I've ever seen," says Roxy.

A super-large structure, this spectacle stretches into the sky with its point. The bottom two-thirds are shiny white, the top third glistens. The base is wide, has steps, and becomes narrower towards the top, with a gold and silver crown that the blazing sun transforms into a tower of fire.

Fritz says, "Maybe there's a pot of gold on top."

They also see smaller structures, triangles that strive for the sky with flickering flames at the top.

"What is it?"

"Where are we?"

Three of them are awestruck; but watch out, Izzy has a frown.

Roxy directs their attention. "Look over there." They move closer and find an elevated spot on some boulders to get a better view of the activity. They see hundreds of milling people, maybe a thousand. Workers, all workers. The Kids hear them grunt and groan. They see the men drenched in sweat, see their muscles protrude as they don't wear anything above their waist. Some workers surround a large platform. There is a massive boulder on top of the platform, rectangular in shape, tied down with some sort of heavy rope. Dozens of workers pull, others push, still others attend to the sides. The wooden platform with its heavy load moves forward ever so slowly, barely inches at a time.

"Look at those guys bringing water." Workers carry buckets, drench the sand in front of the platform, and they pull, push, and guide the platform forward over the wet sand at the slowest pace anyone has ever witnessed.

Others, apparent overseers, wearing some sort of headgear, roar commands in front and back. They shout what seem to be instructions, but definitely not in a friendly manner.

"Look at those guys with whips." Several huge men with whips move about and snarl at workers, submissive creatures with distraught faces. The Kids hear their chorus of moans, an eerie lament of their struggle to survive their fate.

New workers arrive while others leave; it looks like spent workers are continuously being replaced by fresh ones. The system to exchange workers produces a constant flow of bodies in both directions. A line of new bodies swarms in while exhausted bodies struggle out and the platform continues to glide forward.

Fritz ventures, "They are like ants I've watched in the woods. The whole thing looks like the activity of an ant colony, with ants coming and going. I've seen a swarm of worker ants struggle to move a giant captured prize, a centipede or something, plus maybe a few larger overseer ants with the job to keep the prize moving."

But this is not a mass of ants, this is a mass of humanity in misery. Just now, they hear a scream, followed by disruptive commotion. Looks like a human being, not an ant, has been crushed under the platform.

Close by, a long magnificent structure appears to rise out of the ground from below the earth. Zoom keeps staring at it and finally concludes, "It resembles the body of an animal with a human head. The head either has a lot of hair, or, hey, maybe it's a lion's mane."

"And look," says Izzy, "whenever one of the guys who look like supervisors goes by, they bow their head."

Fritz adds, "Yeah, but I've seen a couple of the workers spit at it."

The Kids notice a group of individuals, both men and women, coming towards them. They don't look like workers to Izzy. "Let's get off these boulders and see what they want."

The women are dressed in elaborate gowns; the men are wearing distinctive striped head gear. They surround the youngsters and are definitely curious. Some reach out to touch their clothes, their hair, and skin. They talk about them, gesture towards them.

One of the women advances with something rolled up in her hand. Izzy looks like she is starting to put things together, but Roxy has already assessed the situation and boldly steps forward. "Hi, my name is Roxy," she says, and her eyes dart from one to the other. Incredibly audacious, she starts talking to them, introduces her siblings, and tells them where they are from, namely, "St. Paul, Minnesota, in the USA, on Earth. We have a beautiful river just like you do." Roxy doesn't stop; she wonders who they are, glances at their shoes, their clothes, wants to touch their jewelry. The curious group is amused by the spectacle of this foreign girl taking control.

The woman who had come forward communicates first to Roxy, then to the three others, that her name is Mereret. Her eyes and eyebrows are accented boldly to give her an exotic look. She removes a decorated headband, and places it on Roxy's head. "Ooooh," the group shows their approval, yes, the new girl, Roxy, now looks a little more like them. But she needs to have her face enhanced, and the delighted group leads the Kids away.

They arrive in a large room, comfortably cool, with long tables and cushioned chairs. Rather striking are the walls, boldly decorated with various colorful figures, animals, and designs. Several servers bring a variety of food and place it onto tables.

The Kids are the center of attention; each of them is surrounded by wondrous natives. Of course, since the two groups don't understand each other's language, stories are told with arms and hands, pointing, touching, drawing pictures in the air along with exaggerated facial expressions.

Several women guide Roxy to a corner of the room where Mereret waits. Mereret, who might be a princess, dresses Roxy in a long gown similar to hers, then she motions Roxy to sit and begins to accent Roxy's eyes and eyebrows with distinctive coloring. Roxy now looks like one of them. Mereret smiles a smile of satisfaction. Roxy is succinct, "I like it." Of course, Mereret doesn't know exactly what she said, but she can tell that Roxy is pleased. Roxy adds, "Thank you for making me feel special."

In the midst of all the activity and commotion Zoom has been able to find a quiet spot, and she has gotten out her sketch pad. Of course, wherever she goes, her sketch pad plus drawing utensils come along. Zoom is drawing Mereret in Zoom style—front view, remarkably detailed face, with body long and sleek, the floor-length gown looks to be moving and flowing. Where is the whiff of wind coming from?

Several individuals come to have a look. Their reaction is immediate: they shudder. They show inner turmoil and contort their faces. Zoom frets. "What? You don't like it?"

Others, including Mereret, come, and the room explodes into bedlam. They look at Zoom's drawing, they look at the figures painted onto their wall, in comparison one-dimensional, flat, and wooden. They look back and forth and appear to come to a realization. Mereret moves cautiously towards Zoom and bows her head; they all bow their heads and remain silent. Zoom must be from another world. Is Zoom the goddess of art?

Now Izzy gasps as she realizes they are back in history four or five thousand years! She motions to Fritz. "Come quickly, we have to get out of here. We don't want to get stuck here."

Fritz, relaxed as can be, tries to calm Izzy. "I'll go check outside. I have to look at the horizon."

Izzy grabs Zoom and Roxy. "We're in Egypt. We have to get out of here. Let's follow Fritz."

But hold on, guess what? Roxy wants to stay. "I like it here. They're treating me like a princess."

Zoom also hesitates. "Yeah, I think I'm going to stay a while." Who doesn't like being bowed down to?

Izzy, not one to mess around in critical situations, grabs both and pulls them out. The locals are confused, but the Kids make it outside and Fritz focuses on the horizon . . .

Safely back home, Izzy pulls from her shelf the book she had been studying before. The book about ancient Egypt, the first great civilization, includes pictures of pyramids and explains that when the pyramids were built, the bottom two-thirds appeared white, the top third gold and silver. In our modern era the pyramids have tremendous grandeur, but they have lost their luster, they have become gray. The book, of course, also describes the pharaohs. It includes pictures of Egyptian art, and shows how men and women of the ruling class dressed. But the large, handsome book does not discuss the misery of worker ants.

7

INJUSTICE: THE DOGMATIST AND HIS POODLE

Another year has passed and it's summer again. The wonderful thing about summer is not having a regular schedule that forces you into idiotic conformity, and, as Fritz succinctly expresses, "becomes monotonous from here to eternity." The Kids might look inactive, but they are not bored. Each of them is busy. Izzy reads, Zoom works on her art, Roxy dreams, Fritz does all sorts of things.

One event they do participate in is a 5K race that is part of an annual festival in a small town called North St. Paul. The whole family (yes, everyone) runs the 5K. While they all finish, each of the Kids experiences the race uniquely, based on their distinct personalities.

Zoom does participate willingly and, yes, she does finish, but she only runs about a mile. She is not a jogger, so she walks much of the way. Many bystanders shout encouragement, "Go, girl!" and "You can do it!" But a couple of boys from school are wise guys: "See you next week at the finish line!" Does Zoom care? No, she doesn't. Zoom can't be bothered because she does what is important to Zoom. During her run-walk she focuses on spectators on both sides, looks at their expressions, studies their excited faces, their smiles and the way they laugh. She notices body language, how people cheer, how their arms move. Artists learn by being observant, and Zoom is on the way to becoming an artist. She has a strong will, is confident, and is not easily distracted from what interests her. One of her favorite expressions is, "I know what I want."

We already realize Fritz, lean and agile, is an athlete. He can burst with energy when he has to. He begins the race at full speed and powers himself into the lead. That's good enough for him; he is already satisfied with his performance. Not in any particular hurry, he runs the rest of the race casually, chats with friends in the crowd, and fades into the pack. Except once, when a challenger from his class runs past him and Fritz explodes and leaves the kid in the dust. He makes his point, slows down again, and finishes the race with a nonchalant stride and a smile.

Roxy shows them. Her long legs give her the natural stride of a long-distance runner. She glides across the surface with little friction; her body moves like poetry. Running is effortless for her. As she slides into a trance from the rhyming rhythm of running, her mind empties. But when Roxy is not running, her mind runs continuously, also without effort. This girl is constantly thinking, evaluating, wondering, planning, considering. And then at the finish line of her mental run she announces one of her fantastic ideas.

Izzy runs almost the entire 5 kilometers, but it's a bit of a strain. She does not jog regularly. Running interferes with her thinking. She takes accelerated classes in school and currently is into world history. Lacking the smooth stride of Roxy, Izzy stumbles over the downfall of Rome, has breathing problems when thinking about the Middle Ages, and finally makes the finish line when she reaches the Enlightenment.

Is there anything else they can do together this summer before it ends? Do any of the Kids have a big idea?

In her cozy corner under the slanted roof of the attic, Roxy reaches the finish line of a mental run. Her head springs up and her eyes dart around as she conceives another idea. "Listen, everyone, listen," she commands. "I've got a fantastic plan, the best ever."

The others glance over in wonder.

"Forget about the past," she says. "The past is stuck, forever and ever, we can't change it."

Izzy interjects, "Yeah, but we can learn from it."

Roxy, not to be denied, adds, "Okay, we've been there. But why don't we explore the future? Who knows, maybe we can influence it."

Now they perk up. They all talk at once. "Areyouforreal?" "Ohmygod." "The future?" Zoom is particularly eager. "Traveling to a time to come, that has not happened yet, that's cooler than cool."

Roxy presses her brother, "Fritz, can you do it?"

Fritz is unsure. "The past is easy, it already happened," he says. "The future looks impossible. It hasn't arrived yet." He watches Roxy start to bristle, then adds, "But let me work on it. I'll really try."

Early the next morning, Fritz zips onto the roof. He squints his eyes, concentrates, looks towards the west. Finally, although with a bit of hesitation, he says, "Maybe this way."

Off they go. They don't realize it immediately, but they don't make it into the future.

They walk uncomfortably on a narrow cobblestone street not much wider than a car. Zoom complains, "I should have left my flip-flops at home."

"Where are the cars?" That's what Roxy wants to know. "I'm expecting super modern cars. Maybe flying buses."

Instead, they walk past odd-looking houses on both sides, close together, one or two stories high, with wooden beams built into the houses.

"Look at the filth everywhere. That looks like rotting garbage." While Zoom points to something yucky, she almost steps into horse manure with her skimpy flip-flops.

"Whew. It stinks."

"There is . . . what is that, is that a rat?"

"Watch out!" Someone pours something out a window that splashes on the ground at their feet. Fritz looks at the liquid and coyly states, "Maybe it's not water."

Roxy is definitely confused. "This can't be the future. Did we slip into the past again?"

"I thought . . ." Fritz, with a dejected look on his face, does not finish the sentence.

Zoom asks Izzy, "Any idea where we are?"

"No." But Izzy adds, "I was reading a book about the Middle Ages to Fritz."

Farther ahead they see a crowd. As they come closer, noise from the crowd increases. They reach a large open area surrounded by buildings on all sides, a town square. People mill about, some stand in small groups, they talk, gesture, argue. A larger gathering is in front of the biggest building. The Kids move over to see. Townspeople are boisterous; some throw things at a wooden structure.

Zoom shrieks, "That's a woman stuck there." A woman's head is in one opening, her arms hang out in smaller openings on either side of her head. "She must be in terrible pain. And people spit at her."

A church is on the opposite side of the square, and the throng directs attention to a figure coming through the open main entrance. The figure wears a long dark robe cluttered with embroidery. Because the robe is so oversized, his head appears small.

The figure has a sinister appearance. The townspeople glance away as he walks towards them. They make themselves smaller by bending their knees and sagging their shoulders. Are they trying to hide, to make themselves invisible? Only after he is past them do they straighten up and dare to look at him. They concentrate on his movement, scrutinize his small steps, follow the mysterious motion of his robe, inhale a whiff of the mystifying incense that flows in his magisterial wake. Do they feel adoration or fear?

The figure, perhaps to enhance the size of his head, wears a tall, decorated oval headpiece that looks like a vase. Fritz snickers and asks, "Does the vase hold water? I wonder how it would look with flowers?" Ha, ha.

Izzy hushes him up. "Do you want to get us in trouble?"

Roxy points in the other direction. "Look at that guy coming out of that important looking building."

Someone steps through large, decorated wooden doors. He is dressed differently than the townspeople, looks polished, has curly hair, flaunts a cape, and displays an outrageous looking hat with a plume of feathers. "He must be some sort of official. Maybe he's the mayor," guesses Izzy.

"He looks like a poodle. Let's see what he does." That's Fritz.

The figure coming from the church stops in the middle of the square and examines a fire at the base of a thick post. Apparently satisfied, he squeezes his thin lips tight giving him an uncompromising stern look of, well, why not, a dogmatist.

With imperious gestures he signals to the crowd to spread, and moves with small but irrevocable steps towards the woman stuck in the wooden contraption. As he walks, a few individuals approach him. He holds out a hand, accepts kisses without emotion. The mayor also arrives, and with grandiose gestures takes off his hat, kneels, bows his head, seems to mumble something, and kisses, one after the other, the many rings on both hands of the dogmatist.

Now the dogmatist, with the poodle at his side, stands in front of the doomed captive. He gestures with his hands and begins to speak in monotone. When he raises his arms, the eyes of the crowd follow and look up at the sky. After some snarling, he points to the woman in the wooden structure. He turns his arms downward, and with index fingers pointing emphatically down, the surly dogmatist raises his voice and condemns that thing, that dammed thing. He shuts his eyes and compresses his lips, tightens them as tight as a vise. The poodle raises his hat and the crowd roars and roars. At exactly the same time church bells begin to pound.

A mean-looking hunchback with the bloated face of a pig wobbles through the crowd with a large key and unlocks something behind the wooden structure. The crowd surges forward, surrounding the condemned wretch being dragged towards the fire.

Zoom screams, "They're gonna burn her! We've got to help her!"

Izzy struggles to hold her back. "We can't help her. We can't change history."

Zoom contorts her face into agony. "Maybe we can change the woman's story."

Izzy. "No, no. History is done. The only thing we can influence is the present. Fritz, wegottagetoutahere! Fast! No time to read a book or draw."

Phew! Your narrator brings them back home safely.

The experience leaves quite a mark on Zoom. Her sketch is in charcoal and the tones are gray, dark gray, and black. Flames that look like strands of hair stretching upwards rise from a stack of wood. Above the flames are billows of smoke that reach to the top of her sketch. At the bottom, in the middle, a diminutive hunchbacked figure feeds the fire. Smaller figures that remain unshaped surround the fire. Up on the left, instead of clouds, a large bell with suggested movement swings from side to side. The clapper is visible, also with suggested swings, striking the insides of the bell. A girl in flip-flops stands in a corner, her head bowed.

8

THE AGE OF DICTATORS
WILL END

What's next? Roxy is still obsessed. "What about the future?" Fritz normally prefers action to reading, but he does join Izzy, if somewhat reluctantly, on trips to the library. He checks out books that predict the future. As he expected, they're not much help. Every author has a different idea of what the future might be like, and of course, "They're only making guesses, right?"

Furthermore, none of the books describe how to get to the future. He also glances at science books. They offer possibilities. Perhaps other worlds exist where the same thing happens as here on earth, only faster. Or, could a wormhole provide an opportunity? "I'd love to figure out how to hop on a beam of light and make it burst way beyond its normal speed." There you go, he wants action.

It's the last week of summer vacation. The four of them are seated in a kind of bus, but as they look out the window, Izzy shouts, "Hey, wait a second! There are no windows!" Everything, the top, bottom, right and left sides—it's all made of glass; it's all window!

Roxy is surprised. "And look, we're in the air. We're flying over buildings, but where are the wings?"

Through the glass on all sides they see other airbuses streaking about, this way and that way, all without wings. Izzy goes, "Ohmygod. The sky is full of flying airbuses! Is this a dream?"

The Kids see other kids; in fact, the airbus is full of kids. The bus is alive with chatter. Those kids giggle and goof off; they do what kids on a bus typically do.

Izzy pinches herself. "Ouch." It's not a dream.

A friendly girl smiles at the Kids and greets them with the astonishing statement, "You must be part of the theater group in town," and wishes them good luck with their performance. Part of a theater group? What performance? What is going on?

The girl, pleasant and confident, adds, "I love history. I'm really, really interested in what life was like in the past. A history play is an awesome idea. And you kids are dressed so uniquely. What era do you represent?"

Izzy keeps pinching herself. Perhaps it is a dream, better not be a nightmare.

Silence. Izzy in deep thought. She studies the girl. She notices a faint halo just above her head. Izzy nudges Zoom and Roxy, "Stay alert." Then she slowly turns to Fritz. Fritz grins with the king of all grins and says, "I figured out how to do it."

The girl looks at Izzy, looks at Fritz, shakes her head a bit, and twiddles with her halo. It looks like she is trying to adjust something. More silence.

Izzy makes a bold decision. She leans towards the girl, "We're not actors. We're not wearing costumes. These are our real clothes. We're from your past. We've traveled into our future to see your world, to visit you. Hi, I'm Izzy from the 21st century."

If you step away, close your eyes, and consider the situation, you'll see our four youngsters flying in some unreal flying machine at some moment in the future talking to a girl with a halo. Can this be real? Our Kids together with kids from the future, in the same place, at the same time?

Remember, dear reader, the expanded sense of reality mentioned at the beginning of this tale. Put your disbelief aside. An important point is coming up.

Along with the reader, the Kids naturally have many questions, but they decide to trust the girl. What option do they have? Her name is Marsippa. Why? Because she was born on Mars. Her great-grandparents were part of an early Martian colony.

Marsippa is quite friendly, but it seems she is also a schemer. She has an idea, and what an idea it is. "Why don't the four of you make believe you are actors and put on a kind of show." Her idea is the show should be about life in the past, and of course, "You won't have to act, you can just be yourselves." She and her friends want to know what life was like for kids long ago, and she asks, "Do you still have to go to school, or do you already have learning buttons that help you acquire information? And you don't seem to have a halo, so I can't access your thoughts. Do you still try to read people's faces and have to wonder what they think?"

"Wow! We really are in the future. What do we do now?" Izzy consults with her sisters and brother. Roxy pushes to go ahead and put on a show. "We might as well have some fun in the future, right?"

The sky bus lands inside some sort of a structure also made of see-through material. The Kids follow Marsippa down a hallway into a bubble about the size of the airbus. As the kids from numerous buses storm in—there must be a few hundred or more—the bubble expands, and more and more seats pop up. The bubble becomes a theater, with a stage in front and enough seating to handle this crowd. Marsippa leads the kids behind the stage through one of the stage wings. Alone there, they discuss the situation and develop a plan.

Meanwhile, the kids in the theater look for their friends, scramble to grab the best seats, and become an expectant audience. After a while some start to clap and stomp their feet. More join in as the noise becomes louder. They want the show to start; there is definitely an air of excitement.

What are our Kids planning? What does the audience expect? Marsippa steps through the curtain onto the stage. She is greeted by several calls of encouragement not unlike those you might hear from kids in the 21st century. "Hey, Marsi," and "Way to go, Marsippa." Marsippa is able to calm the audience, except for a hushed cough or two.

"We have the distinct pleasure," she announces, "of having with us today a small theatrical ensemble who call themselves the Kids. They will portray what life was like for kids in the 21st century." She starts to walk off the stage, but quickly scrambles back to the center and adds, "The actors are not wearing halos, so we won't be able to communicate with them mentally."

Boom boom bah, boom boom boom bah. Boom boom bah, boom boom boom bah. Boom boom bah, boom boom boom bah. Out step the Kids, two through the curtain from the middle of the stage, one each from the sides. They clap their hands rhythmically and prance, hip-hop style, to the front of the stage and chant:

> *We're the Kids*
> *Here to perform*
> *What it was like*
> *Before you were born*
>
> *Boom boom bah*
> *Boom boom boom bah*
>
> *We're the Kids*
> *We are cool*
> *We get all A's*
> *When we're in school*
> *We study hard*
> *We love to learn*
> *We also play*
> *That is the Kids way*
>
> *Boom boom bah*
> *Boom boom boom bah*

We're the Kids
We're learning fast
We've got a mess
Can't let that last
It's up to us
To make it right
We need a solution
For political pollution

Boom boom bah
Boom boom boom bah

We're the Kids
From long ago
We sped up the clock
'Twas ticking too slow
We're here to see
What the future is like
Do dictators reign
And still cause pain
Or are the rats gone
Goodbye, so long.

The audience goes wild. The Kids, breathless, bow, smile, and wave to the audience. Then each of them in turn steps forward to show the audience an aspect of life in the 21st century.

Izzy is first. She walks onto the stage to applause, holds up a book, and shows it to the audience. "This is what we still use to learn." She flips the pages so the kids in the future can see what a book was like in the past, and she goes on to read several pages. Then she whips out a writing pad, writes, and reads one of her poems. It ends with: "Learning to read, learning to write, and learning to think take time / But without those skills life in the 21st century does not rhyme."

Zoom is next. She brings forth an easel—where did she get it from?—and begins to sketch. "Maybe you guys can use mental powers to draw, but I still have to manipulate an object to transfer what's in my mind onto paper." While sketching she talks about her techniques and the material she uses, then shows the audience her finished picture of the house the Kids live in. On top of the roof, super large, stands Marsippa with a golden halo that seems to sway and wiggle from an imaginary breeze. The audience hoots and hollers. "Hey, glad you like it."

Then Fritz tumbles across the stage with front flips. He comes to a perfect standstill in the middle of the stage, stretches both arms out, and takes a bow. He follows that up with acrobatic martial arts moves, and finishes off by throwing a frisbee into the audience. He yells, "Watch out!" But, surprise, it comes right back to him. In a soft but convincing voice he tells the audience, "I've learned to mentally communicate with the frisbee." Of course, the audience believes him. Why wouldn't they? He takes another bow and starts to walk off the stage. As Roxy comes onto the stage and passes by Fritz, she says to him, "No way, Fritz. You made that up."

For her performance, Roxy talks passionately about some issues she has to deal with back home such as slow school buses, wretched cafeteria food, and the underfunding of girls' athletics. She also brings up some of her trips into the past. "That's way, way back for you guys," she says.

The Kids' presentation is smashing. Of course, except for Marsippa, no one in the audience is aware that the Kids are not acting, but actually came from their past. The audience enjoys the hip-hop style, a totally new experience for them. Where did they get that from? Is it historical, or did they just make it up? They also want to know where they are from. Earth? Or one of the newer orbs? They ask several questions about the mentioning of "dictators." Could they elaborate on that? Do they have more information?

Afterwards, Marsippa invites the Kids to her capsule in one of the new space communities. The airbus ride from Earth will only take a few minutes. "They fly pretty fast." After they arrive in an oval living space that floats outside of an orb, they have a chance to connect. Two youngsters show up, a couple of years apart in age. Marsippa introduces them as her younger sister and brother. Their names are Sky and River. Both youngsters shake their heads trying to correct the reception from their haloes. Fritz is curious, he wants to get involved with them. They are equally curious and offer to show him around.

The girls and Marsippa want to learn more about their respective eras. Marsippa starts to talk about dictators. They seem to her to be like evil superheroes. She calls them "villains" and talks about "rule by villains." Her grandmother used to tell her "incredible stories about villains from different historical eras. They ruled with the intent of bringing glory to themselves, while the people they powered over suffered. The first dictators she knows about were in ancient Egypt."

Your narrator wants to alert the reader that the first of two key moments in the narrative is coming.

Marsippa, not realizing the significance of her comments, continues casually. She wonders, "You mentioned dictators in your presentation, but wasn't the age of dictators over in your time?"

The question surprises Izzy. Zoom and Roxy are all ears and await the response of their older sister, who is the most knowledgeable in these things. There is a long pause as Izzy considers the question. Marsippa plays with her halo and mutters, "I wish you would wear halos so I could tune in to your thinking."

As Izzy deliberates, she wrinkles her brow and looks down before the strain on her face clears up. "No," she responds emphatically. "No, no, no. The age of dictators is not yet over. We have wannabe dictators again in our era, villains who want glory and power."

"Oh no, how awful, how unfortunate for you," responds Marsippa. "But the good news for humanity," continues Marsippa, "is that by the time your era becomes my era the age of dictators is over."

"Yea, but how long will that take?"

This account taking place in the future is complete. It ends with the point that the endurance of dictators is limited. The narrator can bring the travelers back home safely.

"Hey, what happened?"

"How'd we get back?"

The Kids, back home, back in the 21st century, look at each other, puzzled. Roxy wonders, "We, we were in the future, weren't we?"

Fritz says, "I'm pretty sure I got us there."

Zoom looks at her drawing of a girl with a halo and says, "Yeah, we must have been there."

Izzy shuts the door to uncertainty. "Definitely. We were there!"

Now what? After numerous adventures into the past, the Kids have made an unprecedented leap into the future. Will anyone accept their story? Could they do it again, or is this the end of the adventures for them? Of course, they are the only humans to ever have experienced the future. Roxy suggests, "Someone should make a statue of us. The four of us on a pedestal in downtown St. Paul. We'd become celebrities."

Fritz and Roxy position their feet and start to pose, Fritz casually with a smile, Roxy boldly flexing her muscles, but Izzy brings them back to reality. "Get serious. Who's going to believe we actually visited the future?"

Fritz looks to be thinking behind his casual smile. He comes up with, "When adults don't want to tell us something, they say, 'Oh, you wouldn't understand, you're too young.' Now, if they ask us how we can know something they don't, we can say, 'Oh, you wouldn't understand, you're too old.'"

9

METAMORPHOSIS

After their extraordinary adventures, they have become disillusioned. The Kids are several years older, and they have outgrown the magical ability to travel to the beyond. Several changes have occurred, amongst them is that life has become mundane. The days are too long, nights too short. Zoom yawns in the morning, yawns in the afternoon, and yawns at night. School every day, the same classes, the same homework, the same little irritating issues. A favorite word now is "frustrating." Growing up is frustrating, learning about yourself is frustrating. Time proceeds at a frustratingly slow, slower, the slowest snail's pace. The only way to tell one day from another in Minnesota is glancing out the window at the weather.

Roxy sums up the malaise. "We don't need different names for days of the week if every day is the same. The school week begins on a Sameday, repeats next Sameday, replays the following Sameday, then comes another Sameday, and finally, finally it ends on Sameday in a Samemonth."

Only later, when looking at group photos, can you tell the girls changed from 13 to 14 to 15 to 16 to 17 to 18 to 19. In those photos, Fritz has to keep standing farther in the back, and finally is a head taller than they are. And if we were to put their brains under a microscope, we'd see big changes there also.

On one of the Samedays, Roxy reminisces. "Wouldn't it be great if we could escape into the past like we used to, into a fantastic adventure?" She admits, "There's a lot of stress in school. I'm doing okay, but I need something exciting."

Izzy peeks over her book, studies Roxy, then watches Zoom carefully put her brush down, look up from her painting, and respond. "Yeah, Fritz, can't your magic get us out of these doldrums?"

Fritz, usually laid-back, blurts out that even though he is much taller now, he can't look past the horizon anymore. "Sure, I used to be able to do that. We were all kids then, but now I'm metamorphosing."

Izzy drops her book. "What? You're doing what?"

"Yeah, I'm metamorphosing." Fritz smirks. "We're called teenagers, but that word doesn't describe our situation. People who are over 20 or 30, they're not called twentyagers or thirtyagers, are they?"

"I'm metamorphosing. How cool." Zoom loves it. "I long to become 20 and leave frustration behind. I want to turn into a butterfly, flap my wings, and fly into fabulous sunshine."

But the Kids are not butterflies yet. What distinguishes the ages between 13 and 19 is change, frustratingly slow change. Fritz notes the difference between butterfly and human change. "Butterflies emerge in a couple of weeks. It takes us much too long."

The body changes, the mind changes, and without warning reality can invade. During their metamorphosis our Kids must manage their frustrations, their ups and downs, themselves. Watch out, Izzy! Don't sink, Roxy! Don't crash, Fritz! Frustration, interrupted by unexpected turmoil, has replaced the wonderful innocent escapes of a few years ago. Your narrator can no longer guide their activities and keep them safe.

There's more. Besides their internal metamorphic struggles, chaos zaps them from the outside. Something is happening in the country, thunderclaps and lightning pop up on cloudless days. Their cocoon, their home fortress, cushy and supportive, can no longer keep cultural and political disruption out. Extended family get-togethers are no longer anodyne. Now arguments can flare, or their opposite, the uncomfortable silences that arise when certain topics are avoided. "Shh, don't talk about it. We don't want to disturb a hornet's nest."

Zoom is rattled by news headlines that *provoke* and *scream* and *blast* her mind. These are all her terms. She complains about the "constant noise that makes you pay attention. It controls you."

Roxy adds, "Even at school there's a lot of arguing. You can't tell who's right, who's wrong." She recalls something. "Remember, when we were kids, we'd get into arguments. We couldn't agree who started it, or," she laughs, "even what we were arguing about. One time, I remember this exactly, Grandma Yvonne was knitting and she made a knot. She made a knot on purpose, and then called all of us over. She asked who wants to try to unknot this knot. I tried. I think Zoom tried. But we couldn't do it. It was all tangled up. Then our Grandma said, your argument is like this knot. It's impossible to tease apart."

"I'm not sure I remember that," says Izzy. "But what I notice about the news, as stupid as it is, it's also kinda entertaining. It's like a story that continues from day to day. It's got an erratic plot, and you want to know what happens next. It's a page turner."

The Kids are gaining a pretty good understanding about what is going on in America. Sometimes they talk about the state of affairs. Roxy asks Zoom, "What do you think the key issues are today?"

"It's income disparity, the health care crisis, and the cost of college." Roxy adds, "Yeah, and people are so angry. But what do they do? They just blame others. Does that make sense?"

Izzy expresses the turmoil her way. "It's not a complete poem, but it does rhyme. 'There is wrong and there is right / the views are all black and white / we have the far left and the alt right / everyone is stirred up willing to fight.'"

Zoom just read about a man who killed himself. "The newspaper article quoted someone saying he felt hopeless and just gave up."

During this period of incessant cultural and political pinging—it's like buckshot—the Kids frequently duck, losing their equilibrium. They move through their house like they're in a fog, with eyes closed. They bump into each other. They forgot where they wanted to go. Much of the time they retreat into their own space in the attic and keep to themselves.

Zoom, in her space protected by the slanted ceiling, is quarreling with her art. She can't find her pizzazz. She's intent on figuring out how to portray the future, but says, "I don't know how. I can't get it right. It's so frustrating." Her smile has dried up.

Izzy is also uncommonly quiet. She keeps to herself in her corner and ruminates. If anyone asks her a question, she becomes monosyllabic. She responds with yes or no, mostly no, sometimes NO.

And Roxy, well, her desire but inability to escape has repercussions. Her face is frozen into a frown. She tells anyone who cares to listen, "It was dull yesterday. It's dull today. It'll be dull tomorrow. I'm worried the rest of my life will be dull, dull, dull." She is mentally stuck, in need of a spark.

Fritz slouches around in his dusky area where there is no window, his tight cocoon. His energy remains dormant. He thinks about time and space. He wonders if it could be possible for a kid from the future to travel back to the present, to visit him. He remembers talking about that when he was alone with the two youngsters, Sky and River, while his sisters were with Marsippa. But he never told anyone about it. He's mostly quiet, but he does say out loud to himself, "No one needs to know."

Izzy, not far away, asks, "What? What did you say?"

"Nothing. Never mind."

The girls sometimes also recall their last adventure, the one into the future. Then the memory of their interaction with Marsippa follows them like a shadowy companion. Out of nowhere, while Roxy bumps into Zoom in the hall, Roxy asks, "We were there, weren't we?"

The fog in the house must also contain hidden barbs that cause irritation. In a flash, acrimony can erupt. Roxy spits out at Izzy, "I hate it when you talk to me like that. It's stupid. Just 'cause you're older you think . . . "

"Hey, hey, come on . . . cool it."

"Oh, shut it. I'm sick of this. I'm moving out."

Or Fritz. "No way, I'm not cleaning that. Clean it yourself. Just 'cause I'm the youngest I always get dumped on."

Zoom worries about getting old. She says things like, "I'm forgetting so much," or, "My memory is fading." Her idea of flapping her wings after metamorphosis has taken a hit. "Fly into sunshine? Forget it. More likely into sunset." She tells Izzy, "I can't stand it. I'm starting to forget what we learned in the future."

Izzy mutters, "Stop your complaining. Your age thing is driving me crazy." Then she shouts, "Do something. Do something about it."

"What should I do?"

"I don't know. I don't know anything anymore. The only thing I know is we had an astonishing experience. We are aware of something others aren't, something that could make a difference. We just don't know how to use it. Maybe we'll all forget. Maybe our memories will fade in time."

This malaise must stop. Maybe your narrator can help them.

The source of the motivating kernel that triggers renewed initiative is sometimes mysterious. Izzy eats an apple from the apple tree in their yard and bites into a worm. "Yuck." She spits it out, and with it she spits out her lethargy. She gathers everyone. "Look, I'm struggling. We're all struggling. We've got to stop fighting each other."

No one looks particularly inspired.

"Here are a couple of facts. First of all, we know there will be a future. Our messy world will not end."

She gets some nods.

"Second, some of the problems we currently have in our society will go away. Things will improve. We just don't know exactly . . . "

And now comes the second key moment, the spark that initiates action. Recall, the first one occurred during their discussion with

Marsippa in the future. Izzy had said, "The age of dictators is not yet over." Let's have Izzy repeat the last statement she made just now: "Things will improve. We just don't know exactly . . . "

Zoom leaps up. Her head almost hits the ceiling. She dances around with arms flailing and long hair flying. Zoom experiences a blast of insight. "Optimism!" she shrieks. "It's optimism! Optimism is key. Yeah, things will improve. Optimism means hope." She catches her breath. "No gloom for me!" she shouts. "I want to get involved. I want to initiate change. I want action." The Mississippi is flowing again. Her face radiates. Zoom, not a runner, starts a relay race.

The Kids run with ideas. Roxy grabs the baton. She wonders, "Can we speed up change?"

Fritz, the next runner, blurts out with youthful exuberance, "Can we make the future come quicker?"

Izzy reaches for the baton. "Hey, let me finish my thought. We have the problem of wannabe dictators now, but for how long? We've learned they won't exist in the future, but we don't know when their time will end. Let's see if we can help make them disappear sooner rather than later. Make everyone realize they are rats."

Back to Roxy. "Okay, so no one will build statues to us now, but maybe, just maybe, when we are older, after people realize that we worked to make the future arrive faster, maybe they'll build statues to us then."

Zoom crosses the finish line of the productive discussion. "I'm ready. Let's get to work."

Izzy's conclusion about wannabe dictators dominates the remainder of this tale. The four of them will seek adventures again, but now their focus will be on exposing frauds and fools in the present.

PART 3

The Enigma in America

10

ON THE BUS TO NEW YORK: SIMPLICITY TRUMPS ACCURACY

Where should they begin their activity?

Izzy declares, "Let's explore the center of the action in America right now."

Fritz wants to know, "Where is that?"

"It's in New York City. That's where the Big Guy is making big plans."

It's fall. So off they go to New York on a long weekend. Of course, Fritz can no longer get them there magically; they have to travel like everyone else.

The bus leaves St. Paul early in the morning. After traveling all day and then through the night they will finally arrive in New York before noon the next day. It's a long trip, but Izzy is confident, and the Kids are hungry to experience America. Roxy, the days of dullness behind her, is ready. "Let the adventures begin."

They sit apart so that they each can engage separate travelers. They want to meet people, listen, discuss, learn. They are inquisitive, the first premise of an intellectual undertaking.

Fritz sits back the farthest, he wants to keep an eye on the girls sitting in front of him to make sure they are okay, not being harassed. A noble gesture.

Plopping down next to Izzy is a man with a disheveled appearance. His hair is unkempt, long and greasy, and he has a scraggly beard, but worse is his strong smell. Izzy takes a mint, and turns her nose towards the window, but you can't open bus windows. Help! Time stands still. Izzy must be conscious of every breath of foul air she reluctantly must take to survive. Shall she try to escape to another seat? She also doesn't want to be rude. He asks, "Where you head'n to, missy?"

Poor Izzy is stuck. She is polite, and as she turns her head, she can't help but recognize, there it is, on his soiled sweatshirt, the image of the man all over the news. He notices her stare and says, "That's my man, the Big Guy."

"I'm going to New York."

"Hey, you might run into the Big Guy."

She continues to be polite. "What is your destination?"

The man, maybe 40, maybe 60 or 70, tough to tell, says he's not going anywhere in particular. "I'm just moving around."

Izzy's curiosity overcomes her antipathy towards his appearance as she wants to find out more about him. He calls himself Big Mack. Izzy asks, "Isn't that the name of a hamburger?"

"Yeah, the burger was named after me."

"Where do you live?"

"I've got a small trailer in nowheretown. Vermin livin' there now. I left 'cause there weren't no jobs."

"What do you do now?"

"Oh, I'm constantly on the road. I take a lot of buses." On his own, he starts talking about the bus driver. "I know most of the drivers. Our driver is called The Hound, 'cause he's been with this bus company forever. After he's finished driving, he drinks a case or two of beer to relax. Looky at his belly later. Has two kids, one's in prison, the other, who knows? But he drives good. I frequently sit in the first row and talk to the drivers. They often let me board without a ticket. Us at the bottom gotta work together. That helps me get by."

Big Mack travels across the country, apparently the weather and his brain algorithms determine the direction. His experiences could probably fill a novel, but he doesn't write, he just survives. Life on the road is cheap. He sleeps outside often, sometimes with "my guys," buddies of his, sometimes just on the bus or in bus stations. "There's a lot of guys like me. I know a bunch of 'em. See the guy couple of rows in front with the big hat? His name is Billy Goat. He's mean, gets into lot of fights, but me and him are good."

Izzy wants to focus the conversation. "Why do you wear that sweatshirt?"

"Well, why not? He's the Big Guy."

"What do you like about him?"

"I like what he says."

"Do you like what he does?"

"He don't do much. He don't have to do much. Just has to keep talking big."

Big Mack notices that missy, as he calls her, is attentive. "The other guys on the road like me, we run into each other all the time. They want guys as leaders they can understand. When the guys in Washington say somethin' they gotta be loud, say things over and over, keep poundin' away."

Big Mack lifts a paper bag to his mouth and takes a sip of something. Where did it come from, where did he put it?

Izzy looks away but turns back to him and asks, "Are you saying people don't hear what our leaders say?"

"Yeah, like I say, they gotta be loud. The big guys in history, they were like lions. They didn't pussy around, they roared. And when they roared, people listened."

He continues. "As a kid I did comic books. No, not Mickey Mouse or the dumb duck. I did superheroes—Batman, Superman, Captain America. I wanted action, good guys, bad guys, winners and losers. Nobody paid attention to the details of what happened, that wasn't the thing, but me and my friends got a thrust from the spectacle."

Izzy, with some irritation in her voice, says, "But isn't that stupid stuff?"

"What you call stupid works."

He takes another sip from the paper bag and continues with gusto. "Captain America shows up and BIFF, BAM, BOOM. Then the wrestling guys learnt from the comic book guys, and in the ring in front of raging fans and on the tube it became BIFF, BAM, BOOM. That's why we watched. Same thing today. The Big Guy shows up and BIFF, BAM, BOOM. Me and my guys, we love that about him."

He stops, and looks down. He goes on, but slowly now after he swallows hard. "Wanna know something, missy? Long time ago, hell, maybe when I was as old as you, I did a couple of semesters in college. I read some books, you know, the ones without pictures. But things changed for me and I left." Another drink, then again with assurance, "My people on buses, on the street, in bars, we want superheroes. When I look at TV, when I see talking heads, I wanna enjoy myself, be entertained. So lemme tell you, couple of weeks ago I went into a used bookstore looking for comics, and I came across a little book about wooden characters named Punch and Judy. It also had some pictures. It was all BIFF, BAM, BOOM. Perfect. The guy doin' all the slapping with a long stick and punching and kicking while he's screaming is just like the Big Guy."

Izzy interrupts. "Are you saying that what goes on in Washington is similar to comic books, Punch and Judy stuff?"

"Yeah, missy, you're getting it. It's all about entertainment. Entertainment is a must. But the entertainment has gotta be like comic books." He stops, then slowly adds, "It's gotta be simple."

"But it's gotta be accurate?"

"Nah, accuracy don't matter."

Izzy writes that down. "Simplicity is more important than accuracy."

Wow! He gets off at the next stop. His seat remains empty, but his BO and his comments about entertainment linger.

Fritz's adventure is a bit different. An older woman can't find a seat in the front, walks slowly to the back and asks him, "Is this seat taken, young man?"

"Yes, it's empty."

"Oh, that's too bad."

"No, no. I mean no one's sitting there. Please, you can sit here."

It takes a while for her to get settled. She sets a large travel bag on the floor in front of the seat, rests her supersized pocketbook on the seat, takes off her jacket, folds it carefully, and places it on top of her travel bag. She picks up her pocketbook, but immediately puts it down again, bends down to pick up her jacket, searches for something in the pocket. It's not there.

Fritz asks, "Can I help you find something?"

"Thank you, young man, but you don't know where it is. I know exactly where I put it." She places her jacket on her bag again, picks up her pocketbook, looks at her seat and gives her pocketbook to Fritz. "Please hold it." She gets out a handkerchief and uses it to clean the seat. "Look how dirty it is."

Finally, she sits down. Fritz hands her the pocketbook, she places it on her lap, and takes a deep breath.

"Did you find what you were looking for?"

"It's in my bag. I'll get it later. Why aren't you sitting with your parents?"

"They're not here. They're back home."

"They allow you to travel all alone?"

"I'm with my older sisters."

"How much older are they?"

"Five minutes, a year, and two years."

Fritz is not sure she heard that. She wants to know where they are.

"They're not sitting together. We want to sit apart so we can meet people."

"How absolutely odd. Don't you get along?" She doesn't wait for an answer and asks, "Are you going to visit a relative?"

"No. We're going to New York."

"Oh no. New York City? All alone?"

Fritz doesn't say anything.

"I don't think you should go all alone. The city is dangerous. Are your parents aware of this? Say, are you running away?"

Fritz, struggling, politely says, "Ma'am, I think we'll be okay."

"Oh, young people are so foolish today."

She notices Fritz has a book on his lap, and she wants to have a look. "Is it something maybe you shouldn't be reading yet?"

He shows her the book with a boy on the cover wearing a broad-brimmed hat and without shoes. "It's Tom Sawyer."

"Oh, I suppose that's all right."

"Tom Sawyer is only 12 and he leaves home."

"Young man, don't be impudent. He's in a story, he was made up, but you're real. And those times were much safer. What about the other book?"

"What other book?"

"The one under your leg. Are you trying to hide it?"

"Oh, that one."

"Let me see the cover, young man."

"It's a book my grandfather gave me. He said I should read it. It's important."

"Let me see it."

Fritz shows it to her. It's called *On Bullshit*.

She emits an ugh. "Just what I thought."

Perhaps to soften the blow, Fritz adds, "It's written by a philosopher."

Poor Fritz. It's a long way to the next stop.

Roxy also has an encounter. At one of the bus stops a young woman with a buzz haircut sits down beside her. Her face is unadorned—no makeup on her cheeks or eyebrows, none to lengthen her eyelashes. Her lips are painted neither red, nor blue, nor green, nor black, and nothing dangles from her ears, nose, or neck. She is a total natural. After she sits down and settles in, she turns to Roxy and says, "Hey, I'm Emma, and I've got a dilemma."

"What?"

"I said I'm Emma, and I've got a dilemma. What's your name, and what's your game?"

"What? What did you say?"

"I just want to know your name, don't worry, I'm tame."

Roxy has never been flabbergasted before, but she is now. "Ah, hi, ah, my name's Roxy."

Emma offers a fist bump and says, "I do like your name Roxy, but it does rhyme with foxy."

Roxy looks away, out the window, at the passing highway vista, but she doesn't see anything. Her mind has been hit hard. It seems like an eternity passes, but only seconds go by. She recuperates quickly and offers, "Roxy also rhymes with moxie. I hope I've solved your dilemma, Emma."

The girls look at each other, and both break out in a smile. They've connected.

Emma doesn't adorn her face; she adorns her speech with rhymes. Perhaps her mind is laced with diamonds and jewels. She is passionate and provocative. Emma digs right in. "Roxy, our world's a better place, but America has become an international disgrace. Our senile political leaders shuffle their feet to a discordant, repulsive, and disingenuous beat. They're afraid to show up on main street where the people's rap is upbeat. Ask them to listen, to observe, to reason, to think, they slink into meaningless metaphysical stink. Their brains are petrified, ossified, homogenized, and pulverized."

Roxy can't do anything else but listen.

Emma continues, solemnly. "Who are the losers? We are, you and me, our generation. We're already engulfed by twilight. If we don't want to slide into darkness, we will need to fight back, and we won't use bullets or bazookas. We'll illuminate with reason. We are the future, they are the past. If we have the will, their madness won't last."

Emma gets off at the next stop. She is heading to an anti-gun rally. She and Roxy exchange phone numbers and promise to stay in contact.

Zoom brought her companions along, her sketch pad, and her drawing utensils. Wherever Zoom goes, her companions go along; they need each other. She is always prepared to converse with her pencil, to direct it, to guide it precisely, to embolden its mark, or to allow it to subtly hint at a soft-blowing wind. Sometimes her pencil has knowledge and guides her.

Zoom spends her awake time on the bus drawing faces, her passion right now. She has a magazine and draws one face after another from its pages. She is meticulous, and for the amount of detail she directs her friends to create she has also acquired zen patience. She sits alone for most of the trip, but the last stop before New York a man her grandfather's age sits down beside her. He can't help but notice Zoom's art and says, "You're an artist, do draw a picture of me."

"No, sir, I can't do pictures from memory. I need a photo in front of me."

He faces her. "Well, just look and see. You can draw me directly."

She shakes her head.

"I'm famous. I'm a poet and a singer. Don't you recognize me?"

She shakes her head. "Where are you heading to? What are you going to do?"

"I'm off to New York, just like you. Gotta write a song, I'm overdue."

She asks, "A protest song?"

"No," says he, perhaps wistfully, "My protest anthems are now history."

Before he gets off the bus in New York he tells her to "stay forever young."

11

ASSES IN NEW YORK

So, there they are, four youngsters from the tranquil Midwest, now amongst more commotion and concrete than anywhere else in the world. Fritz, tall back home, says, "Man, it's different, it's so huge. I feel like a lost Lilliputian."

Roxy looks up, up, up. "Yeah, the skyscrapers actually scrape the sky."

The four of them march down 42nd Street towards Fifth Avenue. Then they head north towards Trump Tower. Besides the constant cacophony of cars, cabs, and trucks, with drivers and jaywalkers cursing, frequent sirens, and the rattling of construction activity, the four Kids begin to hear the clamor of protestors chanting and yelling. Raucous demonstrators, a mixed and colorful bunch with and without signs, want to keep America democratic. Many wave American flags, and some are dressed in redwhiteandblue. They protest in front of the entrance to the infamous Trump Tower with fewer floors than advertised. Fritz looks up. It's all glass. He tries to count the floors, but it's impossible. He does want to know, "What happened to the people who rented the floors that vanished?"

Izzy is cautious. She tells them, "Let's stick together. This is chaotic."

Roxy either does not hear or does not want to hear. "Let's squeeze through these people right to the front."

They are now blocked by police officers behind barriers whose job it is to keep the crowd away from the entrance to the tower.

They are not unfriendly, and look like they are handling routine work. One of the cops can tell they are not New Yorkers. "Hey, where you from?"

On the other side some individuals are being let through and allowed to enter. Zoom notices they look different than the people in the crowd. "They're all men, all dressed in black suits, but they have white shirts, red ties, and white faces."

Fritz adds, "Funny, with blue suits they might also look like the flag."

Back to Zoom. "Yeah, they don't look like our flag, though. With all the black complementing the white and red, you don't have a good feeling."

What Zoom is not able to see is that they also have black shoes, black socks, black belts, carrying black, blacker, the blackest bags with résumés inside.

Roxy doesn't like barriers. "Follow me." She's headed to where the men in black, one at a time or in twos and threes, are allowed past the police barrier into the tower. She expects to march right in following them, but a policeman stops her. Before the policeman can speak, Roxy says, "What are you doing? We're part of the youth theater project and we better not be late!"

The policeman looks Roxy over, his face, initially serious, loosens, and he apparently can't suppress a tiny smile. He says, "Oh, okay," and allows them to sneak in through the entry doors. New York cops can be good guys.

The helpful cop moves the plot. If he hadn't let the Kids pass, we wouldn't hear about the painter, his painting, and the two asses.

They enter through the main entrance right into the lobby of the tower. They all speak at the same time. "Wow." "Is this for real?" "A palace of gold!" It's gaudy, glitzy, glamorous, gigantic. "I'm getting goosebumps."

People with "I'm important" stamped on their foreheads mill about in serious black attire. It must be a uniform, but a few blonde, slender women offer a contrast.

Far on the other side of the lobby they see commotion. The Kids move closer. A group of men in blackwhitered surround something. The entire group looks like a knot that rolls forward erratically. Roxy says, "I've heard that mafia bosses use dozens of bodyguards to create confusion."

Izzy is wary, "Stay here."

Zoom and Fritz listen, but Roxy, all too curious, steps closer. She is bluntly shoved back. "Scram, bitch." The jumbled knot disappears behind a guard down a hallway.

The Kids follow another group, try to make out bits of conversation, and the human conveyer belt pulls, pushes, and jostles everyone including the Kids into an elevator, going up, and up, and up. Some of the men inside the packed elevator continue to speak, but in hushed voices. Others stand like statues and stare. It's air conditioned, yet some faces look like they have been in sweatboxes, or their red ties, flaming nooses, are tied too tight. The elevator door opens and out they scramble.

Izzy: "Oh my. Another gaudy, glitzy space."

Zoom: "It's gold. Gold everywhere. One of those chandeliers, and our parents can retire."

The men migrate to one side of the hall and form a ragged line beside a wall laced with gold trimmings. If the wall also had provocative photos or perhaps erotic paintings, this could resemble the waiting area of a high-end bordello. But the men in black wait, fidget, look nervous without that sort of diversion. Fritz, always ready with a quip, wonders, "Maybe they're here for a funeral?"

Ha, ha. Roxy has to laugh. "A funeral way up here? Maybe the body can ascend faster to heaven."

"No. I think they're here to meet with the Big Guy," whispers Izzy. "I overheard some of them earlier talk about interviewing for big jobs."

The men wait in front of a door. As the door opens, they stiffen up and focus. Someone wearing a sneer emerges escorting a blackwhitered type out the door directly to the elevator. When he returns, he brusquely signals to one of those waiting to follow him inside. The door shuts. "Maybe they are allowed to visit with the corpse one at a time." That's still Fritz.

Then the knot from downstairs mysteriously reappears. It must have come up in a different elevator. The men protecting what's inside are now a bit more casual, and the Kids get a glimpse. They see a bloated individual riding on a cart and a woman beside him all in silver. The now loosened knot hustles through the door. The men left waiting outside act irritated. Looks like the knot cut in front of the line. Fritz can't withhold his observation. "Did you see the hair of the silver one? She had silver hair, straight down. Looked like a silver corn broom. And about as long."

The Kids move to the other side of the spacious hall where they notice an open door. They look in and see a painter in front of an easel painting a portrait. The painter, an artist with a brush in each hand, looks at several large photographs posted on a near wall. The painter looks at several of them intently, shrugs his shoulders, and adds a stroke of paint to the portrait. Something covered with brown paper also hangs on the wall. A couple of times the painter goes to it, lifts the brown paper, studies what is underneath, and comes back to add brushstrokes to the painting. The emerging painting is of an older man who looks unnaturally serious. He looks straight ahead with a too-phony blond hairdo for a man his age. Is it a wig?

Roxy speaks up. "Who are you painting?"

The painter turns around. He did not notice that anyone was watching. "Never mind," he responds. "Who are you?"

Roxy quickly adds, "We heard about your painting and wanted to come see. Zoom here, she's a painter also."

"Oh, well, in that case, what do you paint, young lady?"

Zoom responds, at first hesitatingly "I, ah, I, well, I," and then blurts out, "I also paint portraits." She gains a little confidence. "At first I did women, yeah, I specialized in portraits of women, but I also do men now."

The painter says he would love to see some of her work. Zoom adds, "I'm now starting to experiment a bit, yeah. One of my friends, she is a passionate violin player, and I just painted her but formed her body into the shape of a violin. I'm like combining two realities, a human body and a violin. Get it?"

"Clever, quite clever," responds the painter. "Actually, shhh, keep this under your hat, I'm doing something a bit similar." His painting, he says, is of a famous man. "Of course, I'm using actual photos of him, but look, look over there under the brown cover." He walks over, lifts the cover, and reveals a photo of a donkey taken from behind. "I got myself a close-up photo of a donkey's ass. And I'm now incorporating the subtle coloration of the ass into this portrait, using the graybrown for areas of the skin, the face, neck, big ears, and large hands. It's not obvious, but it's there. The serious pose of this, eh, dynamo, features the coloration from the ass of an ass." The painter pauses, then continues, almost whispering, "Of course, no one knows about it. Only I know, and now you kids know. It's our little secret."

The Kids are still in the room with the painter. Four women storm in. They all look alike—tall, thin, and blond. One of them wants to know when the painting will be done. "Time is running short, we have a deadline, hurry up, can't you paint faster, what's taking you so long?" They are irritable and snappish and leave in a huff. They pay no attention to the Kids.

When they are gone, Izzy asks the painter, "Who are they?" The painter says one is the wife of the man he is painting, two are his daughters, and the fourth is, well, a new friend . . .

Fritz wants to know about the knot of dark men who seemed to be concealing someone. "They were hustled through the other door."

The painter puts down his brush, rolls his eyes, puts his fingers across his lips and whispers, "A fraud."

When they arrive back home in St. Paul, the Kids are trying to understand what they saw: the protestors in red, white, and blue; the men in red, white, and black; the strange story about the painting;

the four lookalike women; somebody or something the painter called a fraud. You can tell Izzy has been thinking; she has a way of simplifying things. "I don't like black. The men in black gave me the awful feeling of tragedy, but the painter was like a jester, he broke up the doom and made you laugh."

Zoom, on the other hand, creates a painting of a woman's body in a tight dress with multiple legs. Instead of a head, four balloons hang from the neck. The balloons droop, are dull and motionless. There is no breeze.

12

ON THE BUS TO WASHINGTON, DC: GOOD AMERICAN JOE, BAD AMERICAN JOE

It's almost spring break. Months have passed, but their experience in New York continues to occupy them. The feeling of tragedy, comedy, and yes, farce, coupled with the insipid image of balloon heads, lingers.

Izzy talks about "the darkness amongst us."

Zoom has discovered, "A breeze does not always work for my art. Sometimes oppressive calmness is effective."

Fritz says he's learned about power. "The knot pushed right to the front."

Roxy discovered that a clever story does not have to be true to be effective. "Fiction is entertaining in real life too. Remember, the policeman smiled."

What's next? "Washington, DC, must be next," so says Izzy, and they develop a plan. When to go, what to bring, what to see, where to stay, what to wear. Zoom creates a design for a t-shirt, and Izzy comes up with a text. They have eight made, two for each of them. The front states, "Youth for Truth." The back proclaims, "Don't Lie Behind My Back." Might not be great, but it will do.

Roxy spends hours alone in the woods and fields near her home.

She collects something she wants to use in Washington. "It'll be a tiny surprise," she confides in Fritz, but only in Fritz.

Izzy reads from morning to night. She wants to gain a better understanding, she has so many questions. She also clarifies her thoughts by writing poetry. "It focuses my mind."

And while Fritz no longer has the ability to see farther into the distance than others, he now wants to be able to hear sounds below the normal human hearing range. He has some sort of a plan that he only shares with Roxy. Zoom keeps asking, "What are you guys talking about?" Fritz keeps putting her off. "You might hear about it later."

Just like their trip to New York, they travel by bus. Again, they spread out to engage with other travelers. Fritz sits in the back.

Traveling from St. Paul they must change buses in Chicago. Izzy finds a seat beside a woman who immediately says, "Hallo. Wie gehts?"

"What?"

"I want you to know right away zat I'm from Tschermany. My name is Helga."

The reader has met her before, but Izzy hasn't.

"Oh, nice to meet you. I'm Izzy."

"Zat's an interesting name."

"Guten Tag, Helga. See, I know a little German too."

"Ja, ja. Maybe you can learn more."

"Why do you find my name interesting?"

"Because your last sree letters are from the last two letters of ze alphabet. Zat is unusual."

Helga is on a mission. "I want to help start ze process of change in America. Let me tell you why." She twists in her seat as much as possible towards Izzy and scrutinizes her face. "I don't know anysing about you, but let me tell you a little bit about me. After ze war, you know, ze last world war, in Tschermany we had nossing. America was gut. American soldiers was gut, helped Tschermans wis food and closing. Zey did not have to help us. Tschermany lost ze var. We were ze enemy. My faser was a soldier. Maybe he shot an American."

She stops, perhaps waiting for a reaction from her listener. "I was just a little girl, but I remember exactly a very nice GI, his name was Joe, no, no, not ze toy, zis was a real man mit a real uniform and a real helmet, he was gut, very gut. Whenever he see me he give me somesing. He give me toys, sometimes chocolate. What I like best was gum you could make big bubbles wis. He was really kind. You understand? Kind. Being kind to little girls is a very good sing. Little girls will remember zat."

Helga sounds like she has told this story before. Her sentences flow, even though the Germanized English words splash against rocks in her stream.

"Do you know about ze war and ze role of America afterwards?" Helga quizzes Izzy. "Not enough. I'd like to learn more from you."

"Gut. Very gut. I tell you more later. But first I want to tell you about Joe today in America."

Izzy wonders, "The same guy?"

"No, no, a new Joe. Zere is also John, and Mike, and Ralph, and Mitch, and Mary, and Janet. Zese Americans today wis common names, well, not all American, but too many, zey do not want to help little girls. Zat is bad." Helga makes sure Izzy is still listening. "What I mean is zat people who need help today, ze poor, ze homeless, ze people who come to America wis nossing, zey no get much help. Joe and John and Mary, zey say to hell mit you. Zat is not gut." She looks stern. "I sink America has lost its way."

Helga seems to be about 70 or so. Her hair is gray, her face angular, and she either wears little or no makeup. She has the eyes of a much younger woman; they shine. She avoids small talk and gets right to the matter with determination. All the while she looks straight into Izzy's eyes almost without blinking. Now she straightens back up in her seat and closes her eyes. Is she done talking? Is she going to sleep? Izzy turns to her. She can see her eyes are closed, yet Izzy asks quietly, "What are your plans to change America?"

Helga's eyes pop open and sparkle immediately as she turns her head toward Izzy. "Gut, very gut. It's getting dark outside, but you awake.

Maybe you and I will become friends. America is a big ship. Hard to turn around. Hard to change direction. Ve need very strong wind to blow for a long time. Wis ze breath zat I breathe out talking to you, talking to others, I make a little stir in the air." She raises her arm and with her hand spins circles into the space between her and Izzy. "I try to start a little breeze. Maybe you help. Others will help. We try to convince the Joes and Johns to become gut again and help stir ze air. Maybe all togeser we can make big wind. Maybe we turn ze America ship around."

Izzy wonders, "How do you get people to help?"

"Here is what I do. I tell and I ask. I tell story about good American Joe and bad American Joe. It makes people sink wherever I go."

"But we don't want the boat to sink."

"No, no, I don't mean sink under water, I mean sink as to use brain. Ha, that would be funny. So, when I tell my story people sink wis zeir head." She touches her forehead with her pointer finger.

"And what do you ask?"

"I ask simple question. Which Joe you want to be?"

"And what do people say?"

"Most want to be good Joe. No one wants to be bad Joe. But some want to argue. Zey don't like ze question. It makes zem uncomfortable. You can tell when someone, like a worm, what you call it, when it wiggles?"

Izzy says, "squirm."

"Zat's right, zey squirm. And what I know from people in Tschermany after ze war, when people squirm, zey feel guilt. It forces zem to sink, and zere is gut chance zey become gut." Then Helga says, "Let us rest. We talk more tomorrow."

How is it that Izzy attracts interesting people?

The bus travels through the night. If you can get comfortable in your seat, the hum of the engine and the slight swaying encourage sleep. Izzy closes her eyes, but she's not sleeping yet. The prolonged silence builds its own momentum. Izzy is compelled to touch Helga's wrinkled hand. She speaks in a quiet yet strong voice. "I want to change America too."

Fritz also has an adventure worth describing, but it's not at all what the Kids were hoping for. Well, maybe Fritz was, secretly. At the stop after Chicago, a young woman enters the bus, hesitates, looks around, then swivels all the way to the back of the bus. As she lifts a backpack to the overhead bin and positions it, Fritz, looking up, is blinded by her red tunic with a lace edge that bounces, and bounces, and bounces. She sits down beside him, says, "Hi, how are ya?" "Hi," says Fritz. She is about his age, maybe a little older. After a while she asks him if they could switch seats. She'd like to sit by the window and lean against it. They switch. She closes her eyes. Fritz tries to relax, but can't take his eyes off her red tunic with short sleeves. Is she chilly?

Later, after they get off the bus in Washington, Roxy is annoyed. "What were you doing? You were making out with that girl. You don't even know her." During the night, she had to go to the bathroom at the back of the bus. Fritz was busy, did not notice Roxy.

Fritz resists quietly, but firmly. "She was cold," he says, and walks away.

It's afternoon when they arrive in Washington. It feels good to get out and stretch their legs. Izzy steps out into the sunshine, smiles and bounces around. For her sisters the bus trip was too long and disheartening as many of the travelers looked like characters out of old films depicting the underside of life. It was also hard on the digestive system, junk food, upon junk food, more junk food, and stale salad with wilted edges.

Izzy introduces her siblings to Helga, but Helga has to leave for an appointment—"Wis someone who sinks he is more important san he really is." She says tomorrow she has to take a bus "all ze way to Las Vegas. But I'm sure we see each oser again."

Izzy wants to know why she doesn't fly. "You said you were in New York. You just came from Chicago and then you're headed for Las Vegas. Why don't you fly?"

"What, to see clouds? We haf clouds in Tschermany, too. Ze clouds here come to my country a few days later."

13

FICTION IN WASHINGTON, DC

The Kids are in the capital of the US, the focus of the world right now. But unlike most visitors they are not here as tourists. They have come to investigate what goes on here. And they arrive prepared. The bus trip gave them a lot of time to think of objectives.

Zoom says, "I want to feel my way through the blinding facade of fog to find clarity." Nice alliteration, Zoom!

Fritz has high hopes to "Break right through the obstructing sound barrier of lies and listen for truth."

Roxy simply says, "I fear nothing. Nothing is going to stop me."

Izzy found an inexpensive place to spend the night. They check in, look at their simple rooms, and change into their t-shirts: "Youth for Truth." Their overnights are not interesting, but their encounters during the day are.

Their first encounter is with white nationalists, their second experience is a lunch at a controversial international hotel. Finally, they behold a procession of prominent senators and congressmen marching solemnly from the Capitol Building to the commemoration of a new church. But first they have a look around, get an impression of the US capital.

"This is completely different from New York," says Zoom. "New York is modern, cool. These buildings exude power."

Washington was designed with the intent to convey substance. It is a symbol of an epic past Americans are continually, but selectively, reminded of from kindergarten on. America is exceptional, a beacon, and of course, favored by God. The magnificent structures in the capital reinforce that exceptionalism via their columns, flourishes, and inscriptions. There must be a thousand statues that glorify memorable white heroes.

These awesome structures compel the visitor to methodically take in the size and the grandeur. Look up to the top! Let your eyes glide all the way to one end, then ever so slowly back to the other end! The expanse overwhelms. The building signifies permanence and strength.

The White House, of course, is different. Its whiteness is a symbol of virtue. The individual who resides there has won the trust of the people, and to much of the world becomes a champion of hope and decency.

The people you see are a varied bunch. Those with business here stand out: politicians and their staff members, lobbyists, various dignitaries, power seekers. They walk briskly, look serious, and are typically dressed in blackwhitered.

Zoom goes, "Hey, we've already met these guys in New York."

A few notice the Kids because of their t-shirts. They look back and chuckle, or perhaps snicker at the script on the back, "Don't Lie Behind My Back." After several such occurrences Fritz addresses the next group of blackwhitered types. "Excuse me, gentlemen. Can any of you tell me where I can find some truth?" They seem perturbed, but must be in a hurry and move on quickly. "Maybe they are blackwhitered-clad sons of Tricky Dicky?" Fritz shows off his knowledge of John Lennon lyrics.

Many walk more slowly, stare, appear to be in awe, and cluster at key tourist sites. These are, of course, visitors. They are casually and colorfully dressed, and look flushed with pride.

Sometimes masses of insurgents don't care about the sights. They arrive to leave their imprint on politicians, on the media, on the president. They come with signs and banners and draped in various flags. They bring confetti, balloons, bullhorns; they march, raise fists, form circles, hold hands. Roxy notices a relatively small group that seems to be resting. "Maybe they're getting ready to protest."

There are perhaps several dozen people in a corner of a park, mostly men standing around. They talk, smoke, drink beer. A couple of flags are visible, some signs rest beside trees, a few shields with obscure symbols. Some practice salutes.

Izzy warns, "They look and act a bit weird."

Haircuts distinguish the group. Fritz gives a colorful description. "The sides of their heads look like a lawn mower went radical. Their tops look like greased weeds."

The men seem unsettled. They each regularly grab their crotch with the free hand not holding a beer, pull and tug, making sure everything fits just right, and then a few minutes later the hand goes down again to adjust the goods. Oh, and they are all white.

Roxy takes the initiative. She wants to go and mingle with them. "This is what we came here to see, plus I brought a present for them from back home." She reaches into her pocket and adds, "I've got 'em right here in the box."

Fritz, a bit on the skinny side, speaks quietly. "I'm not sure it's a good idea to mingle with those goons."

"Yeah, they seem creepy," adds Zoom, but "I'm also curious. We just need to be careful."

All four of them cross the street, Roxy in the lead.

"Hey, guys. Can anyone spare a beer?"

Stupefied gazes greet her. Stares and silence. Some fidget nervously. A few hands work on their crotch. There are grunts. Then one of them, let's call him Bobo, he's got to have a name, starts to talk. "What the fuck? Who the fuck are you?" And so it goes. Not very eloquent.

Where do these guys come from? Have they slept in deep caves and only recently ventured out into sunlight? Are they like bacteria that suddenly proliferate as antibiotics become ineffective? Many have tattoos on their arms, but all seem to be a hitching post for ornaments. On their chests and around their necks they display various mysterious emblems, runes, the meaning perhaps known only to them. They wear different types of crosses, and there, a swastika, there, another one hidden within another cross. Fritz mumbles, "I wonder who they voted for?"

Roxy doesn't give up. "What, you guys out of beer?"

Bobo says, "Man, you're just a baby chick with no feathers. You ain't old enough." He continues. "You all got the same t-shirts. What's it mean?"

Roxy doesn't respond. Instead, she says she wants to see some of their emblems. "If I like them, I'll sprinkle some pixie dust on you. I'm from Minnesota, and I want to give you a gift from Minnesota, a little pixie dust."

She steps up to Bobo and examines several crosses around his neck. "Nice," she says. She opens her wooden box, sticks in her hand to get something, and then places that same hand on his head and says,

> *Pixie dust, pixie dust, do your good thing*
> *Give him the gift of the magical red ring.*

She moves to the next fellow, examines his emblem dangling from his chest, gets something out of her box, touches his head, and says,

> *Pixie dust, pixie dust, do your good thing*
> *Surprise him with a magical red ring.*

She does that a dozen times or so. The men look confused at this audacious girl. They're not sure what to make of it. They keep fussing, grunting. Some look nervous and begin to practice salutes again. The salutes must be comfortable. Their arms pop up automatically without any strain. They must also be comforting; the salutes seem to relax them.

The Kids leave. When they are out of sight of the white nationalists, Roxy stops. "Wait. I want to see something." She opens her box, looks inside, and counts. Her sisters must wonder what the thing with the box and the little rhyme was all about. Roxy winks at Fritz and tells everyone, "I've got four left."

Zoom goes, "Four what?"

"Four ticks. I collected them back home and I brought about two dozen. Maybe we can sic the rest on the Big Guy."

Next day—watch out, infamous hotel. Actually, it's called the Trump International Hotel. This is the first visit to this landmark for the Kids. The reader already knows they came a second time for the magnificent costume ball.

They walk right up to the arch, are unceremoniously stopped, and of course Roxy steps up and asserts, "We are the leaders of the Republican Club in our school and we are here to meet our uncle for lunch."

"Who might your uncle be?"

She lifts her hand, and with her pointer finger beckons the fellow in uniform. He steps closer, and she whispers something into his ear.

"Oh, well, of course, go right in. May I guide you in or do you know your way around?" Roxy does not care to respond; she starts to march under the arch and right through the doors as her siblings follow.

It's spacious, airy. Roxy demands a quiet spot. "My uncle, the Vice President, will be a bit late." But they already want to sit down and order something.

Good for you, Roxy. Wouldn't it be great for Emma to be here to witness your moxie?

Other tables are occupied, most with two or three guests. Hushed conversations all around.

Zoom looks at the menu and is aghast. "A single shrimp is more expensive than what we pay at home for an entire lunch." But who cares about the cost. "Let's order," says Roxy.

At the next table sit two men dressed in blackwhitered. "We keep encountering the type. It must be a fashion thing," says Izzy. Initially the men were chatting quietly, but now they have a disagreement and become louder. Fritz sits closest to them and hears some snippets . . . stump . . . removal . . . remote . . . raining . . . or training. Fritz is frustrated. He can't understand, but he came prepared. Out of his pocket he pulls a small gadget, about the size of a quarter. He gets up, walks to the table, and asks them, "Hey guys, could one of you be so kind as to take a photo of our group? We're celebrating a special occasion."

Sure, of course, one of them gets up and takes some pictures with Fritz's phone camera. "Hey, nice t-shirt. I assume you want the right kinda truth." Fritz just smiles.

Fritz thanks him politely, and they both join their respective tables again. Unknown to the other is that Fritz placed a tiny voice recorder into the flowers in the middle of their table.

Fritz winks at Roxy. Izzy and Zoom know something just happened. They look at Fritz with question marks written on their faces. Fritz smiles sheepishly and says, "Like Roxy, I also plan ahead."

The two men at the other table continue their animated conversation. They are soon joined by a third character who looks like he just stepped out of a jungle in Central America still fighting the capitalists. He struts in with a machine gun over his shoulder, swaggers to the table in boots, stands for a while with feet spread wide apart, overlooks the establishment, wants to see if anyone is familiar, and finally sits. A total revolutionary, unkempt hair covered partially by a beret, unshaven for days, wears a worn out, loose-fitting green (or is it a brown?) jacket, and caresses his machine gun.

Izzy notices that the newcomer does all the talking, the other two, now quiet, constantly nod in agreement. She signals for her siblings to lean closer and says quietly, "That's obsequiousness in action. I'm sure we had that in the past, but it seems to be rather common now."

Fritz asks his sisters to slow down eating lunch, "Don't eat so fast, savor it." After about 20 minutes the two guys and the character get up and leave, the character in the lead. He takes long steps, the machine gun tight in his grip. The others follow close behind with quick small steps. The waiter comes to clear their table, and Fritz, as quick as a flash, grabs one of the flowers on that table. He tells the waiter, "I want to give it to someone special."

Your narrator just took some liberties. The account of the previous scene, while accurate in its essence, does include some hyperbole. Of course, the newcomer did not walk into this hotel for the privileged with a machine gun, but in a different era he could have. The machine gun of past revolutionary struggles has been replaced today by more insidious weapons, offshoots of new technologies, tweet, tweet, that are, like machine guns of the past, employed to gain influence and control. Tweets can be used to announce diplomatic action, but they are also used to assassinate opponents. No need to shoot someone on Fifth Avenue. That's the old way of settling scores. The inclusion of the hardcore macho machine gun is but a bit of nostalgia, rat ta ta ta tat!

In the evening, resting on a worn-out mattress, the Kids surround the voice recorder and listen to the conversation multiple times. Izzy and Zoom do research on an iPad to help them understand some of the things mentioned. The conversation they listen to is about a plan to develop a "training center." The issues the three men discuss are where, when, how big, how to sell it, how to fill it. They want to create this "training center" in a desolate area of the west. It "absolutely must" be far from population centers and "absolutely must" be inaccessible. "That means no roads." Access would be via a specially built railroad that would only go as far as that "facility." It's not clear who, but some group would be brought in to build infrastructure, repeatedly referred to as "housing," but once someone said "barracks." They also disagreed about who would function as the "security personnel." "Our military" wouldn't need much training, but if they recruit from various paramilitary groups we have in the country, or perhaps "import" personnel from another country, they would need some training in security protocol. And who would they "protect"? They would "protect" people who were asked, then told to "go back" to "fix the broken and crime-infested places they came from." And this: "We don't want them."

The guy with the machine gun ends the discussion. "Look, word is gonna get out sooner or later. This will be too big to contain, so we gotta be careful how we talk about it." After a few moments he continues. "We're gonna talk about giving people assistance, we're gonna talk about helping those who need help." Finally, "I'm certain our base can be brought along. Rest assured, we know how to motivate 'em."

The Kids don't know what to make of this.

"I'm confused."

"I'm concerned."

"Is this real or a sick trick?"

Izzy has heard about the famous "War of the Worlds" radio broadcast from the '30s that became a sensation. "I wonder if the device recorded the actual conversation at the Trump Hotel, or did the manufacturer stuff it with a fake recording as a marketing gimmick?"

The next morning arrives on time, but they don't want to open their eyes. Izzy has a headache. She had frightening dreams. Fritz wonders, what if. "What if I didn't bring the listening device? Then we wouldn't know."

Zoom says, "Yeah, but it's better to be in the know than to be dumb and happy."

Their unease persists, but this will be their last day in Washington, and another curious event awaits them. "Come on, we have to get going. Maybe this event will change our mood." The Kids head to the Capitol Building where they will witness the scheduled procession. A thousand people or more already mingle in front of the magnificent structure with its many stairs and columns. Some are just tourists without an agenda, but most are here to protest. They have come with signs and slogans, banners and flags. They want to be seen and be heard, they want to make a difference, this is the way democracy works.

Izzy asks one of the women protestors, "What are you guys against?"

She is articulate. "Hey, we want to stop the tight relationship between our government, which is supposed to be secular, you know, and religion." If the reader has to ask which religion, then, dear reader, you better stop reading right here.

A group of senators and congressmen—a faction calling themselves the Spiritual Statesmen—are planning a procession from the Capitol Building to a site several blocks away to bring solemnity to the groundbreaking ceremony of a new church.

The Kids have wiggled themselves into the front. They are right by the ropes placed there to control crowds. And here we go, a door swings open, and out they come. The protestors increase the volume, signs move up and down to grab attention. Some protestors are dressed to be noticed. There is a clown, an Uncle Sam on stilts.

Leading the procession is a man wearing a long black robe. The Kids don't know who he is, but they overhear someone behind them say it's one of the Supreme Court Justices. He is followed by the Spiritual Statesmen, about two dozen of them, all men, all white. They pretty much all wear the same uniform, blackwhitered, with a lapel pin of the American flag. Even though it's cloudy, every single one of them wears black sunglasses.

The shouting of protesters intensifies. The Kids hear a chorus of boos, the occasional slander. A chant begins, at first it's faint, but it becomes stronger. "Faith or laws, you choose, do both, we lose. Faith or laws, you choose, do both, we lose. Faith or laws, you choose, do both, we lose."

The Spiritual Statesmen in their black sunglasses look straight ahead without giving the protestors a glance. Perhaps they also wear earplugs. They seem to be oblivious to the noise. They don't smile, don't flinch. They look serious, and two dozen lips are sealed tight, two dozen vises. Security people protect this procession. They are also dressed in black; they also wear barrier sunglasses. They definitely look intimidating, like bikers in suits, but without their bikes.

The procession comes close to where the Kids stand, and as the Spiritual Statesmen slowly pass, Fritz notices that they walk in sync as if to a beat. Startled, he alerts the others, "There, can you hear that? Right there. They're holding something. There, again. They must have small bells in their hands." While walking—step, step—they shake their hands, and Fritz can hear a faint jingle. It's step, step, jingle, step, step, jingle, step, step, jingle. "Maybe these Spiritual Statesmen are regressing to a time they were altar boys or acolytes."

The procession passes by them, but not a single one of the politicians looks at them or their t-shirts, Youth for Truth. And look, there is also a last solitary individual in this procession. He is also dressed in a long black robe, but a white clergy collar is visible just under his Adam's apple, and an oversized cross dangles from his neck. As the procession moves on, the crowd slowly breaks up, but many protestors follow and continue their rancor.

Izzy turns around and looks for Zoom. "Where is she? Where did she go?"

They find her on the edge of a lawn where she has gotten out her drawing accomplices, always with her. She is intense, focused, her cheeks ruddy. Doesn't say a word, just works. Her sketch is in charcoal, and the tones are gray, dark gray, and black. We've seen Zoom's dark charcoal work before. In the middle of her pad Zoom placed a barrier. On this side of the barrier protesters are indicated only with oval heads and mouths open wide. The protesters are focused on an imposing figure on the other side of the barrier. That figure is dressed in a long dark robe. Is it a judicial or a clerical robe? The figure looks straight ahead past the protesters and taps in front of him with a white cane. To make sure the intent is clear, Zoom adds a seeing-eye dog. From start to finish Zoom works continuously without stopping. She does not hesitate, erase, rethink, or break her trance. The composition just flows out in a continuous stream from inside of her.

Zoom looks up. She does not smile, but nods with her head indicating she is done. Izzy, who had her own reaction to the scene they witnessed, gives Zoom a piece of paper with a poem she just wrote. "Can I add my six lines to your composition?"

Zoom reads it. "I like it. Top left, but write carefully."

Here is Izzy's poem.

I look straight ahead
With blinders on my head
So I don't have to see
Your notion of reality
Just leave me be
With my partiality.

14

OFF TO THE HEARTLAND

The bus trip back to St. Paul is long and boring. They sleep much of the time.

Back home Zoom summarizes her thoughts about our capital. "Washington has an unreal quality about it. What happens there is like fiction."

Izzy has a similar idea, but expresses it differently. "To me Washington is a big stage. Individuals and groups come to perform. But the politicians and their entourage, they also perform. There's something false about them, though. Not sure if they're portraying themselves, or someone else."

In the real city of St. Paul, Roxy and Fritz have some regrets. They had quite an experience in Washington, but let's be honest, they were too adolescent. The surprising episode with the ticks, that's definitely a rapscallion activity, not to be recommended. After a little discussion with your narrator, Roxy admits that unleashing ticks onto individuals you don't like is not right. Her own words: "I'm past the tick thing. Next time I'm gonna sic facts and reason on someone's mind." But she does add some rationalizing: "It's unlikely that any of the ticks will find their way down to the skin, and even if one did, the chance of the tick being infectious is as tiny as the tick."

Fritz also acted underhandedly by secretly planting the listening device. "Nope, don't think I'll do that again," he says. "Gotta stick to what's right."

What do they do with their newfound maturity? Where do they go next? To another city? "Let's explore the hinterlands," suggests Zoom. "Let's find out what life is like there, how people live, what they think. I wanna know what's important to them."

Because they all have drivers' licenses, they plan, get ready, and go, this time in an old Honda Odyssey. They got it from their grandparents who can get by with one car for a while. When Izzy picked it up her grandfather yelled as she was leaving, "Make sure you bring it back in one piece."

It's a minivan and there is plenty of room to slouch and snooze, and plenty of time to draw, read, and think. They've packed camping gear, sleeping bags, art supplies, some books, writing equipment, a chess set, their phones, iPads. No, they don't take the famous highways from the north made memorable by blues and rock and roll legends, Route 66 or Highway 61. They choose obscure country roads, slowly zigzagging south, then west, turning east, then heading south again. They have a lot of time; it's the beginning of summer.

At first, they drive through medium-sized towns. Pleasant main streets with small restaurants, banks, several churches, mostly older grain elevators but also a few new ones that show activity, as well as car dealerships and other businesses with new and used products at the edge of town for the farm economy. But gradually towns become smaller.

It's getting late, the Kids have been hoping for a campground, but there, look, Izzy, who is driving, spots an abandoned farm. "We might be in luck! Let's try it."

A gravel driveway covered with weeds, an old farmhouse plus various outbuildings, all disheveled, some boarded-up windows, other windows broken, things coming apart. A partially open door invites them to enter and check out where people spent decades living, loving, sustaining their lives full of hope for their children and their children's children by working the fields, tending to animals, day in and day out, during hot summers and hard winters.

As they enter, Zoom examines various remains still here and there. She runs her finger over a surface and looks at the thick dust on her finger. She inspects several nails still stuck in the wall above rectangles that stand out because they are lighter. "Look, pictures once hung here. Maybe of a couple. Maybe of grandchildren. They must have provided meaning and turned the house into a warm and safe home." After a moment she adds, "Where do the accumulated memories of the house go?"

Izzy, with a touch of sadness, speaks softly, as if to herself. "Were the people forced to leave? Did they die? Why didn't their children take over the farm?" She adds, "This might make for a touching story, maybe . . ."

"Ohmygod!" Roxy calls out. "Look at these wrappers, look at these crumbs." She is in the kitchen. "Come quick, there might be someone here."

"Whatdowedo?" Nobody is outright scared, but they are tense and probably wonder who, where, how many, friend or foe? Izzy doesn't panic. "It could have been a homeless person, long gone."

But still, they split up into twos and search the whole house without finding anything. Then they hear a muffled sneeze coming from somewhere below. Fritz finds a trap door with a staircase heading down, probably an old root cellar. He calls down, "Come on out. We know you're there."

They hear whispering, then a faint "Okay, I come."

Someone walks up the steps and pops out with his hands held up and says, "Don't shoot, please." Tension. The Kids stand stiffly around the opening to the cellar. They stare at the man emerging. He looks scared. He's dirty, and his clothes are torn. He nervously eyes each of them, one after the other, and as the stress on his face recedes, he quietly calls into the cellar something in Spanish, and slowly, a boy comes up, six or seven, also dirty, also scared. The man puts his hand on the boy's shoulder and says, "It's okay."

He tells the Kids he and his son have been living in the US for years. His son was born here. His name is Diego, and his son is Mario.

He worked as a farm helper, laborer, and in construction, always using the back-entry door, existing in the shadows. "It never was good, but now it's bad." He was working, his son had started to go to school, but "officials," as he called them, had caught some of his friends. And the people he worked with, the people in town, while never particularly welcoming, had become aggressive. While walking his son home from school a week ago, a car screeched to a stop, and several white men emerged, accosted him, and roughed him up. "They said I should go back to the 'shithole' country I came from."

Days later, men with covered faces broke down his apartment door and smashed things. "That's when I say I must leave."

Quick responses from the Kids. Zoom wants to go there. "Let's see for ourselves. Let's see if we can do something about it."

Roxy agrees. "That's what we're here for, right? We want to see if we can change some attitudes."

But Diego warns them. "The whites, they fall into a black hole. At first only some, then more." He continues, "You kids good, but you're also white, watch out the black hole doesn't suck you in."

That's how they spent the evening, the man telling the Kids about his experiences and warning them, the Kids telling the man about their adventures in New York and Washington. He intends to leave during the night so he can escape this town unseen. There are a couple of locals he does not want to run into again. Roxy makes sure to get his phone number, and she expresses her wish out loud: "I want you to make it."

15

HE DON'T BELONG HERE,
HE'S MEXICAN

And then, too early in the morning, while the Kids sleep, a door opens. Voices. Hard boots pound on wood floors and come closer. "Well, look at this. What have we here?"

Fritz jumps up. "Who are you? What do you want?"

"No, no. We're gonna ask the questions. Who in the hell are you?"

For a quick second Fritz looks for something to grab. Then he sees the two young men are both wearing camouflage jackets and holding rifles. The girls scramble to stand up, keeping their sleeping bags wrapped around them.

Looks of disbelief on both sides. The men were hoping to snatch someone. The Kids wanted to stay asleep.

It's dim, not yet daybreak. They stare. And they stare back. There is a light switch, but no electricity. All the players stay frozen in place. The situation remains incoherent.

Brazen Roxy tries a gambit. "I need to get dressed. Can you guys move into the kitchen, please?"

Nothing. The young men, just a couple of years older than the Kids, don't move.

Roxy presses. "Hey, you guys hard of hearing? I want to get dressed."

If there were a clock, the ticking would now be oppressive, tick . . . tick . . . tick . . . tick . . . tick . . . tick. Then one, unnerved by the ticking, pulls the other by the arm, and they both stomp into the kitchen.

Roxy gets dressed quickly, and steps into the kitchen with bare feet. "Got a few leftover donuts from yesterday. Want any?"

"No. Who are you? What are you doing here?" The other: "Did you see a Mexican guy with a kid?"

"Well, I wish I had more to offer you, but I don't."

The others move cautiously towards the kitchen, but remain standing just outside. Roxy points and introduces them. "This is my twin brother, Fritz, and these are my sisters, Izzy and Zoom. I'm Roxy. We're unarmed. After you place your rifles outside, come back in and introduce yourselves."

The men are nonplussed. The clock starts ticking again, tick . . . tick . . . tick . . . They are unsure of what to do.

"Go ahead," Roxy says. "We can talk, but no guns."

Tick . . . tick. One grabs both rifles, walks out the door, comes right back in.

Roxy smiles. She disarmed them.

"Hey," one of the men says, "we've got nothing against you. We're looking for a Mexican. We think he stayed in one of the abandoned houses around here."

It's still Roxy. "Who are you guys? What are your names?"

"I'm Joe, and this is my brother Jeb."

"Hi Joe, hi Jeb. We're traveling through. We couldn't find a campground. So we found this house. Do you know how long it's been empty?"

"Look, I'm asking and you're not answering. Jeb, maybe you should get your rifle and look around. Maybe they're hiding something."

Izzy steps into the kitchen. "He's not here. Why are you looking for him? What did he do?"

"He's a fricking Mexican. A dammed illegal. He stole food from our grocery store in broad daylight."

"How much? I mean, how many dollars' worth?"

"Oh, probably about 20 bucks."

Izzy now tries her own gambit. She walks into the living room, goes to her backpack, comes back. "Here, here's $20."

"What? No, you don't have to pay. He's the guy who stole the food."

"Yeah, but we helped him eat it last night."

"What? You mean . . . ? Right here . . . ? With you . . . ?"

Joe and Jeb are local vigilantes. Outsiders beware. Well, maybe not all outsiders.

"You mean that Mexican was here last night, and you're okay?"

"Yeah, we found him here when we entered the house."

"When did he leave?"

"Well, like I said, he shared the food he had with us, and he was going to leave during the night. Said he wanted to be safe. He had a really nice son, probably about six. Pretty shy, though."

"I can't believe you stayed with him, slept here. He probably stole some of your stuff."

"Well, he didn't steal my wallet. Maybe he took a pair of socks."

Joe and Jeb's faces are stone cold. What do you do when your expectations keep getting iced up?

Fritz steps in from the outside. He boiled some water on his camping stove. "Come on out. You get a choice, hot chocolate or instant coffee." Bare feet scamper out. Boots follow. Zoom brings her drawing pad outside, sits down where she can see everyone.

"So you guys are hunting a guy because he stole food?"

"Yeah, he stole, but it's more than that. He don't belong here. He's Mexican."

Joe is a big guy with broad shoulders. Says he's 21, a good-looking kid in need of a haircut. He wears a red MAGA hat—Make America Great Again—that seems a size too small. His brother is 19 and has a sense of humor. He wears his MAGA hat backwards. He says it stands for Americans Gung-ho Against Mexicans. "Get it? It's kind of a joke," he adds.

"Where are you from, by the way?"

"We're from up north, from St. Paul."

"He's probably also headed north like the others. Probably steal some more."

"Well, maybe. I gave Diego my parents' address. He can stop there and rest. He told us he's headed for Canada."

"You're trying to help a Mexican? Who steals?"

"Yeah, he stole food. He must have been hungry."

"Hey, what's your sister doing?"

"She's drawing. Maybe she's drawing you."

"Can you show me?"

"I'm not done yet, but you can come here to have a look."

"Holy crap, that's us. Man, and you can tell the difference between me and Jeb. Why am I aiming my rifle?"

"At first I thought you were going to shoot us cause we're trespassing or something."

"Sorry about that. I've never shot anybody. Only aimed at Mexicans, but never shot at one."

Izzy asks, "Well, is there a good place in town to get breakfast? Maybe you guys can join us?"

"Yeah, the best place is Greta's. In fact, we gotta head over there now. We both work there. You can't miss it on Main Street. Just look for the biggest American flag right in front." Jeb adds, "Maybe we can make up for scaring you guys and get you a free breakfast."

After Joe and Jeb leave, Roxy is confused. "I thought we were gonna eat here and then continue . . . "

"Yeah, we're still going," responds Izzy. "But let's see what this town is all about. I have an idea. Let's pack and go. I'll tell you all about it."

Greta's restaurant. It's a simple place, a counter and a bunch of tables. There's still a good breakfast crowd. The Kids find an empty table in a corner.

Joe comes to their table smiling. No guns. No boots thudding ominously. Only camo pants. "Hey, glad you made it. I asked my aunt, and, yeah, you can eat for free."

"Your aunt?"

"Yeah, she owns the place."

After a good and free breakfast, and after the breakfast crowd is mostly gone, they have a freewheeling conversation. Joe is the waiter. He works the tables and behind the counter. Jeb works in the kitchen. Both were born here, and they'll die here. "It's not a bad place to live," says Jeb.

"Yeah, we got everything we want. We just don't want others to steal it," adds Joe.

Izzy wants to know, "Do you have everything you need?"

"Yeah, I think so."

"So what about the empty houses? Why aren't they occupied?"

Their aunt comes wearing a camo apron and rolled-up shirt sleeves. She is a woman about 60. Her hair must have been colored brown some time ago because the hair close to her scalp is all gray. Maybe she's trying to look special for an event because her hair is also rolled up into curlers.

She starts to talk and has difficulty stopping. "Hi, I'm Greta and this here's my restaurant and you can call me Aunt Greta 'cause everybody else around here does and whatdoya think of this place 'cause I just fixed it up and I put some new fancy decor on the walls and we got more customers now and that means more business and that's also good for Joe and Jeb and they're good workers and I hear you guys slept in the old Mueller house and Joe tells me you were actually forced to be with a vagrant Mexican and I hope you're not gonna get sick—"

Izzy interjects, "We should be okay—"

"—well I hope so 'cause the Mexicans are sickos especially the men and they're all socialists 'cause they take whatever they want and it don't matter who owns it 'cause they think everything belongs to everybody and you can't trust 'em and they steal kids especially—"

Izzy: "But—"

"—as I was sayin', they steal kids especially little girls those sonofabitches and they don't have no steady jobs 'cause they just work for a couple of weeks and then quit and move on and when they're out of money they maybe work another couple of weeks or maybe they just steal and every time I see one they're dirty 'cause they don't like to wash off the damn germs they carry and maybe everyone is always sick in Mexico and that's why they come here and in this town we want to get rid of 'em right away 'cause—"

Izzy: "But—"

"—lemme finish 'cause we don't wanna be infected with no germs and about a month ago we had an epidemic here from a Mexican 'cause he came here and brought germs and our doctor died a while ago most probably of old age 'cause there wasn't nothin' wrong with him and so I recalled a recipe from my grandma and I cooked it and served it right here in my restaurant and healed a lot of people with chicken soup and white willow bark 'cause that is the medicine my grandma used and poor grandma she's buried right here in our cemetery and I gotta go into the kitchen to have a smoke."

Aunt Greta speaks in a scratchy monotone, not unlike a five-year-old forced to scratch on the violin. Izzy contorts her face; it looks like she's lost the ability to speak.

Roxy had wandered off earlier. She comes back and says she saw a picture of a man with brown skin hung over a dartboard near the bathroom. Joe, with a hint of reflection, says, "Well, Aunt Greta pretty much hates Mexicans."

Joe and Jeb have to get ready for the lunch crowd. Fritz wants to have a look at that dartboard. Izzy and Roxy take a tour through the restaurant looking at the stuff hanging everywhere. The sense of Americana in this restaurant is obvious. Besides the huge American flag outside, Izzy and Roxy examine photos of a couple of presidents, Reagan and one of the Bushes; a picture of an American flag with the word "Freedom" above; a framed photo of four handsome young men in military uniforms, smiling, with arms around each other's shoulders, along with four signatures on the bottom.

The girls move on to look at numerous plaques and framed statements, both offensive and corny:

"I'm obnoxious. So what?"

A picture of a brown face with the inscription, "I've got many problems, but none are mine. I stole 'em all."

A small basket on the counter with this sign, "It'll taste butter if you tip better."

A framed picture featuring close-up photos of a bald angry male beside a bare butt with the comment, "Duck, shit coming."

A framed stitched heart with the inscription, "Bless your heart."

A photocopied sheet of paper pinned to the wall, "My wife gets exhausted from watching me do everything."

A drawing of an ear of corn with the inscription, "Wanna hear a corny joke?"

A large poster depicting various camouflage styles suggesting camo chic.

And finally, a caricature of the Big Guy with bricks, a trowel, and mortar, "Fuck y'all. I'll build it myself."

Back at the table they are joined by Joe, Jeb, and Aunt Greta. "Me and the boys been talking 'cause you think different about Mexicans, and I wanna know—"

"Stop! Stop! I want to say something," Izzy almost yells. That stops Greta. "Aunt Greta, we're not from here, we're outsiders, but . . . but by helping us with food today, you showed you are kind. So, thank you."

Aunt Greta can't stand still. Every few seconds she shifts her weight from one foot to the other, kind of shifting in place. Perhaps she is not used to listening. Aunt Greta stops shifting and is about to speak, but Izzy raises her hand. "No, not yet." Then with more confidence, "Yesterday someone else was kind. His name is Diego. Just like you, he gave us food."

"But he stole it."

"Stealing is better than starving." Izzy is sure of herself. "Okay, he stole it. But once he had it, he didn't have to share it."

"You're giving the Mexican too much credit because—"

"Well, I think it's a little bit like the bread and fish story in the Bible. Who knows where the food came from, but it fed a lot of hungry people."

It's unclear whether Aunt Greta agrees; she looks a little puzzled.

Izzy finishes, "I bet, yeah, I bet the next time a Mexican comes scrambling through town hungry, I bet that if you give him a free meal, he'd wash the dishes for you."

Aunt Greta leaves again for a smoke. Zoom asks if Joe and Jeb smoke. "Nah, we tried it back when we were teens," says Jeb. "We don't wanna wheeze like Aunt Greta."

Aunt Greta is gone just a single cigarette's length, you can see her exhaling smoke as she comes towards them. Get ready, get set, go!

"Been thinking about our town and what we need 'cause it's good here but it's not perfect and I want to get right down to the point 'cause that's the best way to do it we need some new blood how would you young people like to come live here 'cause it's most definitely a good place and maybe you can even stay at the Mueller house temporarily of course only until we can find you a permanent place a little later and—"

Zoom looks worried. "Permanent? What do you mean?"

"—you didn't let me finish young lady and we got a number of young men here really good young men and they are hard workers and know what's right who are looking for wives my nephew Joe for example he'd be a darn good catch 'cause he's got a good job right now and he might inherit this restaurant some day and you three gals could do pretty well and for the young man we've got a couple of pretty young gals Joe and Jeb's cousins with his looks he could probably get the one he wants and these gals aren't libbers no sir 'cause we raise our women right in this town and they're gonna make a darn good home for him."

Four teenagers have their mouths open . . .

Aunt Greta keeps her foot on the gas. "I know I'm being forward but that's the ways I am and if this is a bit sudden for you just go ahead and think about it a bit and the two of you are certainly old enough to marry and the younger one might wait a year you'd have a good life here think about it."

She leaves because she has to get ready for the lunch crowd and probably needs another smoke.

Joe and Jeb, still there, remain silent. Are they embarrassed by their aunt's bluntness? There is a clock on this wall, it doesn't tick, but let's make it tick anyway, tick . . . tick . . . tick . . . tick . . . tick . . . tick. The ticks, spaced equally apart, are unnerving. It takes a lot of ticks before Izzy can regain composure, an eternity when individuals remain silent. "Ah, your aunt is really something. Ah . . . so why don't you guys move to a city? There'd be more opportunity there."

Joe takes a few seconds to respond. "Every once in a while, a guy from here does that. They don't all come back, but those that do say they didn't like it." He stops, seems to reflect. "You know what we like about this town? Things are calm, things pretty much stay the same, things stay conservative. I like that."

"You like the continuity, right? No big changes. No earthquakes, right?" Izzy continues, "I just turned voting age and I'm excited to vote at the next opportunity. Do you think that is a good idea? I mean, do you think women should vote?"

"Of course. Women are people. They should vote."

"But your great-great-grandfather, he probably didn't want women to vote. He wanted women to be tethered to the house like cattle. If he got wind of your opinion, he'd flip over in his grave. Compared to him you're a flaming liberal."

It looks as if Izzy took the rug right out from under Joe and Jeb. They fall down and land on their butts, and along with the rug she also took their speech. Down on the ground they look confused. "There's also another big change. You guys have decided not to smoke like your aunt."

The lunch crowd is building. In no time the place is crowded, and Joe and Jeb have to work again. Just about everyone wears camouflage, not just the men, also the women. The door opens and a couple walks in with two kids, probably kindergarten age, also dressed in camouflage. Fritz makes quick flippant comments. "Man, those kids are ugly. In camo they can hide from their parents." And, "Besides caskets, undertakers here also offer a variety . . . "

"Fritz, stop!"

But Fritz can't stop himself. "Maybe it's a way to hide from the grim reaper." He thinks a moment, then adds, "Seriously, though, I think camouflage unites them. When I was a kid, I had dreams about humans working and moving like ants. Camo is like the chemical scent ants use to identify members of their colony." Fritz, who used to be able to see beyond the horizon, has transposed that ability into a knack for expressing insight.

The kids are getting stares. Izzy says quietly, "Let's get out of here. I'm getting the creeps."

Back in their car, they move on, but definitely not back to the same house. They drive away from town in a daze.

It stays quiet in the van until Roxy mentions the black hole. "Remember, Diego warned us. Don't you think crazy Aunt Greta tried to suck us in?"

"Whaddya mean?"

"She wanted us to stay. And if we'd stayed, we could become like her."

Fritz wakes up and laughs. "Yeah, pretty soon you might be wearing fatigues."

"No way, don't even joke about that."

Zoom says, "Yeah, crazy Greta is most definitely in a black hole. But what about Joe and Jeb?" She pauses, perhaps waiting for a comment from the others, then adds, "Sure, they were chasing Diego, but it might just be wannabe macho rather than serious aggression."

Izzy at the wheel pulls off the road and stops.

"Why are we stopping?"

"Did you see something?"

Izzy leans on the steering wheel and looks straight ahead through the windshield. "I've been thinking, and I want to make sure my thoughts are clear."

She shuts off the motor. "We found an abandoned house, found a guy scared, running with his kid. We woke up with guns in our faces, went into town, got a glimpse of life there." The air conditioning is off, so Izzy opens the window. "We met a woman. A crazy woman." Izzy stops. She corrects herself. "No, she's not crazy, she's not a bad person, she treated us to breakfast."

"But would she offer that to someone with dark skin?" That's Zoom asking.

"No. No, she would not." Izzy turns her head and looks through the open window, and sees what? Just a blur of trees on the other side of the road.

"So, how is Diego different from us?" She pauses in between the next several sentences. "He's from the tropics . . . His skin is brown to protect him from the sun . . . Greta does not understand that . . . She's not wicked, she's misinformed . . . And misinformed means she has wrong information."

Izzy is getting at something. You can tell by the position of the three others. They are at the edge of their seats leaning in towards her.

"And Joe and Jeb, they're not wicked either . . . They chase Mexicans because their father and grandfather probably did it . . . They don't think about it . . . They do it because that's the way things are done . . . Maybe it's a tradition."

"But tradition is supposed to be a good thing? I mean, we have festivals in St. Paul that honor the traditions of the different people who live there."

"Yeah, wearing the folk costume of the country you're from is nice, but still putting real candles on a Christmas tree is stupid . . . And just because spanking is the way kids were disciplined in the past doesn't mean we should do it today . . . I suppose traditions change gradually . . . But Joe and Jeb should jump off of their tradition bandwagon."

Roxy: "Come to think of it, Greta was trying to arrange marriages for us."

Izzy: "And all of us, we could tell, I mean I certainly felt creepy, I couldn't take it, I wanted to escape."

Zoom adds, "Yeah, we ran. We ran away, didn't we?"

Izzy is intense. "Next time we must stay . . . We must overcome our fear and do what is right . . . Forget the black hole . . . Next time . . . We engage."

She starts the car and speeds off.

16

ART THAT ENGAGES

They find a little wayside and stop to have a late lunch. Fritz takes charge of making a fire. They are going to eat sandwiches, but s'mores would be a nice addition. Fritz holds up a match. "I've only got one match. It's do or die."

Roxy counsels him. "Don't use paper and cheat."

While Fritz is on a self-imposed critical quest for dry tinder, the girls chat.

Zoom says she liked a couple of things Izzy said. She mentions the word "engage." She tells Izzy she likes that word. "You used it in the car. You said, 'Next time we engage.'"

"Oh, yeah, definitely."

Zoom didn't leave her drawing of Joe and Jeb even though Joe wanted it. "I didn't feel good about it. It was just a drawing of them, a simple representation."

"Well, what's wrong with that?"

"It didn't engage. I want more. They liked it because it looked like them. It made them feel good, but I want more."

Fritz is ready and wants everyone's attention. He holds up a single match. "Watch this." He lights his match, but . . . but . . . but. But he has a backup plan. "Okay, we're in the wilderness, I'm out of matches, but I happen to have a mirror. Let's see if that can save us."

Izzy and Zoom continue their conversation. Zoom wishes she

had added something interesting to her drawing. "I would love to have something hanging on their restaurant wall. But it would have to be something that engages, makes a statement, maybe changes things there. You know what I mean?"

"Yeah, you want your art to say something, to make a difference. We fled, but a little memento from you on their wall that makes them think would be good."

"Yeah. Exactly. That's what I want."

"What's the other thing I said that you liked?"

"I liked your reference to the bread and fish story. That's quite a story, isn't it? It's completely different from my drawing of Joe and Jeb. I mean, a couple of fish and a pound of bread feeding many. Definitely a tall tale. And it's so effective.

"Imagine if the man had organized an assembly line of fishermen, an assembly line of fish cleaners, and an assembly line of bakers. He might have become known as a master of efficiency, but not a master with magical powers. His feat would get a couple of paragraphs in a book on the history of engineering. But no, the Bible author added magic to make the story compelling.

"So, my drawing of Joe and Jeb is like holding up a mirror to them. It's simply reflecting what I see. But the bread and fish story is not just reflecting, it's adding a creative spark. And that creative spark makes the difference."

Izzy adds, "Maybe the Bible is the first example of magical realism."

Roxy doesn't know what that is. "Well, it's a tale where real things plus magic things that can't happen in real life are mixed into an entertaining story."

"But the Bible is supposed to be real, right?"

"Hey, quick. I'm about to get a flame with the mirror. Look! Look! There it is!" Fritz has also been listening to the girls' conversation. Here's the proof. As he nurtures the fire, he tells Zoom, "But the mirror alone doesn't work, it just reflects. It needs another ingredient, energy. That's the magic. The mirror plus sunlight can create a spark and change things."

"Hey, that's really cool, Fritz. My picture of Joe and Jeb with guns needs energy."

Izzy suggests, "Maybe a wind that blows flowers into their faces. Maybe a Mexican standing in front of them offering a loaf of bread and a fish."

"One day I want to paint something important," says Zoom. "I want my art to make people think, to tell a story that engages. When I get back home, I'm going to paint an entire wall in our house. Maybe two walls. Then invite people in to my own museum."

17

THIS NEWSPAPER STRIVES TO MAKE PEOPLE FEEL GOOD

Back into the minivan and onto the road again. Their aim is to explore the American heartland. Where is it? Did they miss it? They arrive in a town with at least one traffic light. The light is red. As they wait, Fritz watches a man limping to a door. He unlocks the door and steps inside. Fritz notices the sign, City Sentinel. "Hey look, this town has a newspaper. Let's go see if there is any news."

The storefront is interesting enough. A couple of unusual windows, narrow and rounded at the top. Above the windows is a representation of the Statue of Liberty with the word "liberty" on one side and "freedom" on the other. It almost resembles the facade of a church. Roxy tries the door. Is it open? Yep, it is, and the four Kids stare into a slightly darkened room. "Hi, we're from out of town and are just curious."

"Well . . . please, come on in."

The Kids step inside and see a man in a white shirt and tie behind a desk. "If you have an idea for a story, there's a form on the counter. If you want to buy this week's paper, see the stack on the other side. It'll be a dollar. Help yourself."

Izzy asks, "What kind of stories are you looking for?"

"Well, whatever people want to read. Where you from?"

"We're from St. Paul."

"Oh, old St. Paul. I lived there in a previous life. You're far from home. What are you doing here?"

"We're traveling through. Actually, we want to explore the American heartland."

"Well . . . you're close." He's friendly. Smiles. "Where are you kids staying?"

"We don't know yet. Either an abandoned house or a camping spot."

"Well . . . I still have to finish some work. But you can stay at my house. I've got an empty bedroom."

The Kids get his address, head there, and wait in the yard. Roxy looks forward to talking to someone who lived "in old St. Paul. Let's see what he has to say."

But that's not Izzy's focus. "Forget about that. I'm interested in the newspaper. What does he print, and why?"

When he arrives, he shows the Kids the bedroom. "I'm very sorry," he says, "as you can see, there's only one bed. Three of you will have to sleep on the rug."

"That's okay. We'll be fine. But you said it's empty. Someone's obviously living here."

Roxy notices photos of soccer players on the wall. "Is this your son's room?"

"He's not here."

He limps back out of the room.

Roxy asks, "Why are you limping? Did you get hurt?"

"Oh . . . I tripped over something."

They spend some time talking. His name is Doyle. He went to college in St. Paul.

Roxy wants to know, "Did you like your time in St. Paul?"

"Well . . . I don't look back often, but I do suppose it was kind of a golden, glassy era."

"What do you mean?"

"A city for dreamers. Lots of soap bubbles. Problems? What

problems? Everything was going to get better. It snowed and people wore shorts. Nothing could keep smiles off people's faces."

After a few seconds he adds, "You know . . . it was embarrassingly liberal."

"Oh."

"But sometimes I think about what happened to me."

Now Izzy takes over. "What do you mean? What happened?"

"Well . . . you know . . . reality set in."

He's probably in his mid-forties, but when he talks, he sounds older. His words come out slow, methodical. After he says "well," he pauses before going on. His hair is short, turning gray, with a part on his left side. He looks like the businessman he is. His name in St. Paul was Freddy. Who knows, maybe he spoke faster then. He changed his name to Doyle after he came here. "Well . . . I had to adapt."

"Why did you come here?"

"You know, after graduation I roamed around a bit. Maybe kinda like you're doing. I found a job at this here newspaper, and, well . . . before I knew it, I bought it."

"And you changed your name?"

"Well . . . no . . . not right away.

"The paper was doing okay, but, as it turned out, I was still foolish. I hadn't grown up yet, and I wanted to make changes."

"What kind of changes did you make?"

"Well . . . the liberal bubbles from St. Paul hadn't popped off yet. They made me change the contents, change the tone."

"When did you change your name?"

"After I published the cat article. Well . . . at first I wrote articles with the intent to stimulate, address some social issues—poverty, for instance. But sales declined, advertising declined, my investment was threatened. I had to mature fast. And, you know . . . I did. I popped my bubbles. I changed my name. I grew a thick conservative skin."

He gets up, limps to a bookcase, brings back a sizable scrapbook. He opens it to the first page and points to a newspaper article featuring a large photo of a cat with several paragraphs underneath. "That article turned things around."

"An article about a cat?"

"Yep. Somebody brought in a photo of a cat along with a typical cat story. You know . . . I thought about it for a while. Then I put the cat picture on the front page and sales spiked."

Fritz wants to know, "What, cats appeal to conservatives and dogs to liberals?"

The Kids chuckle, but Doyle does not. "No, no, that's not it. You give the people what they want. I mean, if people want a basic hamburger, don't try to sell them a bowl of lettuce. If people want to indulge in cute and cuddly, don't make them read complex stuff. That's the lesson I learned."

"So how is your paper doing now?"

"Well . . . even better than when I bought it. People buy it. Advertisers support it. I'm doing quite well. That's the most significant thing, right?" He stops for a moment, then adds, "I know that's not important to you yet, but someday it will be. You'll learn."

No doubt, the Kids have heard this type of mild admonition before. Who hasn't? The warning tends to knock a person down a notch; it usually stops the conversation. What is the one with less experience supposed to say to "you'll learn"?

Doyle has to step out, and while he's gone Izzy spews out her venom. "Such stupid guidance. Just because they've been around longer, they think they are wiser. But is it wisdom, or is it the result of some defeat? Maybe his hopes and dreams popped."

When Doyle returns, he says that he will have to leave soon. He has to attend a meeting. "I won't be gone long. You can just stay here."

But he wants to build on his previous comments. "We were talking about success, right? Well . . . success is key. You know, they consider me to be an important patriot in the community. I'm involved in quite a few things. I help make decisions about the future of this city. At the next opportunity I plan to run for mayor." He now adds a chuckle with his mouth open so the Kids can see his teeth. They don't chuckle. It seems to be an awkward moment.

Izzy asks again, "What kind of articles do you print?"

"Well . . . like I already said, stuff that people want to read."

Izzy is persistent. "What kind of stuff is that?"

Roxy adds, "My sister might want to become a writer someday. That's why she is asking."

"What do people want? Well, first of all, we inform with community news, weddings, funerals, births. But the thing is, my readers, they want to be entertained."

"But isn't that just basic stuff? How can it be entertaining?" Izzy asks.

"Of course, you have to write that article a certain way. Facts don't entertain. I also feature articles about church stuff, local sports, with longer articles if our team wins. And you probably know that readers respond positively to crime stories, emotional stories like the cat story, happy stories about someone winning a prize. I use photos of people involved in community events smiling for the camera, women holding bake sales, men fishing."

Izzy asks her key question. "Do you also use your newspaper to educate?"

"Well, my job is not to teach. In order for my newspaper to be successful, the articles I print must make my readers feel good. And they feel good when their response to an article is 'I totally agree with that.' You know, people want their opinions reflected. That's the kind of news that engages them."

Zoom perks up upon hearing the word "engages."

Izzy wants to know if there are Mexicans in town. And do they ever make the paper?

"Sure, there are some Mexicans in town. And sure, every so often I include a photo of Mexicans. But, you know, the photos of people with brown skin are different." He flashes his open-mouth chuckle again. "The sun never shines in those photos. And they are always of a larger group that includes something messy, say, a dirty kid."

"You never print pictures of single Mexicans?"

"No, only as mug shots." His face becomes tight and cold.

"I guess you mean like this picture." Fritz holds up the current *Sentinel* and points to the photo of a brown-skinned individual. "Why is he on the front page?"

"That mug shot engages the reader. The guy was caught stealing. The emotional effect on the reader is a little bit like the cat picture."

Zoom is perplexed about the use of his word "engage." She says, "Okay, I draw and paint, and I want to become an artist. But I want my art to engage, to make the viewer think. You know what I mean?"

Fritz adds, "She wants her art to include a spark."

"Here is what creates a spark with my readers." He reaches for his scrapbook and shows Zoom some photos with articles of artwork.

Zoom takes the scrapbook and flips the pages. She sees a drawing of an abandoned farm, a painting of a big blue sky with tufty clouds, a couple of pictures of vintage cars, a nice still life of an old gas station, a number of scenes with American flags.

"See, those pictures engage, they bring back memories, they make the viewer feel good."

Zoom just frowns.

"But, young lady, this is the kind of art people like. This is what's hanging in the barber shop, at the dentist office, in restaurants. And, most important, the artists are making a living."

Izzy wants to know if he would publish a poem she just wrote.

"Let me read it."

Izzy pulls two pages out of her pocket, unfolds them, and gives them to him. While he reads to himself, each of the Kids watch his face, watch his expressions. Especially Izzy is curious to see his reaction. He folds up the sheets again and hands them back to Izzy without a trace of emotion. "Well, look, camo is a means of bonding. People wear camo here to show they are on the same team. They believe in the same things. If I'd publish your poem, the people here would chase me back to bubblemania in St. Paul."

For the benefit of the reader, here is Izzy's poem. She calls it "Camouflage Calamity."

That guy is wearing camo
A wannabe military dude
It allows him to be macho
And hardcore rude

That gal is wearing camo
Catch me if you can
Hiding in broad daylight
From her militarized man

That kid is wearing camo
Being trained to disguise
Mislead and conceal
To avoid truth and tell lies

Even the baby is wearing camo
Is it a laugh or a cry
Use the nibbler in shape of a bullet
The NRA can resupply

The town is bedecked in camo
Can't tell the bank from the bar
Where to drink or borrow money
They look the same from afar

The food is shaped like camo
You've got no idea what you eat
Are you eating green slime
Or brown fatigue meat

Confusion is rampant
Disguise is everywhere
Can't tell a bucket from a hole
It's hard to compare

They've even disguised the kitchen
Is this a sieve or a pot
And the water faucet
Where is cold, where is hot

Besides visual camo
There is camo for you to smell
Your nose can't tell the difference
It's all burned shit from hell

With brains inscribed with camo
Self-deception is the rule
Trying to get facts
Is too tiring and mentally cruel

If language is marked in camo
And words are used to disguise
We're in trouble, my friend
We can't tell truth from lies.

He leaves for his meeting. The Kids go to the room and have to figure out who gets the bed and which three of them do not. Even though he's gone, they talk about Doyle and his newspaper in hushed voices. They're almost whispering. They don't like him. Roxy asks, "Did you see his teeth? When he talks, he moves his lips without opening his mouth much, and when he smiles his mouth stays closed. Except for those two times, it looked like he had fangs."

There's a knock on the window. The window is open; they hear a voice through the screen. "He sold out. That's what he did."

18

JAKE AND THE FAIRY CIRCLE OF MUSHROOMS

The reader needs some help here. The voice at the window to end the last chapter is Doyle's son, Mickey. His name used to be Homer, but he changed it. The conflict between father and son is basic. Doyle became a realist; he adapted to survive. His son is an idealist.

The Kids meet Mickey at the front door. No, he doesn't want to come in. He wants them to come with him to his place. "We have to leave before it gets dark."

He sits in front and gives Izzy, at the wheel, directions. In the van he corrects himself. "It's not my place, but I'm staying there."

He speaks fast, has a lot he wants to share. "Mickey's my third name. I was born as Dylan. After a few years he changed my name to Homer."

"Oh no, why did he do that?"

"It was soon after he ran the story about the cat. He showed you the article, didn't he? He shows it to everyone." He quickly adds, "I never liked my name, but I hated it when I became a teenager. So, about a year ago, I dropped it and became Mickey."

"So why are you not living at home?"

"We got into a fight, him and me. As I struggled with my name more and more, we argued about his newspaper. He wanted me to get involved, probably take it over some day, but I could see that it was a dumbing device. I was developing my own ideas about life, and I was moving further away from his. He always talked about bubbles, said that they were starting to stick to me. So one day things got severe. We pushed and shoved each other, and he fell down some stairs. That's when I moved out."

Roxy mentions that he said he tripped over something.

"Yeah, he says that." They drive along a dirt road still muddy from the last rainfall. Mickey points to a wooden structure and says, "That's it. You can leave the car right here. We're the last shack, and no one ever comes this far." He smiles and seems pleased.

Roxy looks, and grimaces. "This is what you've been talking about? It's tiny. Looks like gnomes used to live there."

Fritz has to laugh. "And they left because it could collapse with the next breeze."

"Come on, bring your sleeping bags."

As the Kids get things out of the car, Mickey moves ahead. They hear him yell, "I'm back. I've brought some friends." A German Shepherd comes to greet them, tail wagging.

Zoom grabs her backpack and says to no one in particular, "I'm gonna draw a picture of this. Call it 'The good old days,' and submit it to the newspaper."

An old man sits in front of the dilapidated structure under a slanted and shabby roof in what looks like a porch. He calls his dog, has him sit. He says, "Welcome," and releases his dog again to smell them.

The old man has the look of a sage with his longish gray hair hanging like tangled vines and a scraggly gray beard like dried moss all around his face. Izzy looks dumbfounded. Like the others, she stands in front of the shack, in front of the old man. She says, "Hello," and stares.

He must have seen visitors stare at him before. "No, this is not a fairy tale, and no, I'm not a sage. When you are older and you've lived in nature for a while, you don't look like a manicured lawn, you start to look natural, maybe a little wild. People then seem to think you have some special insight into the secrets of life."

"After the fight with my father, I met Jake and I've lived here since." Mickey adds, "Jake comes here every year to escape what he calls 'the persistent pressure of civilization.'"

Roxy is incredulous. "You come here, to this place, to escape?"

He speaks clearly. "I do. I come here for the seclusion. I'm able to let go here. Don't shave. Don't have a schedule. Don't do news. Skip the internet." He has a soft laugh. "My culture degrades fast. I turn into a weed and grow in unpredictable directions."

Still, no one moves.

"If you keep standing there holding your backpacks and staring at me, I'll think you are tourists. Come on, put your things down under the roof here. Let's get to know each other. And since it will get dark soon, we'll need a fire. Any volunteers?"

That generates movement. The Kids put their stuff down and introduce themselves. Fritz volunteers. "I'm good at making a fire."

Numerous stumps function as chairs. Zoom and Izzy gaze at the surroundings.

Roxy again. "What do you do here?"

"I write. I read. I spend a lot of time alone. I'm in the woods a lot." Jake is direct and uncomplicated.

"And do you, like, have a regular home?"

"This is my home for about half a year. I also have a house on the outskirts of a city."

"What do you do there?"

"When I return there, I become civilized again, at least to an acceptable level. I shave. I get a haircut. I behave. I act like others. I express opinions again, maybe I argue, maybe I offer advice."

"You don't express your opinions here?"

"Here we talk, like we're talking now. I might say something, but I don't have to win, or have the last word. The tightness of society doesn't pressure us here. Here things are uncomplicated and loose."

"You're saying you act differently depending on where you are?"

"We're at the edge of civilization here. We throw off the so-called norms, the cage of dos and don'ts, the fake smiles, the little lies, the competition, fashion, and all that it implies. We listen to each other."

Roxy is forward. "How old are you?"

He tilts his head and asks, "Why do you think that's important?"

Before Roxy can respond, Mickey says Jake is as old as some of the trees here. "We'd have to cut one down to count the rings. If the tree rots, we'll never find out."

"But you must be older than all of us put together. Shouldn't we listen to your opinions? Shouldn't you be giving us advice?"

"Sure, I'm older. That means I've lived longer. I've seen more things. But that doesn't mean I should give you advice. All of us here, the others who sometimes come here, we all have different experiences, different backgrounds, different abilities, and because of that we also have different ideas. Age is a factor, but not the only one."

The Kids listen. This is something they haven't heard before.

"I wish I could tell you how to live, what to do, make it easier for you. But all I can tell you about are my experiences during my time."

"But doesn't that mean you know more, and that you should give us advice?

"Your name is Roxy, right? Roxy, I like you. Some people are too intimidated to ask questions." He goes on. "You're living in a completely different era. You're involved in things today I don't understand. Let me exaggerate. I come from the horse and buggy era. You are close to doing mental telepathy. Maybe wisdom worked in the past when changes were slow. Today the only suggestions I can give you are to educate yourselves, stay nimble, and grab all the luck you can reach."

Izzy jumps in. "If I tell you about a problem I have and ask you what I should do, what would you say?"

"I would say, let's look at some options. And if you would ask me which option to choose, I would say, 'Oh, I don't know. Your instincts are probably good.'"

Izzy likes that answer. "I really don't like older people always wanting to give me advice. Like Doyle. It's irritating. 'You'll learn,' or 'you'll change,' or 'you should do this,' or 'you should do that.' Or, worst of all, 'Just wait till you get older.'"

By now the sun has set. It's dark, and because it's cloudy, it's getting pitch dark. This shack is without electricity, so there are no lights. But the woodpile is substantial, and Fritz keeps the fire going. They don't need the heat, it's warm enough here, but they need the light. The six of them sit on stumps in a circle around the fire. The configuration resembles a fairy circle of mushrooms. They sit far enough away from the fire and from each other that they appear to be apparitions. Their stumps and their bodies are dark, but the light from the fire gives their faces a ghostly glow.

When someone speaks, the voice leaps over the fire. You have to listen carefully to hear where it comes from.

Jake's voice resonates. "It's not often this dark. You might be tempted to think you're inside a fairy tale illuminated by the fire. But we are real. The darkness is only obscuring us."

Mickey's voice scrambles over the fire. "Sometimes others show up."

A mushroom asks, "Who comes?"

"A few come from this town. Couple from farther away. They usually stay for a few days, then leave."

Jake's voice resonates again, "They return home refreshed."

Another mushroom wants to know, "Why do people come? What are they looking for?"

"Those who come here don't want to go through life sleepwalking. We want to be aware, aware of ourselves, aware of our circumstances."

Roxy rises from her stump and comes into focus as she moves to the center. She can now see him, and she addresses him. "You don't want to give advice, but you give, kinda like, general guidelines, like, 'be aware of things.' I wish you'd add details. Details would be helpful." Roxy moves back into the darkness.

"I can't give you specific advice, but I can talk in general about three things that move society."

A mushroom asks, "Is three the magical number from fairy tales? The three little pigs, the three golden rings, three wishes?" That comment probably comes from Fritz.

His voice rings out with an echo: "No . . . no . . . no." And his laughter that follows adds crackle to the fire. "These are simply the things I'm interested in."

Jake continues. "Money. I don't need much money here, but in society you need money. Once you have the essentials, then what? You want more. We humans compete. So we buy a boat, then a bigger boat, and so on. And we work, we keep toiling for more. Maybe many compromise themselves. Like Mickey's father."

The mushrooms remain silent. They listen.

"Reason. Ever since reason gradually replaced dogmatism and superstition after the Middle Ages, things have improved. Reasoning, using information, applying facts, has lengthened our lives, has gotten us to the moon. The Big Guy is an aberration. He's going against the trend.

"Control. From the beginning of civilization, whips controlled the masses. Monuments to rulers were not built willingly. The masters had scepters in one hand and whips in the other. Today various sleep agents have replaced whips as means of control. Feel-good cat stories come to mind. And debt."

He hasn't heard from the mushrooms. "Are you still out there?"

Individual voices respond immediately. "Yes, I'm wide awake."

"I'm listening."

"Go on."

"What do you mean by debt?"

"Debt makes people docile. Debtors with a mortgage are no longer free."

He knows he's talking to college-age mushrooms, so he adds emphasis to his next statements. He uses a hollow wooden log. "College debt is even worse—thump, thump. The natural idealism—thump, thump—of educated youth—thump, thump—gets channeled—thump, thump—gets channeled, I say—thump, thump—into slave work—thump, thump—to pay off the masters. If you owe money, you no longer rebel—thump, thump. You become docile. You become part of the problem—thump, thump. You can't become part of the solution—thump."

No reaction from the mushrooms. Only silence. So he adds this: "I happen to know the four of you are on a mission. So I hope you will engage with society now, when you're young, when you don't have debt, when you have not yet been lured by money, when you are still awake. But I can't tell you what you should pursue."

They hear shuffling on the ground, then the creaking of wood as he must be walking up several steps onto the porch and into his shack.

19

TEARS OF JOY
AS JESUS APPEARS

They leave the next morning with the night's dialogue still thumping. Izzy, driving, says, "We're leaving this town of opposites. It has a newspaper that dumbs its many readers, and a sage few hear."

Zoom, not fully awake yet, adds, "We never went into the shack. I'd like to see the inside."

Roxy wonders where his house is. "Do you think it could also be in St. Paul?"

"But listen to this." That's Fritz. "He says he doesn't give advice. But he told us to do our stuff while we are still young. Isn't that advice?"

"Yeah, he doesn't give specific advice, but he talks about general guidelines. I like him. Wish he would live in St. Paul so I could visit."

They stick to their plan of looking for the heartland. As they meander along rural roads the small towns become more alike. They feature a couple of gas stations plus convenience stores, several churches with and without steeples, and of course bars, numerous bars. Rusted pickup trucks wait in front of bars, like horses tied to hitching posts in the sweet past, for burly men to come back out refreshed.

Their conversation is not encouraging. Fritz is dejected. "There isn't much here. Lots of abandoned farms and empty warehouses. I hope we don't need anything. We'd have the choice of dollar-type stores or pawnshops."

There are also "cash" stores. Izzy knows about them. "They offer to fill your pocket fast with easy money. Repeat next month, except you now owe hefty interest to the frauds."

Roxy wants to know, "Are we still in America?"

"What do kids do here?" asks Fritz. "The only ball field I've seen was overgrown with grass, and I haven't seen a single playground."

No problem spending the night here. There aren't any campgrounds, but the Kids have their choice of deserted houses.

But it looks like people do have some fun. Town residents create their own entertainment and display it with apparent pride. "Jesus Saves" signs are everywhere. Zoom says it must be an "art form down here," because there are so many variations: "Jesus Saves" with flowers on a post in the lawn; "Jesus Saves" above clouds painted on a barn; "Jesus Saves" pasted on small billboards; "Jesus Saves" in flashing colored neon signs that protrude from buildings on Main Street; a boulder on the side of a road features "Jesus Saves" with stars and stripes. Of course, it's only natural that churches highlight "Jesus Saves" in large lettering. And is that a hedge trimmed to form J E S U S S A V E S, or is that an illusion?

Fritz tells the others later he saw a bank with a sign in front that said "Jesus Saves Here."

"Wait," says Roxy. "You're making that up again. I didn't see any banks."

Okay, there might not be many banks where Jesus could keep his money, but "Jesus Saves" is definitely a favorite pronouncement of enthusiastic local artists. They also have thought up clever variations: "Thank You Jesus," "Jesus Is God," "God Hates Sin," "U Need Jesus," "Trust Jesus," "Turn to Jesus," "Jesus Is Coming," "Jesus Is Here," "Jesus Will Judge." Some signs offer prescient advice: "Repent, While There Is Still Time," and "Repent Or Perish." An alarming prophecy, "Hell Is Real." And finally, the rather depressing "The End Is Near."

Fritz wonders, "Any optimists in this American heartland?"

It's Sunday. They see latecomers rush to a church. The service must be about to begin so the Kids step inside to have a look. A conductor energetically directs the ensemble with a long conducting baton. The ensemble consists of several musicians and a few singers. During the service the congregation also sings several hymns. Quite a few people sing with gusto, others seem less than comfortable and mouth the lyrics somewhat accurately.

The highlight, of course, is the sermon. The preacher, a round man, arrives from the back and methodically glad-hands his way to the front of the congregation. Finally, in front of the congregation, he welcomes everybody effusively, but also finds fault because "Some of your neighbors aren't here who need to be here. You gotta make sure everyone, and I mean everyone, from our greater family comes."

From conversing with the audience, he drifts into his sermon. The solid preacher begins with a nugget of solid truth that everyone can agree with. He underscores the rightfulness of that truth by pounding his right fist into his left palm. He quickly speeds up his delivery, his now acrobatic hands fluttering in the air. Beads of sweat roll down his cheeks. A handkerchief emerges. He leaves it in one hand and regularly pats his brow and neck. Despite his size, he is deceptively agile. He skips around, his glistening head swings back and forth, he keeps his mouth open wide to release an avalanche of words that seem to overwhelm his listeners, pushing them back into their pews. His flirty forefinger at the end of his arm points to individuals in the congregation. He first warns, then cajoles them. Then in a hushed voice, he offers his own personal words of wisdom. Finally, bouncing up and down like a huge rubber ball, he rejoices and rolls to the end. He finishes with flair and waves his wet handkerchief around, "Hallelujahhallelujah. H A L L E L U J A H!" His sermon is a great bit of theater with a simple message. It's about Jesus. If you're a sinner, you'd better repent to avoid a hellish descent!

After the service, the friendly and soaked pastor greets the new-comers, wants to know where they are from and invites them to stay for lunch. The Kids go downstairs into a large hall and sit at an empty table. Lunch is nothing noteworthy: chicken, beans, rice, with too much salt. No one joins them at their table. Roxy notices that some of the parishioners look at them with suspicion. "They're whispering about us."

Zoom says, "Well, it's okay, we're outsiders."

After lunch volunteers fold up the tables and arrange the chairs in rows in preparation for the afternoon entertainment. The first activity warms the audience up. It is called "Light My Candle," and the Kids decide they might as well stay for the event. Before they find a seat, Izzy spots several trays that contain something covered with napkins on a side table. As she walks by her eyes begin to tear. She whispers to Zoom, "I might be allergic to something."

When everyone is settled, someone other than the pastor gets up in front, closes his eyes, and ends his prayer with, "Lord Jesus, help our youth find the proper truth, shine your light to help us choose right. Amen." And with that a theatrical afternoon begins.

"Light My Candle" is a weekly event where individuals talk about how their candle is being lit with the help of Jesus. The first individual to volunteer a tale tells a story about how he stole a watch from the pawnshop because he "wanted to impress my new lady." But after a day, or who knows, maybe it was a week, Jesus had spoken to him directly, so he went back to the pawnshop and left 20 dollars on the counter for the owner without saying a word. He adds, "The watch probably wasn't even worth that much." Someone in the audience approves: "Good going, Freddy! Jesus lit your candle."

Next is a woman who wants to share how she "had to help our precious children learn to think." She was visiting her 12-year-old niece who lives in a city. When the "sweet child" came home from school with a book that showed a timeline of the earth with "millions and millions" of years, it set off a storm. The woman, let's call her Stormy, tells her story. "I snatched the book from my niece and right the next morning, still as mad as could be"—she must have huffed and puffed to school—"I burst straight into the classroom and I told the students, 'You're being taught to think wrong. Here, the Bible here'—I held the Bible up so everyone in the classroom could see—'don't need no graphs, don't need no numbers. The Bible just tells the truth 'cause it's the word of God.'" Then, after the storm abated, came the calm. "I could tell from the faces of the innocent kids that I done right. Finally, I told them, I said, 'Thinking ain't that hard. It's easy if you read the Bible,' and they all smiled and nodded their heads, every single one of them."

Apparently, the school principal and a security officer came into the classroom, but she had said what needed to be said and exited the scene all by herself. Immediate applause and support came from the appreciative audience, along with "Ain't that the truth," and "You showed 'em the light."

There are others, but worth mentioning is a man who at first hesitates, then does rise. His eyes move nervously from side to side, he speaks machine gun style, words coming out of his mouth in a burst followed by moments of silence and another burst. He wants everyone to know, "I did wrong. I did wrong. I did so very wrong." Silence. Someone shouts, "What'ya do?" He goes, "I ain't tellin'." Then a quick burst, "I gotta get back to Jesus." There is some murmuring in the room, then another burst, "I gotta be redeemed." His eyes flit about. He takes a deep, deep breath to clear the agony in his gut, then finally says, "I gotta bear the cross." His plan is to make a cross from two-by-fours and carry it on his back from here to the state capital, "But I gotta make it hard." Pause. Pause. Pause. "I gotta walk backwards." Gasps from the audience. Finally, someone says, "He's goin' to do it, I knows it."

But now comes the climax. Are you ready, reader?

Everyone gets up, stretches their legs, and goes to the table to get what's on the tray. By now it's late afternoon. Someone closes all the window shades and the lights are turned off. The room becomes a theater at dusk.

A shadow glides from somewhere to the front and stands facing the believers. It takes a while, perhaps there is some sort of technical problem. Individuals in the audience become restive and shift about in their metal chairs. Finally, a ceiling light does go on directly above the individual. The light illuminates him. He looks just like the textbook picture: wavy brown hair reaching down on both sides of his head to his shoulders, framing a ruddy face with a full, well-kept beard; he wears a long white robe without a collar so that his neck and a portion of his shoulders are visible; an illuminated cross hangs from his neck; and he holds his arms out towards his audience with his hands open. It's Jesus himself! The audience, now sitting at the edge of their chairs, is obviously ready for this performance. The believers lift the napkins with their contents to their faces. Guess what's inside? Half a peeled onion. With the arrival of Jesus, real tears now fall from their watery eyes. The room explodes into a cacophony of sniveling, sobbing, weeping, even excessive bawling. But the crying is not from pain or sorrow. No, these are tears of joy at the second coming of Jesus to judge. These sinners have all repented; their candles have been lit, and so they will be saved for eternity.

Whew! While the believers hyperventilate, the Kids escape to the bright outside. They need fresh air.

20

MALE BONDING AS THE BIG GUY APPEARS

The Kids previously found an empty farmhouse at the edge of town, and they head there to get some relief. Later, in the evening, they intend to go to an event in town they heard about. Just like at home, each of them crawls into a corner of the abandoned living room to be alone. Izzy writes; Zoom takes out her sketch pad; Roxy makes plans; Fritz studies opening moves on his magnetic chessboard, his reliable travel companion. Alone and with silence the mind can rejuvenate.

Roxy is rejuvenated first and starts a conversation. "Hey, what do you guys think about this place?"

While scorn is normally not her style, Izzy blurts out, "Well, for one thing, we'll be the only ones thinking in this town."

Here comes Zoom. "But you know, the feeling I got in that church is that humans are like herd animals. We flock together, dress alike, think alike, act alike. Not just here, maybe everywhere. We are different than these people, but you know, maybe back home we, too, are part of a herd."

"You really think that? We are alike like these people are alike?"

"Yeah. I think that's possible."

Fritz jumps in and calls the people pawns. He says, "They look alike and act alike. These dudes are carrying a lot of excess weight around. Notice how everyone moves slowly, like pawns with magnets attached to their feet on a magnetic chessboard. If I lived here, I'd be a knight or a bishop dashing around."

Izzy adds, "Maybe all the knights and bishops left town, maybe that's why there are so many empty houses."

"Yeah," goes Roxy. "I'd escape also. Leave everything behind, just get outta here."

Back to Izzy. "Talking about the church, though. There doesn't seem much to do here, yet there is a lot going on in church. I think they go to church for fun. Sure, I bet they watch a lot of TV, but the church thingy is live theater. There's a stage with different performers. And what do they do? They entertain."

"Yeah, maybe. The preacher was cool, and the Jesus thing, man, that was dramatic. The only thing missing were some trumpets."

It's early evening and the Kids want to make sure they don't miss the next event. A crowd is already forming down the road in front of a bar. Of course, the bar has a neon sign, "Jesus Saves." Underneath that is also a neon sign that blinks on and off showing a dancing couple, he with a cowboy hat, she with curves. On the other end of the building is a neon image of a cocktail glass.

The crowd consists of men, mostly in their twenties and thirties, but some are older, and they're all in a good mood. Many of the guys wear camouflage, the military uniform for human ants that bond. Maybe once they read the poem Izzy wrote they will condemn the camo clothing to cleaning rags, but don't bet on it.

Drinking outside the bar is officially not allowed, but beer bottles are everywhere, full ones in hands, empty ones on top of a railing and in trash cans. Who's going to enforce an unpopular and antibusiness ordinance?

The kids learn that this event is being sponsored both by this particular bar and a competing church to the one they'd attended.

Fritz didn't know that churches compete. "They're not part of capitalism, are they?"

Izzy corrects him. "Sure they are. In order to pay their bills each church has to market itself. An empty church will go the way of an abandoned farm."

Zoom: "Yeah, I wonder how this church is going to outdo the reappearance of Jesus."

They split up to mingle with the crowd and learn what is going on. The men greet each other with fist bumps, good-natured slaps on backs, and toasts by clanging beer bottles. The crowd is excited. Bits of conversation with an abundance of common words referring to body parts, body function, and body waste spike above the general tumult. And why not, four letter words can't be printed in a newspaper or used on TV, so it feels good to give them a full, uncensored airing out in the open. And similar to camouflage, being crude helps these guys unite.

Your narrator wants to be cute and insists on referring to these as "goofy" terms. These guys, by using goofy terms right here, loud and clear, entertain themselves by proving that they are real men. They relish being loud and give particular emphasis to goofy expressions. In the past, such dudes would have worn leather vests with cowboy hats and displayed six-shooters in holsters, but now they've traded those in for baseball caps and a paunch.

The girls must be careful here. Hands are everywhere, but they will have to learn to assert themselves. The situation for Fritz is different. He's a guy and locals always look at a new guy sideways. He gets a few stares. Someone asks where he's from. Someone else asks if he needs a beer.

So what do the Kids hear? The men don't really talk directly about policies or political parties. They talk about issues important to them in a ferociously goofy manner. Life has become a goofy bitch. They've got a lot of problems, and it's the fault of the other guys, goofy guys who come here to destroy our goofy country. Those goofholes, they want handouts, not only for themselves, but for their entire goofy clan. They want a lot of goofy things, but they don't want to become

Americans. The men also complain about some goofy Americans who really don't goofy belong here. They're lazy goofs, don't want no work, keep getting goofy freebies from the goofy government. "Hey, those lazy goofy goofholes, they should be put to work to fix goofy roads or build goofy railroad tracks." Yeah, and everyone is guzzling beer. "And then those guys who talk fancy and show goofy graphs, hey, they need to learn common sense." Someone else agrees, "Yeah, goofy common sense."

Yes, common sense is a biggie for this crowd. They have it. It's not particularly complicated—all you have to do is listen to what's in your head.

Somewhere in the crowd, one of the girls yells, "Hey, hands off, creep!"

These guys are disjointed now, but watch out if someone starts to organize them, they could be like army ants moving menacingly in the same direction following a chemical scent.

And now they hear the first sounds of a band. As it approaches, it looks to be made up of kids of different ages and some adults, seemingly from 5 to 105. It is being led by the pastor from another church. He wears a large cross around his neck right beside a small American flag pinned right above his heart. He marches in front of the band and signals the beat as he lifts his baton high up and down so the musicians, with an age span of 100, can follow. And some kind of do.

Immediately behind the band, there he is, it's the Big Guy. He rides on a horse followed by other riders. When the oldest in the band was a kid a century ago, this could have been the sheriff with a posse. Or, going back 20 centuries, it could have been Jesus with his apostles.

The band is followed by the Big Guy and the Big Guy's followers. As they all come closer, the band gets louder, the music a bit painful. At the same time the men in front of the bar whoop it up, yell, cheer, applaud—they love the spectacle. The pastor-bandleader signals the end with his baton—boom pa boom pa boom pa boom! The Big Guy gets some help to get off his horse, and both he and the pastor walk over to a little stage set up in front of the bar. The pastor uses a megaphone, starts with a prayer, "Lord, you gave us common sense, guide us to use it wisely . . . " He then welcomes the crowd, reminds them that this is a special production by his church, and he wants to see "all who are on the right side of truth" in his church next Sunday morning. And without further ado, he then introduces the Big Guy. "Here he is, our savior, let's give him a big hand."

The Big Guy has a booming voice, doesn't need a megaphone. "Tremendous, incredible, very, very incredible. What a crowd! If you're with me, show me your right fist." Yeah, all the fists pump up. "Truly amazing, amazing. We've been losing too long. We've been getting beat. No more." Cheers and fists pumping. "Believe me, I'm a winner. I like winning. We're gonna win big together." Again, fists smash into air. "Gonna clean up the mess. Make America great again. Who is with me?" It's fists, all fists. "And, and this is really, really important. We must have discipline, really important. You all know I love our great military, we have a tremendous military . . . will . . . you . . . be . . . my . . . army?"

Fists pump amid raucous cheers. They shout their approval.

"Yeah, goofy yeah."

"Let's go build the goofy wall."

"And smash anyone who gets in the goofy way."

He continues. "This is a great, very great country, but criminals, gotta get rid of 'em. We're going to send 'em back." A bottle of beer appears, and he wets his throat with a long sip. "And jobs. Important, jobs. And two chickens in every pot. Who said that? Maybe Jesus said that." Somebody from the crowd yells "And two women for every guy," followed by incredible cheers.

He has more to say. "And, believe me, we're gonna build more jails and stick the losers in there." He has to take a breath, and takes another drink. "We're gonna make America totally great again. We want winners, not losers, incredible. Hey, thanks everybody for coming.

Huge, huge turnout. Let's go drink. My friend, the pastor here, is buying the first round."

The pastor and the politician, the divine and the secular. The attentive reader recalls meeting a pair like this in partnership before. These two allies disappear into the bar, followed by the boisterous crowd, where there no doubt is standing room only.

Before he gets off the podium, the Big Guy takes off his wig and wipes the sweat from his brow. Fritz blurts out, "Hey, he looks familiar." That dude, he's a local actor, earns a little cash every Sunday for his portrayals of Jesus and the Big Guy in front of appreciative audiences.

21

VIOLENCE

That evening, after the crowd squeezed into the bar following the performance of the Big Guy, our four main characters head back to their temporary base in the abandoned farmhouse. It's been quite a day for them, and before they call it a night, they make plans to leave this town the next morning. Izzy says, "We've seen enough. Can't help these folks."

Earlier in the evening, three local boys, Hammer, Truck, and America, had also made plans for the next morning. While the four Kids weaved among the men with ears open, asking questions, Hammer, Truck, and America became aware of the nosy outsiders, and followed them back to the farmhouse. Now, Hammer notices the strange license plate he has never seen before. "Looks foreign to me," he tells his two friends.

America chimes in, "Yeah, they definitely look suspicious. Don't act American."

Truck goes, "Hhrrrhhh hhrrrgh haghhtt, yeah, hhrrrhhh."

Hammer doesn't like outsiders. "I've got a plan. Listen to this." He wants to put some dings into that foreign car.

Truck: "Hhrrrhhh hhrrrgh haghhtt, I wanna do it, hhrrrhhh."

Hammer: "Let's blast 'em tomorrow morning."

Who are Hammer, Truck, and America? Let's have them introduce themselves.

"Hi, I'm Hammer. That's my nickname. My real name is Clarence, but because I've got a reputation for decisive action, I've been called Hammer ever since I can remember."

"Hhrrrhhh hhrrrgh haghhtt. Hey guys, I'm Truck. I was born as Coby, but I'm big, have a loud voice, and people sometimes say I'm as rusty as an old pickup truck, so they call me Truck. I like the name. And because I have a lot of phlegm, I have to clear my throat before I speak. I suppose I then sound like I'm revving my engine at a high decibel level, hhrrrhhh hhrrrgh haghhtt."

"America is my real name. I don't have a nickname. Whenever others wanted to make fun of me, they would say my mother gave birth to a country. But that doesn't bother me anymore. In fact, I've not only accepted my name, it's become part of my identity. I always wear clothes in some combination of red, white, and blue. I have a variety of shirts and sweatshirts with the flag, and I wear my Make America Great Again hat with self-assurance. I'm confident, am full of common sense, and I know what is good for the country. Hey, narrator, thanks for letting us introduce ourselves."

These three friends grew up in this town and have hung out together forever. Not many outsiders show up here, but when one does, they pay attention.

It's the next morning. What's going to happen? The night was uneventful, but Fritz wakes up irritated. "If this is the heartland of America, I'd rather live in one of the extremities."

Izzy and Zoom withhold comment and start to pack.

This is the setting. The farmhouse is on the left. The front door opens to the east. Straight ahead, to the north, is the wide side of the barn where a large American flag was painted years ago—proudly, no doubt. The paint has been peeling for quite some time. To the right of the house, and in front of the far side of the barn, stands a shed. The three structures surround the farmyard, and right in the middle is the parked minivan.

The Kids are invisible. They are inside the house still packing and grumbling. At this moment the heads of Hammer, Truck, and America pop up from behind the shed. All three step into view, and Truck alone moves several feet closer to the minivan. He has a bat and a bucket with baseballs. He throws up a ball in front of him and swings his bat hard against a ball. THUD. He does it again. THUD. And again and again. THUD, THUD, THUD. Fritz hears the noise, looks out the window, and in a flash is out the door. "Hey, that's our minivan."

As Fritz comes charging out, Truck stops. Fritz stops charging, stands still. The three boys all stare at Fritz. Fritz and Hammer are maybe six or seven yards apart. The girls come out, one after the other, see what is happening, look aghast, stay close to the house. Roxy screams, "F r i t z, c o m e b a c k."

The two groups stare at each other. No one moves. No one speaks a word. Then Truck, still holding his bat, ever so slowly cocks it, lifts a ball, and starts his powerful swing i n s l o w m o t i o n. A l i n e d r i v e r i g h t i n t o t h e p a s s e n g e r d o o r w i n d o w.

C R A S H.

As everyone catches up to what just happened, America taunts: "G o b a c k t o w h e r e y o u c a m e f r o m. W e d o n't w a n t y o u h e r e."

Let's leave the two groups frozen where they are. What is going on here? They are all white, so it's not racism. Both groups of teenagers are normal, ordinary adolescents. The four Kids grew up in America with a lot of reason to be optimistic. They come from an ideal home where they are secure and loved, and are prepared for a competitive world via the focus on education by their parents. Izzy will be a junior in a competitive college, and will graduate at the end of the year with a B.A.—having done it in three years. Zoom will be a sophomore in the fall, Roxy and Fritz will be seniors in high school. These Kids have become aware of the turmoil in their country and want to understand the reasons for it. They are inquisitive and choose to explore the enigmatic interior of America.

Hammer, Truck, and America are also good kids. They are well liked in town. Aside from a few pranks, they haven't gotten into any trouble. America has a caring mother, she works hard. She's raising America alone, used to have two jobs, but was let go from her part-time fast-food job because of declining business. She still works full-time at a nursing home, but it doesn't pay well. The other two boys have both parents, but there is a lot of fighting at home, perhaps a result of stress. Life is hard. All three boys are doing okay in high school, but what then? They have few plans. They'll get a job, but where? Move to the city? They'd rather stay right here in town, the town they know. They have a sense of loyalty. And of course, they distrust outsiders, especially smart alecks who ask a lot of questions.

Fritz takes a couple of steps back. Truck rests his bat on his shoulders. Hammer and America look at the damaged vehicle, look at the other kids, and also take a step back. The tension breaks. The three boys turn around, glance back once before disappearing behind the shed.

What agony. Our America withering.

Immediately the Kids head into town. They find out the town does not have police, but the mayor owns the local convenience store and works there. As they walk down Main Street, they notice people looking at them askance. Izzy wonders, "Have they already heard?"

The man behind the counter of the store is Bobby Ray Aldridge, the mayor. He wears a baseball cap with the initials BRA in front with a small American flag above. Izzy tells him about the violence. Should they file some sort of report? Call the police?

Bobby Ray listens, looks at each of the four Kids, says, "The cops are 50 miles away, it would take days, maybe weeks for them to get here. Those guys are busy fighting real crime." He wonders what they are doing trespassing on the old farmstead. "The couple who owned it died a while ago, but trespassing is illegal." He's cocksure. "What are you doing here anyway? Where are you from?" He doesn't wait for an answer. "We here in this town are a real community. We're close. We all know each other. We stick together. The boys you mentioned are good kids. They know right from wrong. Besides trespassing, what did you do to them? I already heard yesterday that you were in town snooping around. Did someone send you? Are you here to make trouble?"

Whew! What a mouthful. The Kids are intimidated. Who wouldn't be? They leave without responding to the mayor. Outside Izzy says, "It's no use. Let's get out of here."

They head back. Roxy wants to jog back, but Izzy looks around cautiously and calls her back. "Let's stick together."

Roxy does run the last stretch and arrives first. "Come quick. Look, look at the car. Someone cleaned it up."

It's true, the dings in the van are still there, but the glass is gone, and the broken window is now covered with clear plastic taped to the door frame. Zoom thinks the guys must have had remorse. "So, they cleaned up some, but who is going to pay for a new window, the body work?" Izzy is still anxious. "We have to get out of here. Let's just get our stuff."

Zoom enters the house first and screams. The others run to help her. There is a male standing in the dark far corner of the living room.

"Hey, don't be scared. I-I'm here to help."

He's a teenager with dark skin, speaks softly and slowly, if a bit nervously. "My, my name is Jamal. I-I-I saw what Truck and his goons did to your car. It's not right. So when you headed back into town, I-I saw you leave. I tried to help and cleaned up a bit. At least you can drive." He takes a deep breath and continues, surer of himself. "I saw you guys yesterday. That guy, his name is Dozer, he's as dumb as a donkey. He calls himself an actor. I think he gets 20 bucks and probably free beer from the pastor who bribes people to show up Sundays."

The Kids, still standing by the doorway, don't know what to say. They keep listening as he continues. "This town is the pits. Everybody knows each other, and while people have their differences, all the whites think alike. Plus, I live in a part of town that you guys would probably never see. It's a ways from the center of town. Just a handful of families live there, some black, some brown, some poor whites." He speaks more urgently. "It's like living at the end of the world. There's no hope. Nothing. I gotta get out of here. I just have to."

Izzy pulls the Kids over and whispers something. They listen, Zoom nods her head, Roxy takes a quick glance at the newcomer, Fritz says something, holds up a thumb. Finally, Izzy walks over to the other side of the empty room, reaches out her hand, and says, "Hi, Jamal, I'm Izzy. You can come with us." They all squeeze into the car and, lucky for them, the motor still works, so off they go.

PART 4

Action

22

SHAKE, RATTLE, AND ROLL

They escape down the road, away, away from this town. The Kids experienced uneasy moments here, so they are relieved to get out with only baseball-sized dents to their car. The only good news now is their car blends in with other cars here in the heartland.

Zoom, at the wheel, asks, "Where should we go? What should we do?"

Izzy does not take charge this time. "I don't know. I don't care."

No one can come up with a plan; no one can even think straight. They drive aimlessly along a country road, take one turn, then another. They get to the edge of a wooded area, haven't seen a house for a while. The road turns into a single-lane gravel trail and becomes a bumpy adventure. The trail ends just inside the woods. Fritz, exploring quickly, sees a small lake. "This looks like a good spot. We can fish, maybe find mushrooms."

Roxy adds, "This looks even more desolate than Jake's place. He had a shack and was on the edge of civilization. We've now left it."

"Good. This gives us a chance to relax as hunter-gatherers."

Fritz and Jamal get into a little conversation. Jamal looks around and all he sees are trees. "Are you sure you want to stay here? There's nothing here."

"Hey, Jamal, I've been going to the Boundary Waters since before kindergarten. Have you ever heard of it?"

Jamal shakes his head.

"It's a humungous area with a million lakes in northern Minnesota. There's nothing there but water and woods. You need a canoe to get around. You pack your gear into a canoe and start paddling. You're in a wilderness far from civilization, miles and miles from the nearest road or town."

"So what do you do there?"

"You survive. No slums up there. No discrimination. You might like it."

The basic laws of survival make everyone equal in the Boundary Waters. Everyone who comes there is searching for something. If you're lucky, you might see another canoe or two during the long day. If your canoes pass close enough, you greet the other adventurers, exchange information about the fishing, and wish them good luck. They look as scruffy and exhausted as you do. You might come across a millionaire tired of his millions, perhaps a savvy politician who wants to unsavvy himself, a cop without a gun, a guy without a job, or perhaps a poet looking for a poem. Everyone who comes there is naked. As you can tell, your narrator is fond of the Boundary Waters.

Fritz and the others unpack and set up camp. Everybody gets a job to do, and when tents are set up, it's time to think about a fire and food. This time Fritz goes fishing while Roxy looks for edibles, Zoom gets out her drawing friends, and Izzy and Jamal gather wood for a fire.

Hours later, Fritz brings back a bunch of fish. Roxy couldn't find any mushrooms or berries, but in order to have a complete meal of protein, vegetable, and fruit as a dessert, let's say she did. So, they feast on fish, flavorful forest mushrooms, and wild berries, then sit around the campfire feeling better. It's now story time. Fritz, unusually talkative, reveals his constant desire since "back when I was a kid" of wanting to live like a hunter-gatherer. "I always wanted to go back in time. In bed at night I imagined I was born thousands of years ago. When I closed my eyes, I visited all the places I saw pictures about in books."

Roxy mentions her recurring dreams before sleeping. They were always about traveling. "I put myself into difficult situations somewhere far away." She would help the locals "figure something out."

Jamal is mostly quiet when the Kids talk. Those fantasies must sound foreign to him. He listens and learns.

The Kids encourage him to reveal his dreams. They are different from the dreams of white kids. "I regularly dream about living somewhere else, often I think about Main Street. But that dream never ends well. I become the only black kid in the middle of town, and that turns out not to be such a good thing."

The Kids also listen and learn.

It has gotten dark when Zoom shows up. "Hi, I'm back." The others now realize that she has been gone, wonder where she was and what she did. Zoom says, "I was just out of sight behind some trees, but I could see and hear you." She shows them her contribution. It's a sketch, made with colored pencils, of a single large eye looking through what might be brush or branches. Near the edge of the picture are squiggles in different colors. They float in space and seem to move as if blown by an imaginary wind.

Fritz wants to know, "Why just an eye? Why not a person?"

"I want to focus on the act of seeing. That's why I only need an eye. And the little curls and loops are being blown about by winds of change."

After a while Fritz says, "Oh."

Zoom adds, "I also did something else."

"What? What did you do?"

She shrugs her shoulders and says, "There will be time to see it tomorrow, it's too dark now."

And that is how the trying day ends.

Next morning, Fritz is up first. He leaves Jamal asleep in the tent they shared and begins to gather firewood. The girls wake up slowly in their tent when Fritz comes running. "Quick, get up, come quickly. You've got to see this." Fritz is definitely excited, tries to hurry everyone to get going to come see what he has discovered. He leads them about 50 yards away to some boulders near the lake, and there, he points. "Look at that." Painted on the rock are some very primitive images made sparsely with few lines: a deer with antlers, a large bird, a turtle, a figure with a spear, a circle within a circle that resembles a sun. Also, three human stick figures that are connected. Their arms stretch out and touch each other.

Fritz can't believe his discovery, "Look, people were here thousands of years ago; we're like walking in their footsteps."

Zoom, the last to arrive, has a mischievous look. She asks, "Is my paint already dry?"

Poor Fritz. You should see him.

Back at camp there is a lot of movement, tidying up. The Kids know what to do, and they do it robotically; they don't need to think about it. Jamal, on the other hand, tries to figure out what to do. He wants to look busy. He moves about without accomplishing much.

The Kids' activity, done in silence, becomes a blanket that covers the growing tension. No one looks at anyone else, everyone looks down, does stuff. But minds churn, pressure builds, and then, boom, Roxy blows her top. She SCREAMS. Her eyes are shut, her mouth is ripped open, her head is tilted back, and she SCREAMS a long SCREAM of agony. Her siblings get it immediately. Silently, they scream their own scream in support. They move towards each other, form a circle, and hold hands.

Words are superfluous, everyone knows what must be done. Go back into town and conquer it.

Roxy's eruption is followed by a flow of creativity. Swift suggestions, ideas zip like arrows, propositions and proposals.

"How do we influence people, with logic or with emotion?"

"Why not through entertainment?"

"Skits might work. But they must be sharp and succinct—movement, not stasis."

"And surprises. We have to jolt the mind with the utterly unexpected."

"Use humor, create astonishment."

"Can you achieve clarity and truth using chaotic techniques?"

"Perhaps through silence?"

"Whatever we do, it must be visual, we need signs, lots of signs."

"Certainly also poems, maybe songs."

"We also could use more people."

The plan is to rent an abandoned house. Jamal has one in mind. They will need supplies, paint, clothes, building materials, cardboard, wood, tools, and probably much more.

Izzy is back in her element. "They already rely on theater to communicate religious and political persuasions. We are going to educate the town through the medium of theater."

They will also rock it, beguile it, unnerve it, confront it, delight it, distract it, and entertain it.

Izzy intends to drive to town on a peace mission. She definitely has courage, but not the brash or careless kind. She features poise plus brains, a good combination to confront difficult situations. Jamal comes along. He has to show her the house. The Kids pool their money, and Izzy takes it, all of it. She is not sure how much the house will cost to rent, so not sure how much money will be left over for supplies. Adventures always include uncertainty.

Off they go. The three staying behind are left penniless, but wood is free, and they can fish and perhaps gather.

Jamal directs them to a house he has fantasized about. It has been empty only for a few months and still looks to be in good shape. The owner, a widow, had to move into an assisted-living facility. Izzy goes there to look for her. Jamal says, "I'll wait in the car."

Izzy finds the owner and explains that she wants to rent the house for a while. The widow, her name is Josephine Adair, is by now a diminutive figure with a bowed back, but with penetrating eyes and a surprisingly strong voice. She was born here, and, like Joe and Jeb from a previous town, will regrettably die in this same town because, "Who's gonna wanna take me outta here now? I've always had a hankering to leave, to go somewhere else, but . . . well ya know, I'm not the only one."

Izzy smiles and starts with "Mrs. Adair," but the small woman with a confident voice says, "Just call me Josy. I like you already."

"Well, thank you. Hello Josy. I'd like to rent your house and bring some friends there. We have a project, we want to shake people up in this town with some new ideas, maybe rattle them a bit."

Josy, she must have been a card in her day, says, "You forgot the roll."

Izzy has a puzzled look as Josy continues. "Ha, ha, there was a song when I was young, 'Shake, Rattle, and Roll,' a kinda revolution in music and, ah, some other things. But then things settled down again, and all of us just got old here."

Izzy regains her footing. "I guess we want to shake, rattle, and roll people out of their monotone routines, and we want to start right here in this town."

Josy listens, says, "Fine," but she says it quietly. She looks down, her eyes searching for something on the floor. She speaks to herself barely perceptibly. "How is she going to do that? She needs help." She looks up, looks straight at Izzy, and now in her regular voice full of energy she says, "You're shaking me up, girl. You can rent it for $1 a week."

"Mission accomplished," says Izzy to Jamal, back in the car. "We already shook up a nice old lady."

They drive down Main Street to the house when Jamal calls out, "Look, the three goons." Izzy sees the three guys walking together. She tells Jamal, "Maybe we can ungoon them."

She stops the car, yells out the window, "Hey, don't I know you guys?"

Truck, Hammer, and America stop to look. Truck goes, "Hhrrrgh haghhtt, oh no, hhrrrgh."

America mumbles, "The foreigner."

Hammer is ready to "Bust that car some more."

Izzy steps out of the car and walks across the street to them. The three of them stand numb, three silent statues with disbelief written on their faces, one wrapped in red, white, and blue. "Hey guys, I'm Izzy, and I need some help."

"Hhrrrgh."

"Shut up, Truck," says Hammer. "Let me talk. What kind of help do you need, Lizzy?"

"It's Izzy. I need my van painted. Want to make it look like the coolest car in town."

"Hhrrrgh."

Izzy looks directly at Hammer. "Sounds to me like Truck is interested."

"Is this some sort of a trick, Fizzy?"

"Lizzy, Fizzy, Izzy, I bet you're getting dizzy. Maybe Hammer needs a nail to pound, to clear his head of dizzying sound."

"What?"

"Ha, ha, come on, Hammer, I'm yanking your chain. Hop in the back of the car, all of you."

But Hammer notices Jamal and asks, "What's he doin' in there?"

"What? You're worried? There's three of you and only one of him. Come on, get in."

Pffff, the air from the machismo balloons escapes and Hammer, Truck, and America do as they are told.

In the car they have a chat that turns things around, hopefully for good. "I really like your names. Truck and Hammer are so bold and utterly cool. And America, well, that's the best name of all. I'd like to be friends with you."

Truck goes, "Hhrrrhhh hhrrrgh . . . but we smashed your car, hhrrrgh."

"Yea, I know, but you can make up for it. I'd like you to help make the car look as bold as your names."

Now Hammer stammers. "You, ah, are you saying you don't want us to, eh, fix it?"

"Well, Jamal here, he's already helped you guys out by fixing the most important thing, the window you broke. Go ahead, thank him for it." Jamal, sitting in the front passenger seat, turns around and expresses an awkward smile. "And, no, the rest of the car doesn't need fixing. If you fix it, it will just be an ordinary car again. I want it to be conspicuous. Driving down Main Street, I want people to notice, to stare, to be wowed."

America makes the key contribution. "Maybe we should paint the car like the flag."

"Fantastic idea," says Izzy. "The car will be the visible symbol of our movement."

Hammer goes, "What do you mean by movement?"

Izzy responds with a wink and says, "It's gonna be the biggest thing this town has ever seen, and I want you to be an important part of it."

A while later the van is bursting with supplies they picked up from several different locations. Then Izzy drives them to their homes so they can pick up the things they will need for the next few days at their campsite where the car will be painted.

The boys live in three separate houses, one, two, three, right next to each other. They all look alike, small with a dismal gray appearance. Jamal comments, "This is a nice neighborhood compared to where I live."

Izzy and Jamal wait in the van while they go get their things. As they walk towards the first house, she notices they stop and discuss something, look back at her once or twice, nod and shake their heads, gesture with arms until they finally separate, off to their respective houses. Izzy waits and wonders. After a while one comes out of the house, then another, then the third. They wait for each other and talk again, but this time they have smiles on their faces. When they enter the van, Izzy can sense a positive mood. They bring sleeping gear and fishing rods.

"So what issues did you guys have to resolve before entering your houses, and why did you come out smiling?"

Hammer explains that "We had to get our story straight. I told my mom we got invited to a revival lasting a few days."

23

A DEFINING MOMENT: THE WALL CRUMBLES

The minivan with the three newcomers arrives. Zoom, Fritz, and Roxy uneasily eyeball Truck, Hammer, and America. Izzy tries to reassure, "These guys are okay. Let's get to know them. Let's unpack, go check out all the stuff we bought, and let's organize."

No one moves. Izzy walks around the car, inspects the dents and the plastic window. She makes another attempt. "Look, we've talked about the van. We're going to work it out, plus, we all want the same thing, we all want a better life. Let's work on the future together."

They unload, but the uneasiness persists. Fritz wants to cross the divide. "Hey, why don't you guys help me catch dinner." Great idea, Fritz. Off they all go with their fishing gear. Later, they do return smiling, and Hammer holds up a stringer. "Look. We did real good."

Fritz, happy with the fishing excursion, offers his tale of the importance of fishing to humanity. He reaches into his pocket, pulls out a folded sheet of paper, unfolds it, and starts to read. "Once upon a time there were two ferocious leaders threatening each other with war, but at the last minute they were encouraged to go fishing together. They head off into the wilderness alone, no one knows where they are. After months and months, they finally return as the best of friends, call each other brother, and bring peace to their lands."

Fritz stops reading, looks to make sure everyone is listening, then adds, "I have more. Their long seclusion inspired the imagination of storytellers who created wondrous tales about their exploits. These stories further unified the two peoples, and the peace between them lasted way past the death of the two leaders."

Fritz folds the paper, sticks it back into his pocket, and looks around, perhaps wondering if everyone gets his point. He adds, "There are two lessons here. The first one is obvious. Fishing is not just fun, it leads to friendship." He pauses, perhaps thinking how to phrase the second point. "And the really important second lesson is that stories don't just entertain, they can also unify the world."

Zoom likes that. "Fritz, that is cool. Where did you get that from?"

"I wrote it myself."

In the evening, they gather around the fire. Izzy wants to develop a plan, but attempts at discussion repeatedly hit a barrier. While fishing together earlier helped, the evening's fits and starts mean there is still uneasiness. America identifies the problem. "Look, I think I like you, but you're different. I've been in this town all my life, and I've never met anyone like you."

Now comes one of the highlights of this tale.

Zoom stands up, decisively. She grabs a stick, and as everyone watches she scratches a large circle on the ground. "This is our country," she says. "It's big." Then she draws a line through the middle. "And this is a wall." She bends down and scratches a stick figure on one side of the line and says, "That's me." Then she scratches another stick figure on the other side of the line, looks at America, and says, "That's you."

Zoom straightens up. "I grew up on this side and you on the other side. Let's learn more about each other so we can break through the wall." She waits a moment, and now with a probing but warm voice, continues. "What are your hopes for the future, America? I mean, what do you want to do with your life? Where do you want to go? What do you want to see?"

Some in the group stand, others sit on logs, but all lean forward to listen. They must wonder where this is going. America hesitates and gives Zoom the opportunity to continue. Her voice is now strong. "I want to be an artist. I love to draw and paint. I love how a creative force comes from within me that allows me to shape an image, one brush stroke at a time. I also love the silence when I work. It allows me to dream."

The group is mesmerized. No one moves. All eyes remain focused on Zoom as she continues. "I love new things, new experiences. I want to travel the world to see what is out there, and I expect to convert some experiences into images on canvas. And some day I'm going to create a huge wall mural in my house." Zoom sits down as she got up, decisively.

Roxy jumps up eagerly and begins. "I want to go into business. I'm still undecided about the details. I suppose college will help me figure that out, but I do know that I want to be useful in some important way. I want to make a difference. I'm taking Spanish in school. Maybe that can help me communicate with some people who need help."

Fritz immediately follows. "I'm going to college to challenge myself. I'm not sure yet what I want to major in, but I definitely want to pursue adventures. I want to do unusual things, test myself, climb mountains. I want to do something big. What if I could find a way to make my early longings come true, to time travel? Into the past. Or even into the future. Maybe I'll major in physics to see if there might be a way."

Now Izzy. "All my friends know my calling is theater. I love the stage. I was born to act, to dance, to perform. But I'm also interested in watching others perform. And who knows where the stage will lead me. I feel the world is full of opportunity, it's open, it's grand." Izzy picks up Zoom's stick and scratches out half of the line representing the wall and says, "Now, let's hear from you guys."

"Hhrrrhhh hhrrrgh, all I ever wanted to do was own a truck someday." That's all he says.

Izzy prods, "What do you want to do with it?"

"I just want to drive it, nothing else, hhrrrgh."

"Where do you want to go?"

"Oh, just around town."

"What if you could drive all the way to Minnesota?"

"That's far. Do you think I could do it?"

"Yep, Truck, I think you could, and you should."

Now Jamal stands up and steps into the circle. "As I was growing up, I always felt confined, kinda like stuck in a box. The people I hung out with were all from my end of the town, all of them living in their own boxes. There were so many things I couldn't do, didn't feel a part of. I knew Truck and the other guys, but we really had nothin' in common. When I saw you guys from out of town, something happened and I broke out."

Zoom asks, "How do you feel now?"

"I feel a sense of freedom. I feel ready to try new things. I too want to be an American," and he jumps across half of the line still remaining.

Hammer picks up the stick and scratches out more of the line. Now only a small section remains. "No one talked to me about the future. No one talked to me about options. No one ever talked to me about things I could do or become. College? Never gave it a thought."

Roxy asks, "What are you going to do as an adult?"

"I guess I'll do the same thing the other guys in town do."

"What do they do?"

"I guess . . . I guess they're waiting."

"Why do they wait?"

"Gee, maybe they wait to be saved."

Zoom nudges America. "Come on, America. You're the last one. Get it done."

America has had time to gather his thoughts. He walks into the circle and stands on the stick figure that represents him. "Look, I've never really thought about it, but I guess my view of America is based on my experience right here in this town. Everyone in this town is American. They look American, they think American, they act American. Everyone assumes that anyone who looks, thinks, or acts differently is not American."

Izzy interjects. "What about us? We look like people in town, but we think differently. Are we not American?"

"Well, that's just it. You seem to be American."

"What do you mean 'seem'? Look, America, it will take courage. Tear down the last bit of this wall to open your mind. Then we can all join hands and all be Americans."

America, dressed in red, white, and blue, lifts his right arm up high, and says, "Yeah, we're all Americans." And with that he picks up the stick and scratches out the last remains of the wall.

A defining moment, two groups of American kids connect. They connect in spite of being different in some ways. They whoop it up with cheers and shouts, hugs and high fives.

They spend a long night around the campfire, their faces aglow, sharing experiences. They tell each other stories, some true, others surely seriously exaggerated, recalling dangerous episodes and amazing close calls. Sounds like some of them are lucky to still be alive. Comments like, "You gotta be kidding," or "I don't believe you really did that" follow these stories. Fritz is happy. He says, "Hey, I told you, stories really do unify."

Now they can move to a serious discussion about their future and the future of their generation. Agreed, soon they will be the ones in charge of their community and their country. And they don't want to look to the mythic past, when, of course, everything was always golden, as the stories about the past from grandmothers have soothed children at bedtime forever. Izzy has a way with words. "Leave that fairy tale stuff about how great the past was to the old and mentally infirm. We must look forward."

With the arrival of the first morning light, they agree on a mantra. "We are the future. They are the past."

24

THEY DAZZLE THE TOWN

The future begins the next day. Truck, Hammer, and America work on the car. They have red, white, and blue paint. Jamal goes, "Hey, I want to join you guys."

Zoom looks in every so often. "It's coming along," and she discusses art concepts with the boys. But her main role is to make signs and posters.

Izzy helps Zoom with signs, develops slogans, but she also starts to think about ideas for skits and other shenanigans.

Fritz helps out with the car, but because he is encouraged by the success of his story about how fishing can change attitudes, he is trying to figure out how best to change opinions. He tells no one in particular, "Knowledge is based on hard facts, on real information. Opinions are different, they are beliefs soft as a pillow stuffed with emotional feathers."

Zoom says, "Soft as what?"

"Soft as a pillow." Fritz says, "That means while opinions can be interesting or not, they are basically harmless."

Zoom is pesky and challenges Fritz. "What about opinions derived from false facts that prove to be harmful?"

Looks like Fritz will have to do some more thinking.

Roxy is a jack of all trades. She jumps in to help wherever she is needed. She does spend much of her time working with Izzy. Many of the shenanigans we will hear about later come from her fertile mind. She also calls some people trying to expand the group.

They keep at it. They work, but they also play. They fish for food, fish for fun, fish to bond. In the evening they continue to build their relationship by retelling stories of their personal adventures and fantastic exploits.

It would be nice to hear, years from now, when they are grandmothers and grandfathers, how their memory of these youthful activities might be embellished into wonderful stories for their grandchildren at bedtime. Who knows, perhaps Roxy will reimagine the work on the minivan into a fantastic tale. Shhh, let's imagine the future and listen in. "Back when I was your age, we still drove in cars. They moved on hard surfaces on the ground called roads and were uncomfortable and dangerous. Inside you had to be tied down, you could not move. So I thought and I thought and I thought until I finally came up with a plan. I painted eagle wings on the outside of the van, and I painted them in the colors of our flag. Then I climbed onto the roof, said the three magic words, and the van and I, we left the road and flew through the air. My friends cheered and cheered. They probably wondered why they had not thought of it first. But your grandma did. Now it's time to sleep. Good night, sleep tight."

Two days later they pack up, stuffing everything into the van. Not everyone fits inside. Jamal is already on the roof. "Come on, Hammer, there's still room for you."

Roxy jogs, and Truck volunteers to walk, well, at least part of the way. He wants to lose some weight, a good sign. Just before they reach the town, everyone except Izzy at the wheel gets ready outside of the car.

Here they come. The van slowly enters Main Street. The Kids prance alongside. They start to make noise, and what noise! They chant in unison: "Hidee hidee hidee ho, we've come to say hello. Hidee hidee hidee he, we're here to set you free.

"Fiddle dee dee, fiddle dee dum, we're here to bring this town some fun."

Several people on the sidewalk stop and look. The teenagers wave to them and continue to chant. "Life is hard! times are tough! join us if you've had enough!"

Some people scratch their heads.

"Hi ho! Hi ho! Lies just have to go! Wake up! Get up! Something's going on! Wake up! Rise up! You've been asleep too long! We're American youth! We've come to counter lies with truth!"

A few people come out of buildings looking puzzled, then slide into an easy smile. At the center of it all is the van. It's painted a crazy red, white, and blue. On one side of the entire car length is an uneven flag. The stripes are long and follow the contours of the vehicle. And because the side of the van is slightly bowed with baseball sized indentations, the stripes of the flag are a bit wavy. On the far end of the van are stars in the shape of the peace sign, but insanely unorganized.

More and more townspeople appear and assemble. Cars stop and drivers step out to look.

The other side of the minivan is painted with slogans. "We want better schools." "Let's be friends." "Health insurance for all."

Some of the writing is small so people move closer to the car to read. "History shows the past wasn't so great."

And the kids have signs. Roxy holds hers up. The front says, "The future is coming." The back states, "The past is gone."

Truck has a broad sign hanging from his shoulders, "I'm Learning." As he walks past, a sign on his back becomes legible, "To Dream."

America is of course wearing red, white, and blue. He waves to people as he holds up his sign. "America is better when bigger."

Hammer's sign says, "I too deserve college."

Fritz sprints from one side of the street to the other. The sign he's holding states, "Jump for Joy." He asks someone in the crowd to hold his sign. He does cartwheels, walks on his hands, astonishes and amazes, then takes the sign back and repeats.

Jamal and Zoom wear t-shirts that Zoom designed. The front says, "America Is For All." Both of them move in and out of the crowd, shaking hands and teasing people with, "There's more to come on Saturday," or "The big event is Saturday."

As the minivan and America's youth move slowly down Main Street, the crowd builds. Most people walk along to stay with the wondrous display and join new onlookers further down the street. It's a festive atmosphere, as if a circus had appeared with clowns and dancing bears.

As they approach the driveway of the house they are renting, they turn to the crowd, wave, clap, and yell in unison, "Hip, hip hooray, there's more to come on Saturday."

Once in the house they gush with excitement. "What a success!"

"We pulled it off."

"Wow."

"Can you believe all the people?"

"I was nervous at first when people looked puzzled."

"Me too, but when they started to smile, I knew it was all good."

"Great job, everybody."

"Yeah, we're a team."

"Whew!

"As smooth as a fairy tale."

The reader might ask, weren't there any dissenters in the crowd? The reaction seems too good to be true. Your narrator responds: true, not everyone cheered. A few sneered at the slogans. Several rebuked them as radicals. Some called out the local kids. But our group was way too excited to notice the few dissenters.

25

AGITATORS FOR CHANGE

"Our entrance was smashing, but the first act does not a successful performance make." That's Izzy. "Now comes the real challenge." She sets the goal. "We want to shake people up, rattle their brains, and I suppose, to honor Josy, add 'roll' to the mix. Let's see if we can roll out a little revolution!"

Truck looks confused and stammers, "Hhrrrgh haghhtt, with guns and tanks?"

"No, a revolution of ideas."

Roxy's face turns bright. "How about this? A revolution to end tired thoughts with espresso thinking."

The medium for the revolution will be theater, but not puppy dog shows. No, theater that growls, theater that bites. Even Hammer understands that people here need a jolt. He says, "Folks are broken, they're worn out, it'll be hard to get their attention. We need to sock 'em with homers. Singles won't do!"

Fritz expresses pretty much the same thing. He offers his Fritz wisdom. "Bland opinions won't rattle anyone. Adding plain salt to dull meat and potatoes won't do the trick. You'd have to add some Carolina Reaper."

Zoom asks, "What's that? I'm not sure I like the sound of it."

"It's the hottest pepper in the world. Fire in your mouth. Eat one of those and you're shook up forever."

So what kind of theater? Short, direct, peppery, agitative, out-of-the-park-home-run skits. Izzy, our theater expert, has been thinking about this. She says the most important thing is to keep the audience awake. "You can't change the world if, yawn, yawn, the audience misses the great idea 'cause they're asleep, right?"

America adds, "Yeah, we gotta be entertaining."

"Well, entertainment, yes, and no. Perhaps more important is that we have to keep the audience engaged, keep them on their toes, people should think along and wonder." She continues, "And since we're trying to change minds, the audience has to get it. Complexity is out; clarity is in."

Truck asks, "Hhrrrhhh, so our, haghhtt, play's gonna be like comic books?"

"No." Izzy is sure of herself. She speeds up. "Nonono! Comic books don't contain ideas. They only contain action. Action induces new action, which provokes more action. You get an action chain without meaning."

She stops to breathe.

It certainly sounds like Izzy has assimilated the comments Big Mack made on the bus to New York. He talked about the BIFF, BAM, BOOM action of comic book superheroes and the Punch and Judy characters that the Big Guy in Washington copies.

Izzy continues. "We're after meaning. We want to convey something important. Mindless action makes you lethargic, numb, and dumb, the opposite of what we need for our revolution."

"Hhrrrhhh, okay, I think I get it. No Batman, no Superman."

Izzy finishes. "Finally, the plot has to run into an obstruction, something unexpected has to happen, something uncomfortable, something that shakes people up."

Izzy has a sense of purpose. She is serious about this undertaking. She wants to matter. Her ambition sets a standard. It affects everyone. Of course, her siblings are used to Izzy's intensity, but for the boys from town, this is something they have not been exposed to before, a new experience. Perhaps Truck's single-word expression speaks for all of them. He is able to say it without having to clear his throat: "Wow."

But to paint the car is one thing, to play Shakespeare quite another. Zoom warns everyone this won't be easy. "Creativity doesn't just happen like moonlight falling on your face through a sudden opening in the clouds and you say 'aha.' Creativity requires perspiration and persistence."

Let the perspiration and persistence begin. They divide into small groups. The first suggestions sputter, they don't flow, but as they become more comfortable with the process, they open the spigot in their brains and ideas pour out. Most ideas are tossed, but that's okay. Their brains keep producing.

They generate concepts, jot down proposals, take notes, cross out, toss out, they create heaps of crumbled paper. They act out ideas, try out slogans, draw images, incorporate famous sayings, discard them, try others, suggest historical analogies, and imagine audience responses. Izzy reminds them again and again, "Don't get too complicated, make sure people get the point."

In the afternoon, Diego—from that first abandoned house a long time ago—shows up with his son, Mario. Roxy had called them. She wondered where they were and what they are doing.

The Kids greet them warmly and recall how they separated a while back. Father and son headed north, but Diego soon had second thoughts. "I was running. I don't want to run no more." Diego looks at everyone, his eyes get stuck on the local kids he doesn't know. "I came to America a long time ago to make a better life for myself. I'm glad my son was born here. America is now my home. I stay here. I am a Mexican-American."

The boys from town are uneasy. Truck goes "Hhrrrhhh hhrrrgh haghhtt, but . . ."

Roxy tries to calm him down. "Remember, Truck, we're working on a skit about the palette of colors in America. Brown is a part of that.

Diego is a good guy. Maybe you should take Mario and show him around the house and the yard."

America says, "But wait a second. He's a Mexican."

"Yeah, I know," Izzy butts in. "My grandparents are German. You told me your grandparents came from Ireland. They got a chance here, and you and I are proof that they made it. Let's give this Mexican a chance. If he doesn't hold up his end, we can deal with it." She grabs something from her pocket. "Here's a chocolate bar. See if little Mario is interested."

Another newcomer arrives in the evening after it's already dark to join the growing group. While in the front yard, they see a light in the distance moving to and fro. As it comes closer, they see it's a flashlight.

Roxy moves towards the light. "I can't believe it, you actually came. You made it."

"Hey, Roxy, I'm here to help shine some light on America's sorry plight."

It's Emma. Roxy is happy that she has come to join them. She introduces Emma to her siblings. "We became friends way back on the bus to New York."

Then Emma introduces herself to the others. "Hi guys, my name's Emma. I'm an American with a dilemma. I speak the truth, I don't lie. Cross my heart, hope to die."

The boys from town stand silently and look at this newcomer with the buzz haircut and unadorned face. None of the boys from town are poets, and they don't know that her mind is laced with gold and silver sequins, but they hear something that rattles their brains.

Emma continues to rhyme. "I don't mince words. Against power and lust I declare disgust." She adds with emphasis, "But I can also scream in silence to protest the shameful gun alliance."

Now the heads of the boys must be spinning. They have open mouths but not a word escapes, and their eyes dart about looking for cover.

Roxy holds her hands over her mouth so she doesn't laugh out loud.

"Come on, guys, focus your eyes, you'll get used to me and my repartee."

They shuffle away silently in different directions.

The next morning after breakfast things do work out okay. The three newcomers, Diego, Mario, and Emma, are weaved into the group. Fritz counts, and notes, "There's now 11 of us." And by the afternoon, the group of 11 has identified a handful of ideas for skits that offer some promise. That's progress.

Towards evening, Izzy picks up Josy for a cookout, and Josy is rolled into the yard in her wheelchair.

Emma, always straightforward, starts off the exchange. "Hi, Josy, my name's Emma. I'd like to get to know you better. Your life has been long, what went right, what went wrong?"

Josy looks at Emma. She says, "Well, Emma, you're quite direct, you don't waste any time, do you?"

Josy turns her head slowly one way, then the other way as she studies the faces of the young people that stand around her. She takes her time, repositions herself in her chair, stretches a bit, then begins. "Well," she breathes hard, "I think I got stuck. When I was your age I had resolve and I had speed." She stops and takes another deep breath. "I ran right through things that were in my way. At some point things changed, well . . ." Josy said all of that matter-of-factly, but she now becomes reflective. "Actually, no . . . there wasn't a particular point . . . things evolved so slowly I never became aware of change . . . I must have been moving in molasses." She stops again, waits, then smiles a surprised smile. "Did I really say molasses?" She goes on, "Well, time kept rolling along, but I kept falling farther behind until I got stuck in the past. Now, a lifetime later, I'm stuck in a wheelchair."

Josy's advice for these young people: "Forever do it, forever be nimble, forever keep moving, forever stay young."

The older woman in the wheelchair energizes the younger generation. That evening they talk about the state of the country that seems stuck, the need for fresh ideas, for solutions that work, and they reject the politics of blame.

Hammer shares an anecdote. "My mom is always angry, always at the same things, like she kicks the garbage can because it leaks. But she never does anything about it."

And from America comes this realization: "Yeah, I've always worn the colors of the flag, but I'm starting to realize things aren't all that colorful. There is a lot of gray in America."

Jamal focuses on race. "Whites want to go back to some glorious past, but the past for my family wasn't glorious."

Their discussion moves to diversity, and everyone including Josy agrees, ideas must come from different sources. Diego says, "If the soccer team has good players, but play is poor, why not get new ideas from new foreign players?"

Roxy stands up briskly. Something has been on her mind. "Hey, listen to me, listen everyone. We need a name. We could be stupid and call ourselves something that only exists in zoos here, like lions, tigers, or elephants, or we could be smart and call ourselves by what we want to accomplish. We want change, and to get change we need to shake things up. To me that sounds like agitate. So why not call ourselves 'Young Agitators for Change'?"

"Wait! What about Josy?" Fritz jumps up. "I want Josy to be one of us. Sure, she's older, but she's getting unstuck and might turn back her clock. She would make us 12. So maybe we should drop 'young' and just call ourselves 'Agitators for Change.'"

All smiles, all thumbs are up. Comments reflect that everyone likes being part of this group, being a cog in "our" movement, and that "we need Josy." Roxy looks at Fritz, nods her head ever so slightly, looks pleased, and says, "That's good, nice going, Fritz."

Zoom likes the number 12. "A lot of things come in 12. The months, the hours on my wristwatch. Twelve is kind of a magical number."

America contributes, "Yeah, there were also 12 apostles."

Zoom took a course in Greek literature and she responds, "Well, okay, but first there were the 12 Olympic gods."

Let the action of the 12 Agitators for Change begin! Someone puts on some music. Guess what's playing? It's "Shake, Rattle, and Roll," and the kids get up to move to the rhythm. And guess who also rises. Yep, it's Josy. She pushes herself up, stands erect, takes a few steps from her wheelchair, and begins to sway and swivel her hips. Everyone else claps and forms a circle around her while Josy, unstuck, is rockin' and rollin'.

26

THEATER SHENANIGANS

It's Friday, and they're still struggling with their skits.

Jamal is worried. "I'm still uncertain about the dog thing."

Fritz is not at all comfortable playing the Big Guy. "Maybe Diego should take my place. Or maybe we should just drop that skit."

"I know my lines, but I just can't get the delivery right." Zoom walks off the stage during the final rehearsal almost kicking herself in frustration.

Izzy tries to reassure them. "Good theater," she says, "always breathes stress right up to performance time. You need uneasiness and a bit of chaos for peak delivery. I think you guys are gonna be fine."

Okay, good luck to the 12 of you. May you soar, not crash.

Jamal and Hammer head into town with a stack of flyers. They hand them out to individuals, are allowed to tape some to the inside of store windows, bring some to bars and churches. Unfortunately, the town does not have a newspaper. While the two boys together get some looks, Hammer responds without hesitation, "What's up? He's my buddy." Most people are interested in the event. They look at the flyer, seem puzzled but curious, and ask the boys for more information. The boys cleverly respond with teasers like, "Live theater is unpredictable." "Anything can happen." "Someone might die."

The flyer is simple. The words THEATER SHENANIGANS is on top in bold letters followed by "Presented by Agitators for Change."

Below that reads, "The world premiere of the one-act play MAKE AMERICA GREAT AND BRIGHT AGAIN? plus other mischief."

Near the bottom it says, "Free for town residents," followed by the location, date, and time, plus, "Bring your own chairs."

At the very bottom in small print:

> *Warning! These shenanigans could change you. We are not responsible for your possible mental anguish. If your mind is closed, stay home and lower the shades.*

Saturday arrives. A veranda located in the front of the house with gates on either side will be the stage. Before the veranda is a good-sized lawn, perfect for the audience. The actors place all the chairs they can find on the lawn in front of the stage. America worries, "What if only a few people come? What if . . . " No one hears the rest as they're all busy doing last minute stuff. Anticipation is in the air, critters in stomachs flap their wings.

It's still early, but people start to mill about on the sidewalk in front of the house, a hopeful sign. Izzy goes over to them and asks them to come in and grab a seat. More and more come, soon the lawn is filled with chairs just like at a regular outdoor theater. People seem to be in a pretty good mood. They look around, no doubt wondering about what they're about to see. And the performance begins.

On the left side of the stage stands a table with three chairs. A performer walks on stage and places a large sign in the middle of the stage: "Barry's Bar." He turns to the audience and says, I'm the bartender.

Three performers follow him onto the stage. They wave sluggishly to the audience, take a seat at the table, slouch down, and drink beer.

Two additional performers appear carrying a large tub they place several yards to the right of the table. They smile and also wave to the audience. They are followed by another performer who stands beside the tub, looks gloomily at the audience, strips down to his underpants, and steps into the tub.

Next, three comically dressed performers appear, and one after the other march, clown style, from one side of the stage to the other. They each carry a sign they hold up for the audience to see. The first sign states, "Men without hope," *the second,* "Overdose on drugs," *the last,* "Or drown in beer." *They exit the stage.*

The bartender takes bottles of beer from a table, pops them open, and pours the beer into the tub. The performer in the tub says, What can I do? It's hopeless. Beer is my only escape. *He drowns theatrically.*

The bartender tells the two performers standing by the tub, Get him out of here, quick. We don't want anyone to notice. *They drag the drowned man off the stage. A few seconds pass, then the bartender calls out to the other customers,* Drink, drink, brothers, drink. Don't worry, don't think. One of you come here. The tub is filled with beer.

One of the men leaves the table, walks over to the tub, and steps inside. He says, What can I do? It's hopeless. Beer is my only escape. *He also drowns theatrically.*

The bartender tells the two performers standing by the tub, Get him out of here, quick. We don't want anyone to notice. *They drag the drowned man off the stage. A few seconds pass, then the bartender calls out to the other customers,* Drink, drink, brothers, drink. Don't worry, don't think. One of you come here. The tub is filled with beer.

One of the men leaves the table, he walks halfway to the tub and stops.

There is a long silence, as all performers stand still. Finally, they all exit the stage.

A young woman pursued by a man walks briskly through the audience towards the stage. She says, Hey, you creep, how dare you. Get your hands off me.

He smirks, kisses his hands, and says, Ahh, sweet.

She walks onto the stage and is visibly upset. How dare you touch me without my permission.

He follows close behind. She has to fight him off continuously. He then turns to the audience, gazes at individual men, and speaks directly to them. Hey, I can't help being attracted to beautiful women. How about you? And what about you? Me, I just start kissing them. She'll come around. *He turns to her and blows her a kiss.*

A loud melodious voice is heard from the top of the house. The audience can see a figure on the roof dressed in a robe and with a lot of hair, but the figure is not visible to the man. The figure uses a bullhorn. Don't worry, son, I've got you covered. Those who believe in me also believe in you.

The man continues to look up to the roof and searches. Hey, is that you, God?

The man beckons to the woman with his index finger. *She shakes her head. He pursues her eagerly as she exits the stage.*

An unexpected disturbance erupts from one side of the audience. A scream erupts *and several performers run over behind some bushes beside the lawn.* Ohmygod, another woman. *They pull the woman from the bushes. One of the performers does CPR, but to no avail. Someone covers her face with a cloth.*

There is commotion in the audience, people come to have a look. Another performer says, She was just middle-aged. Looks like we need to call an undertaker. Let's move the body into the house.

The performer addresses the audience. It's another casualty, maybe hopelessness killed her. I hear several women have died in town recently, women without a known illness.

Several other performers carry the motionless body into the house.

The performer continues, Please be seated again. Let's continue with the show.

But several individuals from the audience stay and refuse to sit down. One of them is quite upset and protests. You can't go on with the show, someone just died. *Several others speak at the same time. They look disturbed and agree with him.*

Izzy is forced to rescue the situation. Wait, wait, this is part of the show. The woman didn't die, she just acted. This was a skit. We wanted to also depict the hopelessness of women. *She saves the situation, but it's not clear these people are satisfied. They do finally take a seat, but they are still shaken.*

Izzy steps back onto the stage and announces, It's best if we take a ten-minute intermission.

But again, without warning, another commotion arises in the audience, a woman in a wheelchair (it is actually Josy), yells, Hey, that's my pocketbook. *A white man scampers away with her pocketbook and disappears.*

Izzy goes to Josy to see what happened. One of the young men sitting next to Josy (it's actually Hammer) says a black kid ran off with the pocketbook. I saw it with my own eyes.

Izzy acts unconvinced, but Hammer stammers, Hey, who else saw it? I can't be the only one. It was one of the black troublemakers from outside town. *He looks directly and pleadingly at others close by.*

By now a number of people have surrounded them. One man says, Those black guys are bad. Whenever they come to town, somethin' happens.

Someone else now says, Yea, it was that dude with the weird hair. I saw him near Josy. *Others join in,* We have to get them once and for all.

Izzy says loudly, Okay, let's put this on hold. We'll resolve this after the play, trust me. We'll be back in ten.

During intermission a performer with a pure white face mask walks through the crowd. He pulls two performers with leashes who walk on hands and knees. One wears a brown face mask, the other wears a mask with polka dots. They draw a crowd, and someone asks what this means. They're animals, can't you see? They're subservient to me. *He repeats that several times, walking the grounds.* They're animals, can't you see? They're subservient to me.

The audience is definitely uneasy. Izzy comes back out and bangs on a large old washtub to get attention. What you just saw was a little introduction to our one-act play, *Make America Great and Bright Again?* And please note, there is a question mark at the end of the title. So do take your seats and get ready for the second half.

Make America Great and Bright Again?

All performers wear masks. The Big Guy and his accomplices have Caucasian face masks and wear black jackets, white shirts, and red ties. Except for Steve, who wears three dark shirts, one over the other. They all hold up signs attached to a strip of wood with their names.

Steve: *Saunters arrogantly onto the stage, looks over the audience before speaking.* Hey, pay attention, everyone. Hey you, *he points to someone.* Stop talking and listen. I've got a problem. You've got a problem. *He points to the audience.* We all have a problem. Our country has been compromised. Many don't belong here. We've got to bring back the times when all were white, and all was right. Let me introduce to you . . . *he pauses for dramatic effect . . .* someone . . . who can make that wish come true. *He applauds vigorously as the performer who plays the Big Guy walks with exaggerated confidence to the front of the stage. Steve exits.*

The Big Guy: *Clapping his hands.* Thank you, Steve. Steve is a bit of a rebel, but he is one of my most trusted advisors. I'm the Big Guy, yes I am, and I've got a hellofa plan. I want to make America great again, but we also must make it bright again. Very important. When we were . . . *He coughs . . .* all honest and most of us were white, we had jobs, good money, and TV wrestling at night. I'm white, so stick with me, but I need your pledge of loyalty. *Calls loudly to Steve.* Hey, Steve, my loyal rebel, let's begin. We need to kick someone out.

Reince: *Pulls aggressively on a rope as he comes onto the stage. The rope is tied around the waist of a performer with a black mask.* Steve is gone. I'm here.

The Big Guy: *Surprised.* What happened to Steve?

Reince: You fired him. *He pulls on the rope.* Getoutta here, scum. Back to your huts in Africa where you're from. *Reince drags the individual, who struggles to resist, off the other side of the stage.*

The Big Guy: *Claps.* Nice work, Reince. Let's kick someone else out to make America brighter.

A white individual without a face mask interrupts the play. He wears a hat with a feather and skips onto the stage, jumps back and forth clown like, makes a lot of noise yelling, Yahoo! and Hooray! I'm from Norway, *and skips off the other side of the stage. Other actors come from behind the stage and chase him amid such calls as* Hey, who are you? Get outta here. You don't belong here. *There is confusion, but one actor moves to the front of the stage and apologizes to the audience. The play finally continues.*

The Big Guy: Sorry about that, friends. I'll continue where I left off . . . Nice work, Reince. Let's kick someone else out to make America brighter.

A Lawyer: *Pulls aggressively on a rope as he comes onto the stage. The rope is tied around the waist of a performer with a brown mask.* Reince is gone. I'm here.

The Big Guy: *Surprised.* What happened to Reince?

A Lawyer: You fired him. *He pulls on the rope.* Getoutta here, scum. Back to the jungles where you came from. *The lawyer drags the individual, who struggles to resist, off the other side of the stage.*

The Big Guy: Who's next, my loyal lawyer? We need to kick someone else out. My white supporters demand it. Wait. Did I just say white supporters? Ha, ha. All my supporters are white. I love 'em. *He waves to the audience, points to them, then points to himself, points back to the audience, and gives a thumbs-up sign.*

The General: *Pulls aggressively on a rope as he comes onto the stage. The rope is tied around the waist of a performer with a tan mask.* The lawyer is gone, sir. You fired him. I'm here. *He pulls on the rope.* Getoutta here, you Mediterranean scum. Back to the misery where you came from. *The General drags the individual, who struggles to resist, off the other side of the stage.*

The Big Guy: Hey, General, there must be more who don't belong here. Let's get all of them the hell out.

Mike: *Pulls aggressively on three ropes attached to three performers as he comes onto the stage.* Getoutta here, you Slavic, Irish, and yellow scum. Back to the swamps where you came from. *Mike pulls the performers, who all struggle to resist. The Irish performer unexpectedly calls out with an Irish accent,* Hey, Mike, your grandfather came from Ireland. *Mike stops, scratches* *his head. He takes a knife and cuts the rope from the Irish performer.* Hurry up, beat it, try to blend in. *He then continues to pull the two others off the other side of the stage.*

The Big Guy: *With exaggerated gestures,* Fantastic job, Mike. Thank you for your servitude. *He addresses the audience.* You know, if something happens to me, Mike here, he'll be penced in as the next Big Guy.

Well, we got rid of all the scum. Now that everyone is white, we can all sleep better at night.

Long pause

The Big Guy continues. My white friends, that's the end of a truly fantastic play. Thank you all for coming. *He claps and hurries off the stage.*

A few seconds later all the performers come back on stage without their masks and take a bow.

The audience seems confused. There is limited clapping. Some people start to file out. When unexpectedly . . . the white individual without a face mask but wearing a hat with a feather reappears. He yells out, Hold it, everyone. It's not over. There's more. *He beckons people leaving to come back.* Please, sit down again. *Most people come back and take a seat, some remain standing.* I'm the lucky one, I'm the whitest of them all, hooray, I'm originally from Norway. *He points to someone and asks,* Where are you from? *The woman says,* I'm American. *He asks,* But where are you from originally? *She responds, with hesitation,* Ah, I think my grandparents came from Bulgaria. Aha, then you are not pure white. *He points to someone else and asks the same question. The response is, from Italy.* Aha, rather swarthy. Certainly not white. *He asks,* Is anyone here from Norway? *One hand goes up. Someone else declares they are from Sweden.* Yo, Sweden is also white. You two are pure white, I'm so sorry, but everyone else has a blight.

All the performers come out again and form a line facing the audience. One after the other, each performer recites one line of the poem below. They each speak slowly, clearly, and loudly.

> *You saw a play about power and might*
> *Who gets to tell others what is wrong or right*
> *If you're born with the brightest white skin*
> *You rule, you're automatically in*
> *But if you're born with a freckle or a spot*
> *Your pureness is gone, you've got a blot*
> *Or if you're a guy with a bit of a tan*
> *You lose out to the whiter-skinned man*
> *As you go home tonight*
> *Consider your skin*
> *Are you sure it's pure white?*
> *Thank you all, and good night.*

After the audience leaves, the Agitators for Change get together. Here are various comments.

"How'd we do?"

"Whaddya think?"

"Not much clapping. Some grunts."

"Not sure anyone left happy."

"I saw faces that were totally blank."

"They walked out like zombies."

"Some were in pain."

"Did anyone see angry faces?"

"Yeah, a few."

"We weren't a sensation."

"Yea, but we weren't trying to be."

"The truth hurts."

"I saw somebody who smirked and kinda gave me a tentative thumbs-up."

27

EMMA'S DILEMMA

The next day is Sunday. Roxy and Emma walk around town to try to get a sense of the mood. Emma wants to find a church. "What do we need a church for?"

"I'm determined to sermon."

Roxy finds the church that sponsored the Big Guy. Churchgoers mill about outside. Emma looks around, walks firmly to a bench, steps onto it, and waves for people to come over.

"Good morning, good believers. My name is Emma, and I've got a dilemma." Several individuals dressed in Sunday attire stand close enough to hear her. A couple of the elderly women look at her buzz haircut and up and down her jeans with more frayed gaps than fabric, and frown. Emma smiles at them. "I understand your dismay. Even though I don't look okay, please do come closer and hear what I have to say." Roxy stands off to the side and watches.

Emma wants a larger gathering, gets the attention of others, and when about two dozen individuals surround her, she begins again. "A good Sunday morning to you all. My name is Emma, and I've come to preach about my dilemma. I want to shed some light on America's racial plight."

She points to individuals in the crowd, then points to herself. Her tone of voice becomes matter-of-fact. "All of us here are white. We're the majority, but should we automatically get priority? Are we automatically right?"

She now makes long pauses between her statements. "In America . . . too often we show animosity with stinging ferocity . . . towards those who are not white . . . In America . . . we have this thing with religiosity, yet we lack generosity to those who arrive here as shadows."

She studies the expressions of her listeners, is clearly annoyed, and switches to a stern voice. "As I look around, look at your faces, I see lemon juice traces. You look sour, instead of a nod in agreement, you glower. Perhaps you'd rather I speak of pleasant things, chocolate, football, wedding rings?"

She now speeds up. "My fellow white Americans, you can shrug your shoulders and be smug, sweep your conscience under a rug, escape with a few beers to numb your knowledge of pain and tears. 'Cause when drunk, you can't tell that all is not sweet, all is not well, right now, right here, in our America. You're off to church hoping for redemption. You're asking your God for some personal attention. You're angling for your future heavenly ascension. But you don't give a rip about tension and dissension, right here, right now, in America. My friends and I are on a mission. We want to remove divisive partitions to improve living conditions. Right here, right now, in America . . . We need you. We implore you to help."

Emma is done. She looks up, tears roll down her cheeks. She finishes with, "And remember, my name is Emma, please help resolve my dilemma." She jumps down from the bench and walks away.

28

THE JESUS CHARADE

It's still Sunday, and in the afternoon it's time once again for the weekly "Light My Candle" celebration along with the appearance of Jesus in the basement of the church. The Kids witnessed these astonishing events as passive participants when they first arrived in town. This time the Agitators for Change participate in order to—what else?—agitate.

The room is packed. The Agitators don't sit together, rather they split up, so their presence is not immediately noticeable. Josy, the oldest agitator, is also in the crowd. When everyone is settled, a church member steps to the front and says a prayer similar to the one last week. "Dear Jesus, help all of us find the proper truth, let your shining light guide us on the path to what is good and right. Amen."

America gets up quickly. He wants to be first. "Some of you know me and have seen me grow up. I'm almost done with high school, but your light only points in the direction to what my older brothers and their friends are doing. Nothing. They're blind and grope in the dark." Someone interrupts, "What do ya mean, blind? What about Jesus's light?"

"It shines into a dead end. It doesn't offer them a way out."

Here comes Truck. "Hhrrrhhh hhrrrgh haghhtt. I've always just wanted to own a truck. But now I want more. How do I get it hhrrrhhh?"

Hammer joins in, "I want Jesus to shine the light on some options for college for me."

Each of these three local youngsters stand when they speak. Because they sit in different areas, the regular church members twist around in their seats to look at each speaker, and their astonishment seems to increase with each one.

Bobby Ray Aldridge, the mayor, is also here. He says pleadingly, "Son, you've just got to believe—"

"Oh, shut up." This is Josy now talking. "I've been believing all my life. Believing sounds good on Sunday. But what do we do the rest of the week? Believing doesn't work then."

The mayor holds his hands over his ears. "Stop, Josy. You're blaspheming."

Josy becomes angry. She pushes herself up from her wheelchair and stands. Izzy, sitting next to her, helps her. "Bobby Ray, open your ears. You blasphemed yesterday." She pauses, and looks straight at him. "When someone stole my purse, weren't you one of the first to blame a black kid? Is that what the holy light made you see? A white boy, America, you just heard him speak," she points to America, "he's the one who took my purse. The whole thing was part of a skit, you know. Open your eyes, Bobby Ray, the black kid with the weird hair is also here. Stand up, Jamal."

Jamal hesitates.

"Go ahead, stand up, Jamal."

He gets up, but looks uncomfortable.

"Look at him, Bobby Ray. You see him now, but you never saw him yesterday." She points to him, "You're guilty."

Something big just happened. No one breathes. No one stirs. The clock stops ticking. Everything is frozen.

Josy's guilty verdict reverberates. What she just dared to blare out loud triggers inaudible pandemonium. The room remains frozen. It takes a while before some dare to make the first cautious movement. Individuals lean towards their neighbors. A subdued sound of whispers emerges as heads turn closer together. Gradually, a murmur arises, a faint drum roll builds as the group murmur becomes more pronounced until it reaches a crescendo and finishes with the clashing crash of cymbals. The agitators begin to clap and cheer. Roxy yells "bravo," a few parishioners rise, express elation. After the first few, others also rise. A number of them jostle towards Josy, they greet, embrace, and thank Josy. Their faces look relieved. Who knows, maybe relieved from years of repressed, suppressed, compressed guilt.

The fairy tale continues.

After things settle down the discussion turns productive. Josy broke through the barrier that kept the previous Sunday afternoon discussions in this church mired in deception and delusion. Now the discussion turns to real options for youth: college, trade school, apprenticeships. How about travel?

Various comments emerge.

"You're right, these kids don't have options."

"Yeah, high school alone ain't enough no more."

Fritz suggests, "Maybe we should have some kinda high school exchange here in America. We do student exchanges with other countries, why not here?"

America jumps in. "I learned a lot from these guys from Minnesota. Could probably learn a lot more if I spent a couple of months in school up there."

The mayor, who has shrunk by at least a foot, cautiously tries to regain some stature by saying, "Whose gonna pay for that?"

He quickly gets pounded again by Josy. "Ever since you've been mayor, we quit spending money on anything, and look what we got. We got nothin'. Our kids got nothin'. Our town's got nothin'. If you don't invest, you get nothin'."

And guess what? Jesus was scheduled to make his usual appearance along with the onions to stimulate tears of joy, but Josy put an end to it because "We need to continue our real discussion."

The group breaks up later than usual. Many are reluctant to leave. People remain standing or they drift away ever so slowly in small groups, and there is the continuous buzz of chatter.

The Agitators head back to the house with high-fives. The appearance of the Big Guy in front of the bar is coming up soon. There is not much time.

Your narrator asks, how likely is this sudden shift in sentiment? Is it fantasy, or could such an abrupt change actually happen? If the agitators only consisted of outsiders, the turnaround would be wishful thinking. It couldn't happen. The local boys, while young, are given some credence. They are part of the clan. But it's the outspokenness of Josy, an elder, who makes the transformation of her listeners possible. She is trusted; she has credibility. And she succinctly expresses a clear reason to unlock an old chest and release musty positions long trapped inside because of conventional group think.

29

THE BIG GUY CHARADE

The crowd in front of the bar builds as people wait for the theatrical event featuring the performance of the Big Guy. History is repeating itself here. The men talk, argue, guffaw, and shout, relying on their favorite common goofy words that spike clear and loud above the crowd. It's amazing what happens to a group of men using limited vocabulary. Include but a few choice goofy terms as adjectives and nouns and fellow travelers nod, they get it, and respond in kind. They all went to the same school. They're connected; they agree; they become bros. In another era, they became comrades. Light a match and they could explode into a mob.

They can hear the band now as it comes closer, led by the pastor of the competing church. Right behind the band is the Big Guy on his horse, yet again followed by his posse, or perhaps his apostles, rugged guys on horses instead of their usual monster pickup trucks. Unfortunately, there is no beer drinking today outside the bar. Rumor has it that the sheriff is coming to town this evening, and so the bar wants to do what is right and proper, no drinking on the street.

But watch out, there is another difference. The agitators are dispersed among the crowd, of course, including Josy. And, here is the really encouraging news: some of the adults from the earlier church meeting are also participants, all ready to engage.

The pastor-bandleader signals—boom pa boom pa boom pa boom!—the end with his baton. The Big Guy gets help again to get off his horse, and both he and the pastor walk over to a little stage set up in front of the bar. And just like last time, the pastor uses a megaphone and starts with a prayer, "Lord, help us . . . " He then welcomes the crowd, reminds them that he and his church are sponsors of this event, and invites everyone who seeks truth to reach out to his church. They could even come during the week, "Our gates to heaven are always open." He finally introduces "the guy you all came to see, our savior, the Big Guy."

Amongst whoops and hollers the Big Guy's big voice booms, "Tremendous, incredible, truly incredible, truly. What a crowd, a tremendous crowd. You're beautiful! If you love me, show me your fist." Yeah, the men love this, love to pump their fists up.

A couple of small bottles pop up here and there, and some other illegal stuff. And why not? This is not unlike a rock concert.

"Truly amazing. We've been losing too long. We've been getting beat. No more." Cheers, and fists pumps! "Believe me, I'm a winner. I like winning. We're all gonna win big together, make America great again."

Now comes the unexpected, the undoing of this cozy weekly indulgence. Counter to the usual script a question comes from the audience. "What are you going to win for us?"

Some of the men turn around, they wonder who asked. The Big Guy also searches, but can't find the questioner. He stammers just a bit, "Oh, what? Ah, we're going to make America great again. Who is with me?"

"Wait, what specifically are you going to win?" The question comes from a different area in the crowd. Heads turn again.

The Big Guy tries to continue, "Ah, great again. America, ah, isn't that winning?" Questions and comments now come quickly from different areas.

"Which era in the past will you take us back to?"

"We don't want to go back to the past."

"We want a better future."

"Give us specifics about our future."

The Big Guy looks dumbfounded. He stands there with his mouth wide open.

One of the men howls, "What the goofy is goofying going on? Who are these goofy goofholes?" The reader's imagination can interpret that.

Josy is clamoring to unlock the chest again. This time she wants to stand on her wheelchair, and Roxy and Zoom come over to help her. The girls have to hold on to her, but as she straightens up and rises above the heads of the others, she explodes. "Enough!" she roars. "Young man, you need to expand your vocabulary! So you can expand your mind! So you can expand your horizon!"

He, visibly angry, constrains himself, responds with, "Lady, you gotta leave. This is our weekly thing."

"How very generous of you to choose more refined words," says Josy with exaggerated sweetness.

Now he can't hold his venomous tongue. "Why, you old goofy witch, come on guys, help me get her the goof out of here."

Some of the men grumble. Finally, a brave voice speaks out. "Let her stay. Let her speak."

The guy hesitates, looks around, hesitates some more, then decides to leave. He coaxes a couple of other guys to also leave, but most of the men stay.

Josy says, "Thank you for staying. I know, the Big Guy is entertaining, but he is like a fake Santa Claus full of bluster. He makes promises of gifts he won't keep, he can't deliver. Don't you men want real solutions that work?"

As Zoom and Roxy help Josy down from her pedestal, Izzy hops to the front. She nudges the Big Guy aside. "Hi everybody, I'm Izzy, I'm from Minnesota. I've been here for a while and I'm interested in your town."

Somebody yells out, "Whaddya like about our town?"

"I didn't say like, I said interested."

Someone else moans, "Yeah, what's to like here."

Izzy: "But wouldn't you want to make it better?"

A shout from somewhere, "Hey, little girl, who the goofy are you?"

Roxy scrambles to the front, gnashing her teeth, stands up straight and tall right next to Izzy. "The age of little girls is over, big boy. You have an option. You can leave silently with Billy, or stay and be part of a conversation. We demand respect."

The Agitators for Change are getting somewhere. A discussion follows, well, it's not a real back-and-forth discussion, just statements kind of loosely connected. Hammer says something, so does America. Some of the men speak up, and individuals who were present at church in the afternoon join in. A few comments are pro the Big Guy, others not, but these snippets of conversation become blocks that build interest and confidence.

"As a businessman he's created swamps, so maybe he can get us out."

"He don't know nothin' about us average folks."

"Yeah, but at least he promises stuff. The other guys don't promise nothin'."

"Come on, man, he says the same stuff over and over again, and we fall for it."

"With all respect to the pastor here, but thoughts and prayers don't mean all that much."

"He's talked about jobs, but what about goofy pay? Oops, sorry. I just meant to say what about pay."

Izzy, still in front, says this is a promising start, but, "We need to keep the talk going." She invites everyone to a jamboree. Tomorrow, 6 p.m., at Josy's house. "You're all invited. Bring your friends."

Roxy, still in front, yells, "Bring bongos, drums, pots, tambourines, anything to pound on. We're gonna have a mass drumming, a drumming for democracy."

Izzy: "We'll supply some food and, listen to this, you guys can bring beer." She gets surprised faces and a lot of smiles.

30

DRUMMING FOR DEMOCRACY

The next evening represents a culmination. The Kids have been working towards this for quite a while, wanting to make a difference. They are pumped. Izzy says, "I'll be over the moon with happiness if this works."

It's sweltering hot with stagnant air, but people arrive early and keep coming. The crowd grows larger than expected. Everyone, absolutely everyone, carries something. Fritz works two grills—no, wait, correction, he actually operates three grills. One came with the house. He had to go borrow one from a neighbor, and who knows where the other came from. Burgers, brats, buns, chips, soda, water, even beer— the works. It's a picnic. Izzy has to send Diego to the convenience store for more food. Of course, Diego takes Mario along.

But more important than the food are the percussion instruments. There might be more drums than people. Even before anything gets started, there are various unconnected and discordant drum sounds, bum bum rat tat tat bum. Humans love to bang on something, listen to the thud. It's a universal pleasure, been around since our hunter-gatherer days. And when you start to bang, you quickly create a sequence, you repeat, it pushes itself forward, your heartbeat, ba bum, ba bum, ba bum, ba bum, ba bum, ba bum.

Somewhere in the crowd someone with magical hands on bongos taps out, bah bah bum, bah bum, bah bah bum, bah bum, bah bah bum, bah bum. It catches on, and others join in. At first, it's a bit uneven, but quickly the sweating drummers drum in sync bah bah bum, bah bum, bah bah bum, bah bum, bah bah bum, bah bum.

"Just look at that crowd!" Izzy might just have to jump over the moon.

"I've seen so many bongos," says Roxy, "but I've also seen a snare drum, several congas, and would you believe a bass drum?"

There are also homemade instruments, a pair of decorated coffee cans, shakers, and a unique tambourine.

Hammer points out that an ingenious drummer bangs with a hammer on an empty beer keg that is cut open. "No, it's not one of my relatives."

The beat resonates and mesmerizes, bah bah bum, bah bum, bah bah bum, bah bum, bah bah bum, bah bum. The sound bounces off the wall of the house, shakes the tress, infiltrates the shrubs, and glides off the ground. Izzy bangs on a pot. Fritz tends to the grills with seemingly three hands, and somehow manages to bang on a log he hollowed out for the occasion. Jamal has an African djembe. He's really into it, contributes a high-pitched yell to the first beat hui bah bah bum, bah bum, hui bah bah bum, bah bum, hui bah bah bum, bah bum. Other shouts and yelps skip and jump through the throng. Drumming is intense; drumming is primitive; drumming brings us back to our roots; drumming satisfies; drumming unifies; drumming unifies; drumming unifies; bah bah bum, bah bum, bah bah bum, bah bum, bah bah bum, bah bum. Drumming unifies.

The beat changes from time to time. Now it's a thumping bum bum, debumpadebum, bum bum, debumpadebum, bum bum, debump-adebum, bum bum, debumpadebum, bum bum, debumpadebum, hui bum bum, debumpadebum, hui bum bum, debumpadebum.

The drumming keeps rolling, but individuals get up at times to stretch their legs, get food, sip on a beer, bump fists. Small groups stand around. People smile, chat, nod their heads. The chatting is sober, only an occasional goofy expletive.

There is a wide banner attached to the house, "Drumming for Democracy." The Agitators for Change take turns circulating with their drums. The Kids from Minnesota introduce themselves to individuals and small groups, talk about where they've been, what they're doing, why they're here, what they are for. The locals, Hammer, Truck, Jamal, and America, all of them, eagerly talk about their newfound longing for more.

All the while drummers pound away in unison, drumming, drumming, drumming, drumming, drumming bum bum, debumpadebum sending dopamine to drummers' sweaty brains.

Emma moves around and talks to the men about her Emma dilemma, namely, a "Collection of protection." Emma's use of rhymes immediately puts the men on the defensive, but they bounce back with vigor after she asks if there's a gun at home. Sure, you bet, almost all of the men have at least one. She follows up with "For protection, right?" She then asks, "What about dental insurance? What about health insurance? Are your kids protected or neglected?" The face of the other dives into confusion. She keeps the pressure on and asks about unions. "Are you protected by a union?" Puzzled looks. "You know your employer has a bunch of lawyers to protect the might of the company, right?" Mental turbulence. "Hey, take this from me, Emma. Sounds like you have a serious dilemma."

Izzy bangs on the old washtub. It's huge and produces a loud brash thud. That stops the drumming. Izzy smiles broadly, says she has some news. Diego walks up with his son, Mario, on his shoulders. He sets Mario down, and holds his hands. "I'm brown, most of you don't like me, most of you don't trust me. But I stay. I make this town my home."

The crowd remains silent. Someone asks, "Where will you live?"

"Right here in Josy's house. Gonna rent."

"But you'll need a job."

Diego nods his head. "I have a job. I will work for Bobby Ray, the mayor, in his store." He points to the mayor in the crowd. Heads turn to look.

The mayor steps through the crowd and comes to the front. He starts to speak thoughtfully, hesitating between sentences. "We need to make some changes . . . Maybe some of us have to learn a few things . . . Maybe some of us got stuck . . . like Josy says she got stuck . . . I like the drumming . . . I like some of the stuff we're talking about . . . Maybe we can figure out how to do some of that stuff." The crowd is abuzz.

Izzy steps forward again and says she has more news. America walks up to the front. He looks a little nervous, swallows hard. "I know the town, always been here, but don't know much about America. Planning to spend half a year in a high school in St. Paul, Minnesota, starting in January. My friends helped make arrangements, and Josy here will help with some money."

Again, the crowd is quiet, but as clapping begins and quickly grows stronger a breeze also emerges. There are yells. "Attaboy." "Good for you." Individuals come up to congratulate him, others shake the hands of the mayor, the Kids get hugs, and now drum sounds begin again with a new beat, dat da, dat da, dat dat dah, dat da, dat da, dat dat dah, dat da, dat da, dat dat dah, dat da, dat da, dat dat dah. It throbs and pulsates, full of passion, faces of drummers are intense, dat da, dat da, dat dat dah. Voices join in, a few at first, then more and more—it's contagious, mysterious, unifying, DRUM MING FOR DE MO CRA CY, DAT DA, DAT DA, DAT DAT DAH, DRUM MING FOR DE MO CRA CY, DAT DA, DAT DA, DAT DAT DAH, DRUM MING FOR DE MO CRA CY, DAT DA, DAT DA, DAT DAT DAH, DRUM MING FOR DE MO CRA CY, DAT DA, DAT DA, DAT DAT DAH, it goes on and on, the drumming flowing and the wind blowing long into the night.

31

A HELLUVA PLAN

What a night! Zoom is up much too early. She surveys the grounds. The area looks like what you'd expect after humanity reveled. The grass is matted. Used plates, utensils, cups, and bottles of all kinds clutter tables and the ground next to chairs. The ashes from the campfire are still hot. Zoom combs through the embers with a stick and finds a couple of sweet potatoes, now completely burned. Fritz had thrown them in for a late-night hunter-gatherer type of snack. And over there, an errant drum someone left behind. All by itself it raps a beat that Zoom must hear as she hip-hops around.

What a week! It's over, all the planning activities, the discussions and ideas that lead to the entrance into the town, the preparations for the theater shenanigans, the hijacking of the men who let themselves be entertained by the Big Guy, and then the actual Drumming for Democracy. And who will ever forget the feats of Josy. She broke barriers, twice standing up to controlling men and forcing retreat. In the Middle Ages, Josy might have been burned at the stake, but today she speaks truth that overcomes injustice.

What do these Agitators for Change do now? They move about aimlessly searching for something, their energy sapped. Izzy knows the feeling. She tries to cheer up individual agitators who are idling about. "This letdown is normal. After the run of a play, actors often flounder with a feeling of emptiness."

The next couple of days they just hang around, clean up, talk some, and get themselves ready to move on. Jamal, Truck, and Hammer are in limbo. Josy is back in her nursing home. Emma is still around. Zoom seems to have disappeared, probably working on some art project. Izzy, Fritz, and Roxy are, well, zombies. Only America and Diego are upbeat. America will head north later to live with the Kids. Diego is about to start his new job and make this his new home.

The Kids wonder to what extent they succeeded with their high hopes. Izzy is somber, "Yeah, we put on a show, wanted a revolution of ideas. We tried to energize everyone."

Roxy responds, somewhat dejected, "Yeah, we did energize some, but not enough."

Fritz sums it up: "Turns out that changing people's minds is as hard as trying to push a thread though the eye of a needle."

Here is a rhyme Izzy wrote expressing her disappointment:

Something is wrong / I wanna make it right / My ideas come strong / My mind takes flight / I reach for the moon / Reach for the stars / But far too soon / I'm left with scars / Those who are wrong / They hold on tight.

So, how much has changed? Will life go on like before? Who knows? Will Jesus continue to appear weekly? And will the other church continue with the Big Guy in their marketing stunt? Sure, perhaps a few hundred people saw their theater performance, and another sizable group participated in the Drumming for Democracy. Those are some small victories, but they only reached a portion of the town's population. A thousand or more did not come for any of their events.

In the midst of this discontent, someone shows up who revives their spirits and brings a new opportunity to agitate. You'll never guess who it is.

It's The Actor who performs as Jesus and the Big Guy! Even though he has a name, he wants to be called by his profession. To respect his wish, we will continue to refer to him here as The Actor.

The Actor walks through the gate into the yard and insists to meet with the "theater director." Izzy, and the others who are here, come to see what the newcomer wants. He's more than a bit longwinded. He introduces himself as The Actor. He has always loved make-believe. Even as a kid, he knocked on people's doors impersonating cops, "Hello in there, this is the police, open up," or a tax collector, "Knock, knock, I'm from the IRS, you're in trouble." Since junior high, he's been "starring" in plays. In high school, he acted "all the major roles" to "standing ovations," he "rocked the auditorium," he "knows" he has the unique "gift" of not just "playing" a character. He actually "becomes" the character, which is a sign of "really, really good acting." He has to take a breath. He heard this group did a play where the Big Guy was portrayed. He heard the acting was bad, and he has come to offer his "assistance" for future performances.

Well, no one is quite sure what to make of this. They don't have any further plans to perform Make America Great and Bright Again? but Roxy quickly asks The Actor to sit down. Would he like something to drink? She hurries into the house, but takes a long time to come out again. When she finally does, you can tell her mind is abuzz. She hands him a drink and tells him to sit tight. She has to have a discussion with her friends "about offering you a job."

The young people move off to the side. The Actor is left alone to wait. He looks at the group but he can't hear them. To him, individuals must look like characters in a silent movie. Suggestive body language, heads turning his way. Perhaps he wonders what is going on. He watches the girl who brought him a bottle of water engage the others. She seems super excited as the others stand around her and listen to her talk. Full of energy, she stops for at most two seconds to allow someone to say a word, only to power ahead again, her mouth in constant motion. Her face is expressive. She must have a big idea. Maybe the girl is trying to convince the others.

Roxy comes alone to him and says, "You can come back tomorrow at this time. I think we will have made a decision." And with that she goes back to the group, and they disappear into the house.

The next day arrives and so does The Actor. The group greets him warmly. They all introduce themselves, welcome him, shake his hand, and yes, they want to hire him. They have an idea. It could be the biggest role he has ever performed, no, not here, and yes, they would have to prepare and rehearse for a couple of days. Is he interested? You bet, of course he is.

The other members of the Agitators for Change all come aboard. The four local kids definitely want to participate. Emma was planning to leave, but now, no way, she will stay. "This idea is unbelievable. Leaving now is inconceivable." Josy is all in also. Diego was to begin his new job at the convenience store, but Bobby Ray Aldridge, the mayor and convenience store owner, wants him to delay his start so he can participate in a "helluva plan."

The next few days they spend in seclusion with The Actor. Even the men of his posse come several times. They will play an important role.

Without a doubt, this will be a challenge for The Actor because he will perform without a specific script. Unable to rely on memorized lines, he'll have to ad lib on the big stage and be ready for anything. Does he have the skills to be nimble?

They have planned all that can possibly be planned for. Tomorrow they leave in a procession of vehicles. They will drive about 100 miles to the state capital, a medium-sized city. And then?

32

PEOPLE WANT PIE

Everyone gathers early in the afternoon. There is nervous anticipation. Maybe the stifling temperature is a factor. You can hear snippets of concern from the posse members.

"These kids are crazy."

"We're only doing this for The Actor."

"But we also gotta protect the youngsters, right?"

"We'll see."

Everyone realizes this is an undertaking with an uncertain outcome. They all know how the adventure will begin—13 vehicles will have to be aligned, but there is concern about how it will end.

Zoom, Fritz, and the local kids, Truck, Hammer, and America, ride in the minivan. It's in the lead and, of course, is still decorated with the zany American flag made wavy with the help of baseball-sized dents. Various inscriptions remain on the other side, including a plea for health care and better schools.

A caravan of 12 pickup trucks follows. The Actor, along with Roxy and Izzy, rides in a black truck in the middle of the caravan. A posse member drives. That truck is dressed up with four American flags, two attached to the front, one on each side, two in the back. Posse members drive the other vehicles. Emma, Jamal, and Diego each ride with different posse members. Josy does not go because of her wheelchair. Also, Diego does not take Mario; it's too dangerous. Bobby Ray is going to watch him in his store.

The trip takes a couple of hours. The caravan arrives at the outskirts of this regional hub by late afternoon and comes to a stop in the parking lot of a large shopping center. The agitators in the minivan want to coordinate with the others exactly what they are going to do.

It's Saturday, and people are out and about. Some come closer to see what the odd-looking lineup of vehicles is all about when the unexpected happens. Someone points and shrieks, "That's him!"

In a flash people appear and surround the truck. "Holy goof, he's here. It's the Big Guy." Some wave to others coming out of the shopping center, "Here, over here, quick."

The Actor, suddenly recognized, seizes the opportunity. He steps out of the truck, has to laugh, shakes hands, "Hey, how are ya, good to see ya." Posse members help him climb into the cargo bed. The Actor rises. He's in his element. He smiles broadly, waves, what a thrill.

People can't believe their good fortune, they cheer and holler, phone cameras come out in force, selfies with him in the background, evidence for ever and ever that they were at the same place at the same time.

Somebody in the crowd surely says, "This trumps everything I've ever experienced."

Someone yells, "Where's your limo?"

The Actor yells back, "I dumped it. Don't need it. Just need a pickup truck. I'm one of you."

The growing throng crowding around him is bewildered. "Is it really you?"

"Yeah, it's me."

But others stay away. They look, shake their heads. "What the goof is going on here?"

The commotion attracts the scrutiny of a cop standing beyond the crowd who looks confused. One hand is on his belt with all his policing equipment, and the other hand is rubbing his face. Perhaps he's wondering if he missed the announcement of some scheduled public activity. One of the posse members walks over to speak with him, points to The Actor in the pickup truck, pokes a finger into the cop's chest, and gives him a thumbs-up as the officer hurries back to his squad car to call in to headquarters. Within minutes a dozen squad cars arrive, sirens blaring. The Actor, still standing in the back of the truck, says "Hey, thank you, America's finest. We are going to win with you. Come on, let's give these incredible policemen a hand," and with that people raise a cheer for the cops.

A couple of the posse members call some of the cops over. They do all the talking; the cops do all the listening. When back in their respective trucks, the caravan starts to roll again, now with the additional and altogether unexpected protection from the police department of this state capital.

The caravan has now become a motorcade. It moves slowly, walking speed, so that the people from the shopping center can keep up on both sides of the street. As the police cars with flashing lights—followed by the minivan, followed by 12 pickup trucks, followed by more police cars—move deeper into the city, the delighted crowd accompanying this fabulous procession keeps building. What a sight!

Here is the view from inside the minivan. Truck gushes hhrrrgh, "Look, look, look at those lights, guys, hhrrrgh blue red blue red blueredblueredbluered, awesome, man."

Hammer, the dude responsible for the dents, is thrilled that the minivan is getting so much attention. "Man, our car's a hit. People point at the flag and take photos."

Fritz advises, "Open the window, yell out you are the artist and offer autographs."

But what's with Zoom? She turns philosophical, or maybe it could be better described as fuzzysophical. "The surprising and totally unexpected appearance of The Actor, ah, I mean the Big Guy, is having a humongous influence on these people. It's given them a jolt, maybe it's cleared their minds, uncluttered them, giving them a spring cleaning."

What? The silence of the others indicates they have no idea what she is talking about, so she adds, "Never mind. I've been working on something. You'll see it later."

The mood from within the pickup truck containing The Actor is tense, filled with anticipation. Izzy and Roxy try to remain disciplined. They compliment The Actor for his composure at the parking lot, but they remind him that the biggest challenge is to come. They want to review various situations that could arise along with his best responses to them. "Hey, Actor, are you listening?"

"Yeah, sure," but he is infatuated by the crowd, keeps looking out the window, completely giddy. He keeps waving to his supporters and mouthing, "I love you too."

As they get close to downtown the crowd changes. The locals from the shopping center and residents from along the motorcade route are joined by boisterous followers of the Big Guy who have come from far and wide. It's now a foaming swell of red Make America Great Again hats, emblazoned Big Guy shirts, an abundance of American flags, pro-America slogans, camo outfits, chants and cheers, and provocative faces with itchy fists searching for infiltrators from other clans.

Even more cops escort the motorcade now. They walk beside the pickup trucks looking serious and keeping people at a distance. Finally, everything comes to a stop in front of the convention center. Izzy tells The Actor, "You're on. Remember our objective," and she adds a quick reminder, "Stop smiling, you have to look stern." She whispers to Roxy, "If they think he's an imposter, we're doomed."

The Actor steps out of the truck. Police officers immediately surround him, but the posse members know what to do. They move the cops aside, and help The Actor onto the truck bed. A couple of posse members talk to the cops. They again do all the talking. The cops listen and nod. Several posse members take positions inside the truck bed at the edges and stare into the army of tumultuous followers.

Izzy and Roxy climb onto the truck without help. Roxy notices a wooden box and gets The Actor to step on it, so he can grow by a couple of feet. Izzy reminds him again: "Give 'em your most serious look."

He feigns a scowl, steps onto the box, and gradually turns 360 degrees, barely shuffling his feet. While turning, he keeps his right arm stretched, repeatedly pumping into the air, saluting his admirers all around him.

Let your mind wander, dear reader, and imagine a small vintage music box with a rotating wooden figure. That little figurine, colorfully painted, turns 360 degrees to lovely chimes. Compared to that dummy, our Actor, turning on his wooden box and performing as the Big Guy, represents a contemporary, live version. But he does not rotate to jingles, he rotates to a cacophony of roars and shouts that make his head swell with pride and dreams of power.

Izzy and Roxy standing beside him on the truck must have goosebumps that tingle. Their eyes are open wide. What do they see? They see a mass of humanity in a spacious area with raw and sweaty faces trying to squeeze closer. They see signs held high with various messages of support and cops protected by riot gear. Farther away, they see groups confronting each other, someone with a large camera and others, perhaps reporters, threatened with flying fists and fast kicks. They see pandemonium.

But as Izzy later recounts, she sees more. She sees pent up frustration; she sees despair; she sees anger. She also sees frauds, sweet swindlers, paid provokers, and yes, fanatics. She sees fanatics out to spread fanaticism, and with that she sees visions of blackwhitered that once decorated a fascist flag in the last century. She sees madness; she sees danger.

The Actor is perspiring and might be a little nervous. He waves his hat back and forth near his face to move the air and says exactly the same thing he said previously. "Hey, how are ya, good to see ya," and he praises the police, "Thank you, America's finest." Not sure anyone heard what he just said. Someone forgot to give him a microphone. "Hello out there, can you hear me now?" Yeah. Wahoo. The response from the crowd builds his confidence. "Hey, listen, listen to me. I've got some really, really big news." While rotating on his pedestal similar to the wooden dummy in the music box, he theatrically points with one hand to different areas of the crowd. At the same time, he places the forefinger of his other hand conspicuously over his lips. Someone in the crowd yells, "Shut up and listen."

"Do you want to be the first to hear gigantic news?"

Yeah, yeah, loud cheers. "Is it about the wall?"

"No, not the wall."

He now pauses dramatically between each statement. "I've got a plan . . . my own personal plan . . . to give something back."

Loud cheers. Long pause.

Roxy nudges him with her hand and says, "Go ahead, say it."

"I . . . I'm making a sacrifice . . . I will give . . . give up . . . give up all of my real estate . . . I will donate it all to you."

The crowd barely reacts.

"My towers . . . my hotels . . . I'm donating them all to the USA."

This unexpected revelation still only gets a limited reaction.

He adds, "I'll even throw in my golf courses!"

Maybe his supporters do not fully understand what he means. Roxy, like turning the mechanism to restart the wooden figure in the music box again, nudges him. "Keep going, don't stop, go to PIE."

"There is more . . . I am here to announce a new program."

The crowd is unsettled. They are not getting the entertainment they expect, the Big Guy's regular insults and abuses.

Roxy nudges him again, "Faster. Now, say it now."

"First, pay. Listen to this new program. I will double the minimum wage."

Whoa! That gets the crowd's attention.

"Second, insurance. All Americans will get the same health insurance elected politicians get—and listen, listen, at a lower, a much lower cost."

Now there's a definite buzz.

"And finally, education. Free education and reeducation for all workers. Community colleges will come to rural America."

That arouses the crowd. Excitement is definitely building as people begin to understand these new developments. A refreshing breeze arrives that fans the growing enthusiasm.

Meanwhile, members of the Agitators for Change are dispersed in the crowd handing out stickers.

The Actor reaches for his MAGA hat, takes it off, holds it up high. "Everyone take off your hats. Punch the top down and turn them inside out, like this. Now apply this new sticker to the front of your hat, like this." The Actor continues. "Your hat should look like this." He holds up his hat with a PIE sticker in front, then places it onto his head. On his wooden pedestal he slowly turns around again 360 degrees pointing to his hat.

As a breeze builds pushing the stifling oppression out, Izzy grabs the microphone. She holds up a hat with the PIE sticker. "Ladies and Gentlemen, this PIE program is for you. It will improve your life. 'P' is for pay. You will earn more. 'I' is for insurance. You'll be insured. And 'E' is for education. You can improve job skills. Who likes this PIE?"

Cheers.

"Who wants some PIE?"

Tumultuous cheers.

"What do you want?"

The crowd screams, "PIE."

"Can't hear you."

"PIE."

"When do you want PIE? Now or later?"

"Now! We want PIE now! PIE now! PIE now! PIE now!"

"What do all Americans deserve?"

"PIE!"

"Who wants a slice of PIE?"

The crowd, refreshed, rejuvenated, invigorated, is delirious.

The Actor again: "There is more." He quiets the crowd only with his finger across his lips. They watch him, follow him. It's a different crowd now. It's positive; the edge is gone. PIE is good for everyone.

He continues, "How we gonna pay for it?"

The crowd becomes expectant.

"There will be higher taxes for high earners, higher taxes on luxury goods, higher taxes on some businesses. And, listen to this, lower taxes on the middle class."

The scene becomes crazy, difficult to describe.

Roxy nudges him again. "Okay, that's it. Finish."

He ends by saying, "I'll see you inside the convention center."

Roxy takes the mic from him as the wind picks up. "Listen, listen everyone. When you go inside, chant, 'I want PIE.' And don't let him forget. Remind him, keep reminding him, you want PIE."

Posse members tell the cops that they can handle things now. "See you guys inside." And they depart.

33

A SURPRISE GUEST

The following afternoon they celebrate. Of course, Josy's house is the venue, and pie is on the menu. Emma went to the bakery first thing in the morning and ordered dozens of "people's pies."

"What kind of pies do you want?"

"I want people's pies decorated with the words 'Pay, Insurance, and Education.' It's a new rallying cry for a hungry nation. Trademark it and your bakery will become a sensation."

Everyone who went along for the adventure yesterday shows up, and they bring genuine excitement. Hugs, hand slaps, fist bumps, crazy new hand greetings. The posse members hang together at a couple of picnic tables and enjoy coconut people's pie, lemon meringue people's pie, and apple crisp people's pie washed down with beer.

Josy had to stay behind yesterday, but she is now eager to hear from others about what she refers to as "your fairy tale."

They tell her and give her various details about the cops, the motorcade, the adoring fans of the Big Guy, and, of course, the PIE episode.

Josy is so proud of everyone. "Tell me again, Roxy, how you saved the situation from ruin."

"Sure. When The Actor said that he would donate everything, his skyscrapers, his jewels, his golf empires, the people didn't react. I was standing right next to him and noticed he did not know what to do. He looked nervous. Afraid all would be lost, that we could be exposed, I took charge. I screamed into his ear, 'Pie, pie, move onto pie,' and he regained his composure." Roxy squeezes out a smile and slightly nods her head. "And that did it. People went crazy."

The Actor stands tall, a little bit off to the side. He probably did not hear Roxy's retelling. He looks dignified and gushes about how "my people" cheered for him. "I said, 'I'm one of you,' and they loved me. And when I declared with confidence, 'Pie, pie for all,' they became delirious. They threw kisses, some cried, I had them in my grasp. I could have said 'charge,' and they would have . . . "

Izzy jumps in with, "Yeah, you were awesome. You became the Big Guy."

The Actor continues. "And just before we left, when I shook the hands of a couple of policemen and said they were 'the greatest,' a couple of guys in front called me Caesar. And they yelled, 'Hail Caesar.' Then I heard them shout something I didn't understand. They shouted a couple of times, 'Give him the Bellamy salute.' But then we quickly left, and I didn't see what happened after that."

At exactly this moment a woman steps through the gate into Josy's yard. "You know what ze Bellamy salute is, right?"

Heads turn around. Izzy goes, "Ohmygod."

"Guten Tag, Helga here." She comes with a plan to snare frauds.

She walks to the group, greets Izzy and the Kids first, "Hallo Izzy, I remember our conversation in the bus. Now I'm wis you again." She shakes everyone's hand, one after the other, and says each time, "I am Helga, very nice to meet you." To The Actor she says, "You must be very gut. I hear what you just said." She waves to the posse still eating pie and drinking beer, "Hallo, Helga here. I sink you are heroes."

If ever there was an entrance that stopped everyone cold, this was it. Izzy and the Kids, who have seen her before, and as the reader knows, will see her again, scratch their heads. The others don't move, don't say anything. The members of the posse stop eating and drinking and watch.

Helga asks, "Does anyone know what ze Bellamy salute is?"

No one replies.

"It's ze Heil Hitler salute." She raises her right arm straight out. "Zat's it."

She gets wrinkled brows and open mouths.

"You did it in America to salute ze flag."

A shy sounding voice, it's Izzy's, asks, "The Nazi flag?"

"Nein, ze American flag. When you did your Pledge of Allegiance before ze war you did ze Bellamy salute."

Everyone stands around awkwardly. They look like submissive pupils in school.

"Zen when ze fascists in Europe used ze raised arm to say hallo to zere dictators, you changed and started to say hallo to your flag by crossing your heart." She waits, looks at individuals, "Did you not know zat?"

Izzy, again quietly, says, "No, I did not know that."

"Ja, ja. And now ze Bellamy salute is coming back mit some people. Nein, not to say hallo to ze flag, but to say hallo to zeir white friends and to Caesar. Zat is not gut."

After the shock wears off and they are able to speak again, there are so many questions. "How did you get here?"

"I come here vis limo. Look." She points to a black limousine beyond the hedge parked on the street. "I come in zat."

"How did you find us?"

"I sink I told you in ze bus. Maybe I forgot. I know how to open doors, find out zings."

"I can't believe it."

"Maybe it is a dream."

Fritz whispers to Izzy, "Maybe she's a fake, like the actor."

"No, it's Helga all right."

After they engage in some small talk, Helga asks where she can lie down. She wants to rest a bit. Zoom immediately offers her room. The others take notice as Zoom has been peculiar of late. No one has been allowed into her room. Both Zoom and Helga leave with Helga getting the final word in, "Oh, zat pie is gut. Ve don't haf pie in Tschermany."

In the evening, everyone but The Actor and his posse gathers for what turns out to be entertainment from Helga. First someone has to buy wine. White wine from the Rhine. "Ja, ja, zat's ze best wine. Please get a couple of bottles for me."

Glass in hand, Helga offers a toast to friendship and to "working togeser, ja?" She takes a sip. "Nein, zat is not wine from ze Rhein wis its beautiful castles."

Fritz says, "Sorry, but . . ."

"I suppose it will have to do. I want to drink a little bit so I can sleep on my vay to Washington later."

"You're leaving for Washington?"

"Ja, ja. I go wis ze limousine later tonight. I must be zere tomorrow morning. You come sree days later, right?"

"You want us to come to Washington?"

"Ja, ja, I tell you why later. It's very important."

Helga the enigma. "I was in a novel once. I'm still zere, ze novel is still zere, but I'm now here."

"What do you mean?"

"A riter made me a karacter in a novel long time ago. He put me into one of his big books and pushed me back in history, way before ze second world war. Ze real me was born at ze end of ze war."

"Who is the writer?"

"I tell you later. First, sis. I was a quiet girl, a little shy. But in ze novel he made me strong. He made me into a fighter, not afraid of anysing. He made me take chances, do what was forbidden. He made me unlock zings and peek inside."

That strikes a chord with Izzy. "That must be weird. Being made into a character who is different, at a different time, doing different things."

"Ja, ja. I wasn't even born yet, and I was already getting in trouble. So now I haf two lives. One in ze book and one right here."

Zoom wants to know which one is more interesting.

"If I would haf stayed shy, my life would be boring. But as I got older, I became more like ze karacter in ze novel. Ze karacter is a little imp. Uses tricks to expose criminals and crooks. Isn't zat funny? Today I haf no fear. I am strong. Sometimes I feel zat I haf magical powers. So I haf come to change America."

"Please, Fritz, anozer glass."

Josy clears her throat. "I'm not in a book, but a long time ago someone wrote a poem about me."

Zoom wants to know if she kept it—does she remember any lines?

Josy stands up from her wheelchair. She steadies herself. As her eyes look past everyone towards the horizon a slight smile crosses her lips. "I solemnly swear / Your beauty is rare / And I'll forever be true / For I love only you."

"That is so sweet. What happened to him?"

"Oh, it was just puppy love. But I still have the poem."

Helga takes a sip, then, "Ze sing about good riters is zat zey make sings up. Poets too. You never know what is true and what is not. My riter was much older zan me. I visited him a lot. He was like an uncle, and he told me stories all ze time. He would say something like, 'Zis actually happened,' or 'It's true, I was zere myself.' But many of his stories are not true, they are lies."

Izzy jumps in, "But isn't that the way of fiction? I mean, fiction is a story that is made up."

"Ja, ja, of course. It doesn't matter if a story is true or not. What's important is zat ze riter, and ze poet also, uses imagination to make ze story gut. And if it's very gut you remember it. Like Josy."

Helga has a plan. After another sip of wine, she says, "Ze wine now tastes a little better. Now we are slowly getting to why I come.

"Who rites poems, who tells stories? Poets and riters who are dreamers do. If ze story is gut, it's a little bit like a dream, we don't care if it actually happened." She takes another sip. "Accountants don't. From accountants, we don't want dreams of debits and credits. We must haf facts, real information about money, of where zings stand.

Just imagine if an accountant were a dreamer, or perhaps a schemer." Helga stops. Looks at her audience. She waits. Is she waiting for a response, or a question?

Josy asks Fritz to pour Helga another glass. "I want you to talk some more."

Helga chuckles and says, "Sank you.

"Poets and accountants. Where do your American rulers fit in? Do zey use facts and figures, rely on information to govern? Nein, we get fiction from zem. Love poems wisout rhyme. Lies."

Helga has half a glass of wine left. "I've had enough. I will be able to sleep." She pours the rest out.

"And now, listen to zis." She stops. With her pointer finger, she beckons for everyone to come closer. She continues in a whisper, "I too will become a dreamer. I will create fiction zat traps zem."

Back to her normal voice. "I want you, Izzy, and definitely Zoom . . ." She stops to interject, "By ze way, you all haf a nice surprise coming tomorrow from Zoom."

Zoom is caught off guard. She looks down and her cheeks blush.

Helga continues, "So Izzy, ja, and definitely Zoom, you must come. But I also want Fritz to be zere. I haf a feeling zat Fritz will become Tom Sawyer. We will see. And also Roxy, who has been quiet, but I sink zat you will not be so quiet at ze costume ball in Washington. You all must come."

It's entirely Helga's show. No one knows what to say.

"And now I must go. Ze limousine is vaiting." She shakes everyone's hand, says "Gut bye." She moves close to Josy and speaks into her ear. She says, "Your lover was a dreamer."

Emma watches Helga step into her limo. She says to no one in particular, "It looks like she is one of a kind. There is no rhyme to Helga, I've searched my mind."

34

THE CITADEL OF ART

A wind is blowing in the small bedroom upstairs. Zoom is holed up there with the door closed. She has been there for days interrupted only by the caravan adventure to the state capital and when Helga visited.

Zoom and Roxy shared the bedroom, but Zoom asked Roxy to leave. She needed to be alone. She leaves the room for quick meals, then a sign remains on her door: KEEP OUT.

The others wonder what's going on. Is she depressed? Does she have some sort of ailment? Is she in love? Swooning over someone? Roxy is sure Zoom is working on an art project. "She always isolates herself when she is consumed by an idea."

But, but . . . there is uncertainty.

"It's been so long."

"Hhrrrhhh hhrrrgh, I saw her bring tons of gallons of paint, hhr-rrgh, into the house a week ago. Maybe, hhrrrgh, she's painting the room real thick like."

The day before the Kids plan to depart for Washington, Zoom invites everyone to come to her room in the evening. "Come near sunset, about 8 p.m."

"Why so late?"

"The wind dies down then. I don't want the competition."

Everyone gathers close to 8 p.m. Josy also arrives and is helped upstairs. Someone knocks on Zoom's door, but Zoom yells, "Not yet, another couple of minutes."

They remain standing in the hallway with the KEEP OUT sign on the door still attached. Normally this group is full of chatter, but the mood is uneasy. Josy volunteers, "She asked me if she could paint the room. I said sure. She also asked if she could pick the colors and the design."

Zoom opens the door. She has a smile as wide as, well you know, the Mississippi in St. Paul. "Come on in."

As they follow Zoom and cross over the threshold they step into another dimension. They come into a citadel of art, surrounded by Zoom art.

A wall mural takes up the entire long inside wall and stretches to include the shorter perpendicular wall of the rectangular room. On the other side of the room, on the outside wall, an abstract creation takes up the space between the two windows.

The mural contains numerous illustrations. Many of the illustrations have historical significance and consist of groups of human figures and various objects.

Looking at the mural, you are overcome by the amount of detail. Your eyes move from one image to the next and keep moving, unable to find a place to rest.

The painting includes the depiction of a number of portals. These portals are openings, perhaps better described as passageways. They feature captions that note the historical import of the particular portal. One portal contains the caption, "1920. We Can Vote." Another one close by states, "1924. Citizenship for Native Americans." Another illustration shows several figures moving through the portal passageway inscribed with "1965."

In the spaces between these and other islands of images, Zoom added splashes of paint in the shape of fluid streaks and swirls that seem to move. Someone asks, "How come the little squiggles are in motion?"

Zoom laughs; she's been waiting for exactly this question. "That's the sign of the wind." She grabs something hanging from a nail in the wall. It's a document within a plastic sheet protector. She begins to read. "The persistent breeze evident in this mural is the wind of progress. It blows away dust, particles of lies, and flawed schemes of the past. The wind has been blowing away superstition and ignorance for centuries. It's not a mythic wind, there is no wind goddess, nor is it a heavenly wind. This wind is a secular wind. It has rid us of forces that constrain and constrict. It transports ships, seeds, and ideas. This wind is responsible for the growth of humanism and democracy, our current state of well-being." She looks at Izzy and smiles.

Izzy, listening intently, nods her head and says, "Good."

Zoom hangs the document back onto the nail. "I'd like to show you some features." She steps to the mural and points to the three portals, "Here, here, and there. Notice the angry faces in front of each portal. Notice, they are all male and all white. They represent oppressive forces trying to keep people from moving through the passageway."

She steps back and watches her audience look closely at the detail.

"Then, look. Look at the faces of the people on the other side of the opening. They're all happy, they made it through with the help of the wind of progress. See how their hair is flying?"

Her audience studies the portals closely.

"I tried to make the faces show triumph, but that's really hard to do."

Fritz notices that the faces of the people past the first portal are all women. "Well yes. That portal gave women the right to vote. And the faces past the second portal are all Native Americans. And those past the third portal are all African-Americans."

The mural shows more, much more. A portal represents the first amendment and press freedom. Another one depicts the Universal Declaration of Human Rights from 1948. Zoom points to her favorite, "The 26th amendment, 1971." She says, "Hooray! I'll be able to vote."

In another area a graph shows education levels from 1800 to today. A thick line starts at the bottom and stretches straight up. Another graph shows life expectancy along with medical images. There is a section that contains only written words: "Tolerance," "Peace," "Interdependence."

The painting also includes a depiction of several walls. They show various activities in front, but on the other side of these walls is empty space, a void. Zoom explains: "Those are barriers, dead ends. That wall over there is nationalism early in the 20th century. And notice those swirls painted in black, white, and red? That implies fascism to me. Those swirls turn counterclockwise. And this small head, right there, with the mouth ripped open, that's the big mouth of a fascist.

"So yes, progress was interrupted several times by explosions that turned out to be squalls. They were ultimately blocked by walls, and the breeze of progress always reasserted itself." Zoom adds, "As we all know, we are currently in the midst of a little squall blustering straight at us. That's why I'm a proud Agitator for Change trying to reverse it."

Fritz has been looking at a particular area for a while and yells out, "Hey, that's us, right? That must be Josy in her wheelchair, and I count 11 small figures for a total of 12. You should add our names, Zoom."

It also looks like Zoom has incorporated a private note. In a corner is a drawing of a mouth, the face covered by a touch of blue-gray paint, with the phrase, "Quick, take my breath." Someone asks her about it, but Zoom only volunteers that it's a line from one of her poems.

Zoom now points to the other side of the room, to the space between the two windows. "That's also entirely my own creation. I love it."

The blank faces of these museum visitors tell you they don't have a clue what they are looking at. They see an outline of a human head with just a few strokes of paint below the head suggesting neck and shoulders. The head is partially covered with two different materials, black tape, an inch wide, and wool. Strips of tape in various lengths crisscross the head seemingly every which way. The strips are not contained within the head but project past the outline of the head well into the white space of the wall. Then there is wool. The wool is coiled into several separate clusters, but there are also single strands.

It is thickest inside the head, and, like the tape, strands of wool stretch beyond the head. The color of the wool is blue. So the composition consists of black tape and blue wool positioned on, over, across, and beyond the outline of a human head.

After looking at this for an eternity, Fritz is the first to overcome his misgivings. He probably is seeking a considerate way to ask, but finally blurts out, "What the heck is it?"

That allows others to mumble incomplete comments that trail off into a hard swallow. "Yeah, yeah, what . . . ?"

"Oh my . . . "

"Why . . . "

"Love, you love . . . ?"

It's good that no one makes a snide comment.

Zoom explains. "It's called, 'The Thinker.'" She reads from another sheet attached to the wall hanging beside her art object. "This could be a troubled individual sitting in a coffee shop thinking to the ends of the universe and back. The wool and tape represent external forces that tug and pull at our minds." With her free hand Zoom pulls imaginary clutter away from her head. "Information, disinformation, conflicting ideas, all of this becomes an uncontrollable influx that threatens to occupy our brain. By carefully placing the material in and around the brain the artist creates a feeling of tension. What do we do? How do we deal with this turmoil?" Zoom reads slowly and stresses enunciation. She obviously wants the group to follow, but after the last sentence she pauses and looks up. Perhaps she wonders how this is going over. Izzy reassures her. "Go on, we're listening."

Zoom gives a quick nod and continues. "How does an individual deal with this invasion? By doing spring cleaning. In order to avoid being blocked by the wall we must rid our mind of all that is false and dangerous. Spring cleaning allows us to start fresh."

Zoom finishes reading and quickly asks, "Do you see the connection?"

"Connection, connection to what?"

"To my mural."

Individuals turn around, look at the expansive wall mural, look back to "The Thinker," back to the mural. But perhaps Izzy gets it. "Yeah, I think you're saying it's easy to get misled by bad ideas, get stuck behind an immovable wall. So we have to empty our heads and start fresh."

Zoom smiles. "Yeah, Izzy. Thanks. That's exactly what I'm saying."

Fritz wonders, "But how do you know that the same bad ideas might not enter your head again?"

Izzy responds. "Yeah, they could. But our record over the last couple hundred years has been pretty good. Not perfect, but we've had steady progress."

Zoom finishes with, "So I think that after spring cleaning we have a good chance to get it right."

35

LEVELS OF HOMELESSNESS, LEVELS OF WEALTH

They depart the next day in their minivan with an inclination to reminisce. Izzy asks, "Who remembers crazy Aunt Greta?"

Zoom does. "That seems like years ago. We got out of there fast."

So does Fritz. "Glad we did, otherwise you both might already be married."

Izzy disregards Fritz. "Yeah, we ran away back then, but we didn't run from this town."

Roxy corrects her. "We ran at first, but we ran right back."

Izzy remembers. "When we came here, I said I wanted to conquer it. I was so much younger then. I've become a bit wiser now. But we did zing the town a bit, right?"

After a while of driving, Izzy says to no one in particular, "I'm going to really miss Josy. I love her audacity to call out what is false—she is so savvy and astute."

Zoom perks up and wonders about Diego. "Do you think she will keep him as a renter?" Izzy leaps to a bit of fantasy. "Maybe she can regain her youth and be reborn as a truth goddess, a secular one. And perhaps, hey, why not, Diego will become her disciple." Zoom offers a soliloquy to anyone who cares to listen. "I asked Diego last night what he's going to do with the room after he moves into the house. Of course, I'm concerned about my art I'm leaving behind. Will someone paint over it, paint the walls white? Remember, I wanted to leave something behind in Aunt Greta's restaurant, art that engages, right? Well, listen to this. Diego said he'll try to use my art to make friends. Can you believe that? He'll invite people to have a look. He'll explain my painting and 'The Thinker' to them. Isn't that awesome? Yeah, that's really what he said." After no one responds, Zoom, totally uncharacteristically, shrieks out, "That's exactly what I want."

Izzy whispers, "What did you say?" And she smiles.

"Here's what I want." That's Roxy. "I want to stumble upon another adventure." Zoom tries to comment, but Roxy quickly follows with "I need new challenges. I want to do stuff. Helga and I talked. She gave me some pointers. She said confidence is key. If you're confident, people will sense that and pay attention to you."

Finally Zoom gets a chance. "Helga said she could open doors. Let's see if you can open any."

"I opened the door to the Trump Hotel, didn't I?"

"Yeah, but that was a while ago. Let's see if you can still do it."

Heading to Washington, they still have several days, so they might as well zigzag and not race. Again, they choose rural roads, not highways. And again, as they drive through small towns in our heartland, they see occasional "Jesus Saves" signs. Out of the blue, Fritz screams, "Look, a PIE sign." Izzy brings the vehicle to a screeching halt. Cheers and high fives in the car.

"There's proof. We're leaving a legacy."

Zoom, "Yeah, we did that. It's our little breeze."

Roxy: "I want to knock on the door and introduce us."

"Come on. We don't have to do that. You'll get another chance." Izzy adds, "It's enough that within the sea of Jesus signs the single PIE sign is a lighthouse. It gives us hope."

At this moment, these blossoming young adults speeding out of their metamorphosis stage feel good about themselves. They have a right to sport satisfied expressions. After a long summer traveling, packed tight with adventures, they accomplished quite a bit. Might as well sit back, relax, enjoy the countryside passing by, watch for more PIE signs. Zoom, our optimist, says, "Things will only get better. I think the wannabe dictator is gonna be undone by this PIE thing. And if he falls, the other mini dictators in the world will fall also. The wind of progress will blow them away."

Well, okay, let's hope so.

But after reliving some highlights, the excitement fades. Patting yourself on the back does not give you a new way forward. Surveying trees and terrain through car windows becomes tedious. Because they don't have a goal in mind, boredom creeps in.

When the road splits without a sign to offer direction, Izzy asks, "Which way should I go?"

Fritz gets them out of their funk. "Didn't Josy tell us about a crazy cousin?"

Izzy corrects him. "Josy called him 'eccentric,' not crazy."

"Well okay. What's the difference?"

"She told me he inherited a lot money, and then she said something amusing. She said, 'He likes to stand on his growing stack of hun-dred-dollar bills and measure how much he's grown in stature.'"

"Let's go look him up. Let's see if he needs a ladder now." You know who said that? Of course, Fritz.

Good. They have a goal again. They have his address, so they redi-rect to a small city a couple of hours away in search of Josy's cousin. Is he still alive? Is he crazy or eccentric? Does he need a ladder to count his money?

They arrive in town early in the evening. Two experiences await them here. Meeting the cousin is the second one.

Because it's getting late, they stop at a small plaza that also turns out to include a Greyhound bus station. The building includes a restaurant, bathrooms, a waiting area for Greyhound passengers with a large map on the wall, several vending machines for snacks and soda, one with candy, another one with miscellaneous items: comb, toothbrush, weird pen, and various plastic junk. Since it's too late to look for an empty house and they can't afford a motel, they will try to spend the night here. They see others slouching with their belongings against a wall. A couple of benches and chairs have slumping individuals in them. The Kids spread out and do their own thing for a while.

Izzy buys a stale sandwich and finds a seat in the waiting area. She has a book but first takes in the scene, looks at the various individuals camping out here. Several travelers seem to wait for their connection, perhaps some will wait all night. Others are definitely scruffy; they must be homeless people trying to survive here. She studies individuals who are unkempt. Someone looks at her. Their eyes meet. Quickly she looks away. After a few seconds, she tries a furtive glance. Is that specter still looking at her?

Traveling isn't always an excursion into sunshine. You can stumble onto murky bits of reality that usually remain invisible, the dirt under the rug. But when the rug is lifted, when you are forced to witness the foulness, your eyes want to shut. Mysteriously, you then become aware of a gnawing ache within you. You become queasy. But while you look away because you don't want to see it, a part of you peeks.

"Hey missy, is that you?"

She freezes. She recognizes something. The smell. She must remember, "Simplicity is more important than accuracy." She looks up, and there he is, Big Mack. He sits down next to her. "Hey, how ya doin? Remember me?"

Izzy waits a few seconds. She has to adjust her breathing, but she gets over it. "I remember. Big Mack, right? How have you been?"

He doesn't respond to her question. But Big Mack is social; he likes to talk. He starts to tell Izzy a story from his recent travels, but then he stops. "Ya know, Missy, I remember ya, and, I gotta be honest, Missy, I thought about ya once or maybe even twice. Ya don't care for the details, ya wanna get right to the essence." He pauses a few seconds, then says, "So I'll come right out and say it. Things have gotten worse."

"I'd like to give you some money, but I don't have much. I'll share my sandwich with you, though."

"You don't have to feel sorry for me. I'm okay. Feel sorry for those worse off than me."

"You're not wearing your Big Guy shirt."

"Yeah, it's gone."

He does accept her half sandwich, and they sit next to each other in hard plastic seats and eat.

"Why did you get rid of it?"

"Yeah, like I said, things got worse. At my level there are now more. They're coming so fast I can't keep track of 'em. No one's building more benches, but more people want 'em."

"What do you mean by your level?"

"Well, how can I explain it? Maybe like this. Ya got different levels in America. Ya got the rich, ya got the middle, and ya got workers. And it's funny, but I think the rich don't know the workers. Well, it's kinda like that with us. We also got levels."

"So what level are you?"

"Hey, I'm at the top, the highest level. Ya can see me, right? Ya can see my guys, right? We sleep on benches, in buses; we stand on corners with signs and go to soup kitchens if they have one. Ya can see us. Once a year they count us. Whatever number comes up probably satisfies 'em. They only count my level, though."

"Come on, Big Mack. You can't be right about that. When the government takes a census, they want to make certain it's accurate. And when they count the homeless, they also want the count to be accurate."

"Are ya certain, Missy? The next level down are hard to see. They live where no one looks for 'em. They keep to themselves. They're hard to know. They live in the shadows. They're like vermin."

"I'm not sure I understand. How do they survive?"

"Well, like I say, it's hard to know. Ya don't see 'em much. They don't come out to get unemployment checks. Them and us, we don't really get together much. But there's another level below 'em."

"I can't believe that. Humans even worse off?"

"I knew a guy at my level once who dropped down a level. I saw him a few years later, and he told me a bit about life as a second level scum. I didn't see him again 'til his body was found in a sewer, mutilated. They only found him because of the stink. He must 'ave dropped down another level. It's hard to know. You never see the guys at the lowest level alive. They are phantoms, ya only see 'em dead. They must live in holes and sewers. When ya find 'em, their bodies are mutilated. Maybe they fight for scraps of leather to chew on until blood flows."

Izzy looks away. "I never heard any of this."

"Well, missy, you're hearing it now. Papers don't report on 'em. People don't wanna know. The second and third levels are never counted. It's too complicated. Those counting in the government want to count fast, and they want to keep it simple."

Big Mack continues. "Maybe the room at each level is limited. So people are pushed down to the next level. A couple of my guys disappeared. I know they're not dead, they must 'ave dropped to a lower level. Now they won't be counted no more."

Izzy looks pale. She holds her tummy. Perhaps her half sandwich feels like an anchor. She can't move. How do you deal with information that burdens your gut?

She has to step out and struggles to get up. Big Mack stays and waits. After she returns, she asks again, "What about your sweatshirt?"

"Didn't want to give it to nobody. I tossed it into a dumpster."

It proved to be a miserable night for Fritz and Izzy. They spent the night in the waiting area. There weren't any benches free, and most of the ground near the walls was taken, so they slouched in plastic chairs. Does it need to be pointed out that plastic is uncomfortable? Zoom and Roxy did better in the car.

Izzy, stiff and barely awake, surveys the area in the morning. Big

Mack is gone. Several bodies she recognizes from yesterday are still spread out on a floor against the wall. New travelers she has not seen before sit or stand around, no doubt waiting. The Kids get something to eat and head out.

They are off to look up Josy's cousin. "I want to see his ladder."

"What if he doesn't want to see us?"

"What if he's dead?"

Roxy drives up a winding road to the address they have. At the top of a hill they come to an impressive-looking mansion. The kids step out of the minivan and see a number of prominent turrets. Fritz counts, "There are one, two, three, four, five, six perfect cones in the front, maybe more in the back." And while most of the other houses in this state are made of wood, this one is all stone.

A car comes from the house down the long driveway. The driver asks them what they're looking for. Roxy responds. "Josy, Sedrick's cousin, sent us. We are friends of hers."

"I didn't know Mr. Sandstone had a cousin. But go ahead. See if you can get in."

"Are you related to him?"

"No, I'm his doctor. He's a bit of a hypochondriac."

"Oh."

They have to get past two sentries; the first is a security guard who controls a gate from a small security booth, the second a maid. Let's see if Roxy can open the doors.

Roxy drives up to the security booth. A guard steps out. He wants to know who they are, what they want. Roxy explains the situation to him. "Mr. Sandstone's esteemed cousin Josy heard he was quite ill. I know his doctor is also concerned. She entrusted us with some recently uncovered information regarding family heritage that will no doubt be of interest to the great man."

The security guard gives her a crafty once over. He looks like he has seen it all. Perhaps he thinks this is one of the better ones, so he allows the van to pass. But, "Hey, what's with your car?"

"Long story. Tell you about it some time. We were part of a motor-cade with the Big Guy."

"You're kidding."

"No. Really. He handed out pies."

"Does he also bake?"

Roxy gives the same explanation about newly uncovered heritage information to the maid, who just says, "Oh, well in that case, please come this way."

Roxy nods her head ever so slightly and says, "Let's go."

The maid leads the four of them up two floors into a room where a man is slumped in a large leather armchair looking out the window.

"Hello, Mr. Sandstone. We bring greetings from your cousin Josy."

He turns his head and sees four young adults. "Ah, Josy. She never forgets to send me birthday wishes and a Christmas card. I also have Christmas cards sent to her."

While they small talk, albeit haltingly, about Josy and the past, Zoom makes a sketch of him. She repeatedly looks up at her subject as her fingers guide her pencil. It's surprising how quickly she creates a replica of the image she sees. He notices and asks her what she is doing. "I'm drawing you."

"Oh, let me see."

He looks at the drawing, promptly says, "You're pretty good, but you're drawing me how I am. You should draw me how I long to be."

"How would I do that?"

"Don't make me appear satisfied, draw me searching, longing. Have me gaze into the distance, look towards the future." Thus begins a revealing conversation.

"But aren't you satisfied with what you have?"

"Can one ever be satisfied? Maybe you have heard of the song 'Satisfaction' from years ago? Most everyone took the meaning to be about ephemeral carnal pleasures. To me the song was about a much different desire, the longing for substantive and enduring recognition. That is the satisfaction I long for, recognition. I've never been one to seek pedestrian thrills."

"What?"

"I don't understand. You must be super wealthy."

"Just look at this house."

Fritz can't help but say, and even manages to say it with a straight face, "You must have quite a ladder to get to the turrets."

"A ladder?"

"You have such a huge house. The maid said you have 22 rooms. And I counted the turrets. You must have a very tall pile of . . . I mean, you must be very rich."

"That's deceiving. Sure, I have some money, however my wealth has only gotten me to the first level."

"What? What do you mean by first level?"

"We have a history museum in this town to which I've donated much money. But all it's gotten me is a wing in the building named after me. Only a wing. And what's more, how many people are aware of it? Teachers take entire classes to the museum, but do the kids know? Would they care? How many of the 50,000 people in this city are aware of the Sandstone Collection in the Sedrick Sandstone Wing?"

"Wow! Doesn't that give you a lot of power in this city?"

"I don't like the word 'power.' I prefer the word 'recognition.' Sure, I have some recognition, I can get some favors, but it's rather minuscule, and it's not from the individuals I want to cultivate."

None of the Kids know what to say. They sit quietly. An unhappy millionaire!

"Do you see that picture on the wall of the yacht? Get up and have a good look at it." The four visitors politely get up and look at the framed close-up photo of a yacht. "It's magnificent, isn't it? You can admire the vessel from the outside, but what transpires inside remains veiled. I was on it once, my only penetration ever into the second level. Pool. Helicopter pad. Theater. Beautiful people who glide on air. The owner is a patrician, you don't hear his name much. He shuns conventional publicity, keeps within his own circle, a level above mine.

"I don't know why I'm telling you kids all of this. My doctor is always worried about my health, so maybe it's good that I get this off my chest. Who else am I going to tell it to?"

Izzy: "Why don't you do something for the homeless? Fund a soup kitchen or something? They'd put your name on it."

"He, he. Give the poor a ham sandwich. They wolf it down. Then what?"

"But they need the help."

"You get dragged down donating to the plebeians. I'm trying to elevate myself with my philanthropy. I want a university named after me. Or at least a college."

"What happens when you get to the second level?"

"That's the right question, young lady. It certainly would be nice to know, but I'm not really sure. I am pretty sure though that those few fortunate and beautiful individuals do strive for the even higher level, the third level. When I was on the yacht, I overheard the patrician mention the word 'icon.' He yearns to have his name elevated to an icon. Who knows, perhaps if your name is an icon, you have attained the third level.

"Look at this." He gets a magazine the Kids have never heard of and shows them the full-page ad on the back of the front page. "Look at this diva. She must have been born in heaven. Her delicate wrist and her long slender fingers feature exquisite jewelry. Her skin is satin, you can smell the Baccarat perfume, and she looks into the distance, yearning. What is her desire? She wants more. There is only a single word in the ad, the name of the exquisite brand.

"Here's another one. This good-looking man has everything it is possible to own. But he's missing something. He looks into the future. He yearns. For what? To have his name become an icon.

"It looks to me like they are yearning, yearning for a third level. Of course, I could have taken the direct approach instead of indirect philanthropy to gain recognition."

"What's the direct approach?"

"Straightforward activity to benefit yourself. Build monuments to yourself. Create today's equivalent of the pyramids, golden skyscrapers or golden golf paradises, and attach your name in gold to them. Then use your fame to gain recognition as a statesman. Of course, you get a much different kind of recognition with the direct approach. Your name doesn't float in the halls of higher learning. Your name could get burdened with weight from quarreling about the minimum wage. That's why I opted for philanthropy. I wanted my name to stay exalted."

That's it. There isn't much more to tell. They are invited to spend the night, but they intend to leave early the next morning. Sandstone says he won't see them tomorrow, he usually sleeps late. "Say hello to Josy when you see her again."

"Thanks, we will."

No, they don't try a dozen bedrooms. The girls all decide to stay in one room. Fritz gets his own bedroom. The maid makes sleeping arrangements for them. The security person, who must also have other responsibilities, knocks on the door Fritz is in. He asks the young man if he should arrange for some female companionship. Fritz, dumbfounded, says, "No, no, I'm, I'm, I'm okay."

36

A MIND AS VARIABLE AS THE TERRAIN IN AMERICA

Four savvy travelers are on the road again at sunrise in their crazy minivan that resembles the flying American flag. "Sorry we had to get up so early." That's Izzy, and she yawns. "We've gotta be in Washington by early afternoon. And I don't want to rush. The last thing we need is a speeding ticket."

Fritz, with eyes closed, asks, "What are we going to do there?"

The Kids might not have a clue, but the reader does. Just as the Kids traveled to the future as youngsters and learned about developments to come, namely that dictators are on the way out, the reader learned of developments to come, namely that frauds are on the way out.

Roxy wonders out loud, "Is she planning a protest?"

Zoom opens her eyes and adds, "She hinted she might commission me to paint something. Maybe she wants me to paint the Capitol Building, or the White House. I'd love to do that. But I would add my own touch, make it engaging in some way."

Izzy: "I guess she's planning something with costumes. She wants us to stop at a costume shop. I have the name and address. They are supposed to know what costumes to give us."

Fritz, his eyes barely open, smirks and adds a sour note. "Does Halloween come early in our capital? Or, is trick or treat a regular . . . "

Izzy doesn't suppress the edge in her voice. "Come on, Fritz. I'm barely awake. Cut the jokes."

The conversation about what might happen in Washington does not go much further. They remain quiet for long stretches, looking out the window, maybe into their own minds. When their reflection is interrupted by a short burst of conversation, it's about their recent past. Like yesterday, they reminisce. But reminiscing means they don't have anything specific to look forward to. They are heading into an unknown and can't make plans.

Two separate incidents in the next town force them to focus on the present again. They drive through an expensive-looking area of large old houses, some featuring wrought iron fences. In front of one of them a group of protesters with signs make a racket, and the Kids notice. They stop to have a look. Guess what signs they are holding. Round PIE signs.

"Can you believe that? Our influence is humungous!" cries Roxy.

Wow! Everyone is excited. They find a place to park and head over to the chanting group.

At the same time the protestors also notice something. "Hey, look at that minivan!"

"Goof, I remember. The van was there when we saw the Big Guy!"

"Get those guys from the goofy car over here."

"They're already coming this way."

"Maybe they know what's going on."

The Kids find themselves surrounded by men and women, several talking at once. They are annoyed, frustrated, distressed. They thought they had something, something that would improve their lives. Then it was taken away.

"You guys were there when the Big Guy showed up. What happened to his promises?"

"Outside we got PIE, inside the convention center we got nothin'!"

The Kids have to be careful here. These people are quite upset.

"I know what happened." That's Roxy speaking up. Her voice is confident.

Whoa! What does Roxy know? What's on her mind?

Roxy with a straight face: "We didn't make it into the convention center, but you guys obviously did. Tell us what you saw there."

One of the protesters, his name is Mike, takes a deep breath and begins. "Me and Mary here, and most of the others, we raced into the building in a fantastic mood. There were already a hell of a lot of people inside. They looked puzzled that we turned our MAGA hats inside out. I told everyone I could about what happened outside, that the Big Guy showed up. And I told them about his three promises. The other guys who came from the outside probably did the same. So, the news spread like wildfire in the hall. The place became electric. Not with the usual rowdiness at the Big Guy's events. No, the place started to buzz with real anticipation. You know, a lot of us are tired of his rhetoric, so now we're ready for news we can use."

Roxy asks, "So what did the Big Guy do and say when he showed up?"

"Yeah, I'll tell ya," Mike continues. "Me, I was standing close to the stage when the Big Guy enters. Mary was right next to me. There was pushing and shoving, and we had to work to stay together. So the Big Guy makes his entrance. He enters majestically, like a ruler. I've seen it before. The place is absolutely packed. The cheering is incredible. It was the loudest I ever heard. But this time everyone's yelling, 'PIE me,' 'PIE me.' People got into this cool thing. They held an imaginary pie, moved their arm out in front holding the pie with an open hand, and quickly brought their hand close to their face smashing the make-believe pie right into their kisser. 'PIE me,' 'PIE me,' with arms stretched out, and open hands brought back again and again close to their face." He demonstrates the "PIE me" arm movement several times.

"So I remember this exactly. The Big Guy takes a couple of steps back and says to someone behind him, he says, 'What the fuck is going on here?' That's what he says. Then he says, 'What are these assholes doing?' I heard him say exactly that. He probably thought the microphone wasn't on, but it was. Then he says, 'Why do they keep calling me Hymie? I'm not a fucking Jew.'"

Mike addresses the teenagers. "So how are you involved with this? Do you guys work for him? Here we're protesting in front of our representative's house. He claims to know nothin'."

Roxy boldly takes charge. "So, yes, we're all aware the Big Guy is volatile. He listens to different advisors. So we know he can change his mind. His mind is big, his mind encompasses all of America. He has a right to be as variable as the terrain in our country. We have the Rockies, the five Great Lakes, huge prairies, there's the Grand Canyon, the Mississippi River, we have Texas, flat Kansas, and tiny Delaware. And that's not even including the diversity of our people. If he's gonna reflect our country, he must encompass all that, he must be adaptable, even volatile, and yes, he can change his mind just as our America changes its mood via its landscape."

During Roxy's speech Izzy watches her intensely. Fritz and Zoom glance at individual protesters and nod their heads in support of Roxy's explanation. After Roxy said "flat Kansas and tiny Delaware," Fritz interjected, "That's right."

Mike can't do anything but listen. You can see on his face he is increasing his concentration. When Roxy is done, he still doesn't speak, but his face says, "Huh?"

Roxy continues, "But, hey, listen. This is really important. Hold him to what he promised outside, not inside. You deserve PIE. If the Big Guy forgets what he promised, and if your representative claims amnesia, vote them out next chance. Stick with PIE. Keep demanding PIE."

Roxy starts to move away and says, "Let's go."

They quickly walk back to their van. No one says a word. Just before they reach the van, Izzy puts her arm around her. She says, "Little sis, you are amazing."

Roxy must be feeling good again. She can't suppress the Roxy nod and look of success.

Now comes their second experience. After about a mile, flashing lights follow them. They pull over to the right expecting the police car to speed by, but no, it stops right behind them, the lights going crazy. Izzy is at the wheel. She opens the window as a policeman comes and says, "Out of the car. Everyone. Out."

Izzy: "I don't think I was speeding, officer."

"Did you hear? I said everyone out."

So they all get out of the car.

"Over there! Spread out! More! Let's go! And don't move. Keep your hands where I can see 'em."

Now a second policeman arrives with a German Shepherd. He guides the dog around the car. The dog does what he is trained to do— smell—but he doesn't stop anywhere. The policeman then leads the dog past the four suspects. As the dog passes him, Fritz wants to touch the dog. The cop yells, "Hey, wise guy, don't touch. He bites."

But the German Shepherd seems disappointed. He did not find what he is trained to find in order to get his treat.

The first cop stands in front of the four. "Spread out more. More. Hands to the side." They do as they are told.

"Where is it? Where's the stuff?"

"What stuff?"

"You know what I mean."

"No I don't."

"Okay, little lady. Don't play games with me. The dog smelled it."

"No he didn't. He didn't stop anywhere, he didn't give the alert signal."

"You're hiding drugs. I know it. With a car looking like that."

"You might think you know, but your dog doesn't. And your dog is right. That makes you wrong."

Cop number one comes. He wants to frisk them. First he checks Fritz, but then . . .

"Hey, get your hands off me. Only a woman can check me. Careful, I bite." Roxy said that.

The two cops retreat a few steps. They converse, look at the Kids, shake their heads, bite their lips, talk some more. One of them comes back and says, "Okay, we gotta let you go. We got an emergency in town. Get back in the car and get outta here."

This is exactly how it happened. Fritz still has his recording device. He was able to turn it on to record the entire conversation. They listen and laugh. They laugh because they are relieved. Izzy then says, "You know, it's actually not funny. The cops stopped us only because our car looks different."

Back in the minivan they are quiet, everyone no doubt occupied with their own thoughts.

They leave the heartland and are now close to Washington. It's been quite an adventure. But there is one more little thing worth telling. Close to Washington on a rural stretch of flat highway that allows everyone to daydream without missing anything, Fritz, without warning, wants Izzy to turn around. "Hey, that billboard? Go back, I gotta see it."

Zoom is getting restless. "What? Go back? I want to finally arrive. What can be so interesting about a billboard?"

Izzy does turn around, and she stops where they can get a good look at the billboard.

"Rather incredible."

"It's the biggest help wanted sign in the world."

"Ha, ha, ha, can you believe that?"

"Whoever's responsible for that is definitely not wearing a MAGA hat."

HELP WANTED

THE BIG GUY IS HIRING

FRAUDS, FOOLS, OPPORTUNISTS, GRIFTERS

MUST BE AMORAL, SHAMELESS, GREEDY, DECEPTIVE

APPLY AT THE WHITE HOUSE

37

BACK TO THE BEGINNING

We're back at the beginning. It's the morning after the costume ball. Zoom didn't get a chance to paint the United States Capitol Building or the White House. Helga commissioned her to paint the demise of the rats who work there. And Izzy wrote the poem "It's Time to Set Traps." Let's place the Kids and Helga back into the scene where we left them on a bank of the Potomac River. Recall, Helga invited them to lunch.

"Today I must leave, I go to ze airport in the afternoon."

"Why?"

"I'm done, at least for now. I go back home. But first I must go to Hameln. It is called Hamelin in English. Zat's where I learned my craft. So let's celebrate our victory over ze rats wis a nice lunch."

Walking away Helga turns around and yells, "Don't forget to bring ze painting. Also bring ze poem."

After the Kids gather their things, they drive to the restaurant Helga mentioned. It's quite European, white tablecloths, beautiful paintings on the walls. They find Helga already sitting at a large table. There are two women with her, they look to be 30 or so. Helga objects, "Nein. No narrator here. Zat's not allowed."

Izzy says, "He won't be able to tell the world about our lunch discussion."

"When ze women are ready to tell ze world, zey will find ze right way to do it. We don't need big news hidden in some small novel. Who knows, ze novel may flop, and ze only readers will be the four of you, and maybe me. We haf important sings to discuss. Please escort ze narrator out."

Roxy walks back to the entrance, steps out, and says, "Wait here." She goes back inside alone.

Later, the Kids come out of the restaurant along with Helga but without the two women. Helga just steps out to wave. The Kids walk away and turn around several times to wave back. As Helga continues to wave, it starts to become misty. Helga yells, "America is too important. Keep fighting ze rats." A fog descends, and Helga, still standing and waving, slowly disappears in the fog.

As the Kids look for their car a conversation ensues.

The narrator asks, *Did you enjoy lunch?*

Smiles. "Yeah, it was great."

What did you eat, Izzy?

"I had salmon with a kind of honey-mustard sauce. It was really good."

Fritz says he had goulash soup. "My grandfather also makes it. This had more meat, though."

How about you, Zoom?

"Oh, I had a large salad. It was really different, but I liked it."

Roxy volunteers: "My favorite used to be schnitzel, but I turned vegetarian. So I ordered kartoffelpuffer."

Oh, potato pancakes.

"They were nice and crispy."

Who were the women with Helga, Roxy?

"They are women who plan to run for Congress next chance."

What are they like?

"We need more people like them. They are full of ideas. I think they'll definitely make a difference. I've got their phone info."

Who are they?

Roxy doesn't answer.

What are their names?

Roxy has a blank look.

What district are they from?

"Wow, it's foggy. It's tough to find the car."

Izzy says, "They're good, really good. I bet we'll hear about them soon."

38

A BURIAL IN THE
WASHINGTON FOG

After the costume ball, after Helga exposes the frauds as rats, after the sunny morning by the Potomac, and after the lunch, an unusual weather event occurs. A thick fog envelopes Washington.

The Kids locate their car, but trying to find their way out they get lost. It's best if they stop to reassess where they are. The car slips them past the entrance of a cemetery through open wrought iron gates attached to two solid stone pillars. It's a safe place to rest away from traffic and other hazards of life.

The car doors open. One after the other they step out into the morbid silence of the fog. They can make out a few obscure gravestones close by, but not much beyond.

"Never before have I seen fog this thick."

"It could be a brazen Washington trick."

"To sneak out facts and bury them quick."

"Look, there, someone goes."

"Without shoes, with ragged clothes."

"Let's see how this tale unfolds."

"That specter emits a painful groan."

"Maybe a burden for which he must atone."

"He's also dragging something all alone."

"Is it a dead body? Is it a full chest?"

"He's pulling hard. He's in distress."

"Hello over there. Do you need help?"

An echo sounds.

"Dodo youyou needeed helelhelp?"

"No, no. Away, away, away from me me me, no one can be here, no one can see see. I must do this alone alone, alone, the grave I choose must remain unknown unknown unknown unknown."

The sound rebounds.

"Maybe it's part of a funeral."

"Maybe it's a secret meeting."

"Maybe it's an illegal activity."

The specter kneels down. He pushes and pushes until there's a thump, thump, thump.

He sneers. "It's my ace in the hole, my final trump, trump, trump."

With shovels of dirt he covers the spot.

He cries out, "Facts and figures, decay, go rot. Fie on you, pursuers, foes, phantoms I so deplore, you will burden me no more. What's gone is gone, goodbye, so long. It's been a load for far too long. I'm in the clear, no one will ever see what's buried here."

The fog lifts. The Kids go to where they saw the specter last. They search for fresh dug earth. They search for a shovel.

Nothing.

Finally, they leave.

39

UNEXPECTED VISITORS

They make it back to St. Paul, so this summer's adventures are over. Izzy and Zoom begin their next year in college. Fritz and Roxy are seniors in high school. You might wonder what their essays will be like when they write about "How I Spent My Summer Vacation."

It's the last weekend before classes begin. At home, they rediscover their own comfortable spaces and their cherished stuff. Their stuff hasn't changed, but they have. They left as inquisitive youngsters; they've returned savvy with a wealth of experiences. And they made a difference. The question remains, how much of a difference?

Fritz must be relishing some time alone, as he has been secluded all day. In the evening the girls hang out together in the living room and Fritz joins them. Zoom wants to talk. "The Big Guy is a rat, we've exposed him. And it also looks like we'll soon get a couple of new representatives."

Roxy interjects. "Wait. We don't want to talk about that here."

"Oh yeah. But here is what we should talk about. I want to figure out how to improve life for Americans." She mentions the signs they saw, the small PIE sign and the giant "Help Wanted" billboard on their way to Washington. "What if? What if we could put the PIE message on billboards? A thousand billboards all across the country. Wouldn't that change things? Maybe even immediately?"

Roxy likes that. "Yeah, and we'd get some of the credit." But she wonders, "Where's the money going to come from?"

Back to Zoom. It becomes clear she's been thinking about this. "Do we in America have enough resources to get PIE for everyone? Sure, aren't we the richest country? PIEs baked onto a thousand billboards could create an unstoppable movement." Zoom looks to see if anyone has figured out where she is going with this. "And guess who can get it done? Sedrick Sandstone. He could become the hero, yeah." She continues. "I wonder, I wonder if we could devise a plan to make the Sandstone name into . . . " At precisely this moment Izzy joins her, and they both together say, " . . . into an icon."

That's their idea, elevate Sandstone's name into icon status in return for his financing the PIE drive.

It's a clever idea, and it's nice that you're in sync, but how do you get that done?

Zoom offers more. "When he inherited money, he got stuck. He wanted more money, wanted recognition."

Izzy adds, "But only from those who are also wealthy."

"Right," says Zoom. "His entire life he's been stuck on the same thing. It's a tragedy he's not even aware of. He's fabricated his own dead end."

Izzy guesses, "You're thinking about your wall painting, right?"

"Yep, I am. Maybe I should go back and add another wall with Sedrick Sandstone banging his head against it."

This discussion ends abruptly for the evening. It turns out this summer's adventures aren't over just yet.

Fritz has been uncommonly quiet. He hasn't said anything at all. And he's looking . . . well, he doesn't look right. Roxy asks, "Anything wrong, Fritz?"

"Not really."

"What do you mean, not really?"

Fritz now has his own room. It is tiny, might have been a pantry when this old farmhouse was built over a hundred years ago, and his door opens to the living room. Fritz keeps staring at the closed door.

Since he is not good at faking things, his face reveals a troubling tale. Roxy tries to lift his spirits. "Hey, if your room's a mess, don't worry. So is mine."

But it's not the state of his room that's on his mind. Without warning the mystery starts to unravel. A loud CRASH comes from his room. Fritz jumps up, moans, "Oh, no," runs to the door, opens it. "Hey, you all right?"

A bookcase has fallen over and spilled its contents onto the floor—books, gadgets, odds and ends. And in the corner, unable to hide, two kids. The girl quietly says, "Sorry." The boy has a grin on his face that won't come off. "We climbed," he says.

Fritz whispers, "Quick, put on your hats."

The others stand and look. They look at the kids. They turn to Fritz. They look back at the kids. He takes each by the hand, walks to the couch, and sits down, the kids beside him, one on each side.

His sisters glare at him. Fritz glares back. "What?" He waits a moment, then follows with, "The bookcase fell."

The girl smiles and looks at everyone inquisitively. "These are your sisters, right Fritz? I remember them." Because no one responds, the girl continues, "Maybe you don't like us visiting. We can go back to our time soon. Fritz just has to show us how."

Zoom tightens her face.

Roxy contorts her face into a question mark.

Izzy covers her face with both hands.

Gradually Roxy's face straightens itself into an exclamation point. "Why don't you take off your hats? Go ahead, just take 'em off."

Both the girl and the boy look at Fritz. Fritz must know the cat is out of the bag; he just nods. As they remove their hats their halos become visible. Izzy is unnerved. She stutters, "You, you, you mean, you. No way. That can't be."

The girl, her name is Sky, and she is nine years old, explains. "When you came to visit us, Fritz came into our room, and he told us some really good stories, and . . . "

The boy, named River, is six, and he interrupts. "The stories happened a long time ago."

"River, I'm talking, I want to explain it."

River says, "Oohhhkay, go ahead." But you can already read in his face he's thinking about his next interruption.

Sky continues. "Fritz explained what we have to do to travel to the past. And I'm already nine. So pretty soon I might no longer be able to travel back in time. That's why we decided to try it now."

River adds, "Yeah, but you couldn't do it. I had to do it."

"River, you didn't have to say that. That's mean."

"No, it's not."

Fritz confesses. "I vaguely remember telling them the trick in traveling to the past. I guess they were able to do it." He hesitates, then adds, "I guess they're here."

Izzy: "You guess?"

"I'm glad America is coming next term. If he were here, he would think he's in a madhouse. How could we explain this?" Izzy contorts her face and explains to an imaginary America. "Two kids show up. They're from the future. We were there once. They traveled to their past, which is our present. They wear halos. They can access each other's thoughts. But they can't access ours, because we lack halos."

Izzy, now with wrinkles on her forehead, asks, "What do we do now?"

Fritz gets up, says, "Don't worry. I'll handle it. Come on, kids. Let's go and clean up the room." He takes the kids into his room and shuts the door.

Roxy knocks on the door. "Can I come in?"

"No."

40

STORIES

It's the next morning. Sky and River are up early. They scurry around the house while everyone else is still asleep. They open bedroom doors, peek in. They want to get the day started. It takes a while, but our heroes do make it to the living room. Fritz is again on the couch with Sky and River.

The kids are not shy. River walks up to Zoom and asks, "What's your name?"

"I'm Zoom."

"I heard you snoring this morning."

"What? I don't snore."

He has the look of a rascal. "Yes you do, like this," and he makes a loud snoring sound. Izzy has to laugh. "He's right, I've heard you snore before."

The shock is over. The two kids have the uncanny ability to entertain. Our young adults have accepted them because, well, they're kids. Human nature has not changed. They are fun to have around, and they are shaking things up.

Here is a conversation between Roxy and Sky. Roxy starts it off.

"So, why did you decide to come?"

"When you visited our time, Fritz told us about his time. My brother loves the adventure stories Fritz told us. I like to hear about the daily things he does. It's different from what we do. It is really funny that he has to use a small broom to brush his teeth."

Roxy wonders, "But you could probably read a book or watch a TV show to learn about our time, right?"

"Oh, those are obsolete. We don't obtain information that way anymore. That's why I like to actually visit your wonderland of antiquity."

That unnerves Roxy. "Hold on, you're calling the present, the time I live in, a what, a land of wondrous antiquity?"

"Well, I know it's not the real antiquity, classical antiquity was the Greeks and the Romans. But the time you live in is still pretty backwards."

"Oh, I see."

"You probably also notice that I have more knowledge than a nine-year-old has in your time. We learn much faster. I probably know about as much as you do."

"Oh."

"Maybe even more."

Roxy is silent. Her face speaks.

The others listen to this conversation and marvel. Sky continues. "River and I, we love stories. History is dead, it's just fact, after fact, after fact." She sighs. "But stories are alive, they move, they connect things, they include surprises, and, if they're really interesting, they have openings and secret passageways. The passageways sometimes lead to things you haven't seen before."

River spurts out, "And they tickle . . . "

"Stop, River, let me finish. But what's even better than hearing a story is being right inside it. And that's why River and I are here. We want to be a part of your story, live in it." She becomes fervent, "Maybe we can influence your story, or even change it. Didn't you also do that? Fritz told us you lived with hunter-gatherers for a while." She stops. "Okay, River. Now it's your turn."

River says, "Oohhh kay. They tickle my thinking."

"You mean your imagination. They tickle your imagination."

"That's what I said. My imagination. Now it's your turn again."

"I'm done."

Izzy must have just swallowed a nugget of golden wisdom; her face is ablaze. She takes a deep breath, exhales, and explodes. "Did you hear what she said? She wants to be active in our narrative. She wants to function inside—inside!—our story. She doesn't want to just passively listen to a story about us, no, she wants to be active as a character within our story! Do you get it?" She spins around. "To Sky, we are a story. All of us here are characters in one big story."

Something is happening here. Izzy dances around the room, moves from person to person, as her arms and hands fly.

"But guess what? Besides our communal story, we also have our individual stories. Isn't my life its own separate story? Am I not my own hero with all of you existing in my story as minor characters? And since I also exist in your stories, that means we each live in multiple stories at the same time."

Zoom gets it. "I've never thought of it that way. I do think of my art as storytelling. But my life a story? That makes me responsible for my own plot." She reflects. "But there's a difference. When I paint, I control everything on the canvas. I have only limited control over other characters that pop into my story."

Back to Izzy. "And the characterization will be slightly different. In my story, I'm me, I see myself from the inside. In your story you only know me from the outside, so I'm slightly different than in my story. And in Roxy's story, I'll be a bit different again. So, is 'me' the character in my story? Are there multiple versions of 'me'? Is my existence the sum of all stories I'm in?"

Fritz: "Maybe it's a little bit like what physicists think of the multiverse. Our universe is one story. The multiverse would represent many different plots, but they would somehow be interconnected."

Fritz can tell that talking about the multiverse impresses his sisters. He goes on to say, "Not sure if I shared this with you, but I think I'm going to study physics in college. Maybe become a cosmologist." He puts on a serious mien. "I definitely want to see if travel between universes could be possible."

Sky is watching these developments. Roxy asks, "So you want to participate in our story, do you?"

"I don't just want to, I am in your story, and I'm already having an influence."

"She's right. She might even become responsible for the next development of the Agitators for Change. Listen to this." Izzy spins around her stage again. "I'm in college, I'm a theater major, I'm fussy about my music, I write poetry, I have certain ideas about life. But guess what? I'm open to change. I could become interested in anthropology, move to Peru, or join the Peace Corps." She raises her arms and moves them out wide. "Yeah, I'm open. I'm open to the world." She spins around. "And now back to Sandstone. He's closed. He's been stuck within a certain narrative his entire life. He doesn't know how to change his plot."

Zoom asks, "What if we enter his story. Could we get him unstuck and make his name into an icon?"

"You know," responds Izzy, "we've actually done this before, changing people's narratives. We just didn't think of it that way. Our shenanigans and our drumming changed a few minds. Let's make plans to change Sandstone's plot and give him a happy ending."

"Hey, everybody." That's Zoom. "What do you think of your individual stories? I love the plot I'm in. I'm living a great story."

Fritz comes up with a Fritz idea. "Next girl I like I'll say I'm interested in her life story, and I'd love to play a tiny role, be part of her fantasy."

Izzy laughs, "Yeah, but my counter to a guy who tries that is, 'Hey, you're just a stand-in. You don't actually get to appear in my story.'"

Fritz asks River and Sky, "Since school starts tomorrow, when do you want to get back?"

Sky hesitates, says, "Oh, I don't know. I'll tell you later."

River blurts out, "I'm staying. I like it here."

"Well, if you're staying, I'm staying too." Sky looks at Fritz. "You haven't had a woman be president, right?"

"No, not yet."

"Well, okay, then I've got something to look forward to."

River says, "If you run for president, I'll vote for you."

41

WHAT ABOUT THE FUTURE?

It's already fall. An election is coming up, and your narrator wonders if the activities described here can make a contribution.

This narrative began with the Kids' quest to accelerate the final demise of dictators. That continues to be their goal. Zoom's idea to convince the forlorn Sandstone to fund a PIE initiative has become their new focal point. The reader might assume their activities must wait until next summer, but for Roxy that's too late. "We must get to Sandstone before the end of the year." Because they are separated—Izzy and Zoom are away in college, Fritz and Roxy are at home in high school—Roxy is taking charge.

The narrator asks, *What's your plan, Roxy?*

"My plan is to shock Sandstone out of his socks and rattle his brain."

How are you going to accomplish that?

"By dunking his head in ice water. Plain and simple. We're gonna funnel facts into his ice-cold brain. Then warm him with appeals to his emotions."

Who's going to do that?

"Me and the others. Josy is gonna shake him up with family matters. Izzy will do her thing. America is bringing the guys. Of course, my friend Emma will also be here. Zoom is working on concepts to portray him as the most noble icon."

Please be more specific. Exactly how are you going to . . .

"We're gonna do the same thing we did before. It worked, didn't it? We're going to develop skits again, convert his living room into a theater, perform right to his face. Every shenanigan will be directed specifically at him."

It might be difficult to convince him. He's set in his ways with a one-track mind.

"We can do it. Emma has already sent me a poem that throws ice on his soppy yearnings."

Can I have a copy of her poem? Might want to include it in the book.

"Sure, I'll give it to you later."

You also mentioned facts earlier. What kind of facts?

"I'm going to talk to him about financial facts."

What do you know about finance?

"Not much yet. But I picked up a couple of books from the library."

Well, how do you plan to use finance?

"It's simple. I'm gonna figure out how spending money on PIE now will be a financial positive for him. And along with those facts, Fritz is gonna build a special ladder for him."

A ladder? To count money?

"No. To count prestige. Each rung will represent a higher level of recognition. Right now, Sandstone sees himself on the first rung, and he wants to reach the second and third rungs. But those two rungs will be less supportive, maybe made out of plywood. The ladder will have additional rungs made of solid oak. We want him to reach the fourth or fifth rung."

Oh. Can I see it?

"No, Fritz hasn't built it yet. Zoom might also include a ladder in her portrait.

"Look, I have to leave. Keep in touch."

What about Emma's poem?

"Oh." Roxy reaches into her pocket and unfolds a sheet of paper. "Here's a copy."

Before leaving, Roxy adds, "Once we succeed and get Sandstone to invest in PIE billboards, we're hoping the thing will take off and become a movement. That's what we want, we want a movement."

So, there you have it. That's their plan for the near future. And here is Emma's poem.

>*Hey, Mr. Sandstone*
>*My name is Emma*
>*I come to you with a dilemma*
>*I hear you're all alone*
>*Without even anyone to disown*
>*Ha, ha*
>*Hey, Mr. Sandstone*
>*You could be buried with your gold*
>*Like pharaohs and kings of old*
>*Your gold nowhere to found*
>*Gold's glitter frozen underground*
>*Or, Mr. Sandstone*
>*You could do heavenly deeds*
>*Help people with persistent needs*
>*Become an iconic living hero*
>*Instead of a gilded dead zero*
>*Hey, Mr. Sandstone*
>*What do you choose, what will it be*
>*Forgotten with your gold for eternity*
>*Or iconic to your billionaire fraternity?*

But just as important as their activities in the near future is how they will comport themselves later, what contribution they can make to America emerging in the 2020s and 2030s.

Will these youngsters stay engaged as the years roll on? Imagine, if Josy hadn't gotten stuck way back as a young woman and instead had continued to shake up her surroundings, perhaps her town could have rattled and rolled in a slightly different direction. Right now, our heroes give us good reason to believe that life in these United States can continue to progress. But the 2020s are 100 years after the emergence of fascism in Europe. Of course, we also learned from an early adventure that we will eliminate dictators at some point in the future. Will they be gone within the next decade? Will democracy in America survive?

ACKNOWLEDGMENTS

Early readers of this manuscript proved to be more helpful than they perhaps realize. They each found shortcomings, and, most importantly, they encouraged me to keep writing. Thank you, Susan Barghini, John Crea, Hilary Frye, Colette Roche, and Regina Snyder.

I also must thank members of a writers group. In particular, Pam Fricke, Sherry Gergen, Linda Koch, Tylor Mintz, Reeve Lasky, and Marilyn Jess each helped with their questions and comments.

Finally, Jim Guhl, Chuck Rang, and Jerri Rang read the manuscript and stimulated polish. Thank you for your diligent reading and guidance.

I am gratified that Yvonne, my wife, stayed with me all the way, morning, noon, and sometimes at night. Never did she waver.

While I received a good deal of support, I take full responsibility for the ideas expressed in the novel.

ABOUT THE AUTHOR

RAINER LINK rejuvenates from the daily fatigue caused by our political turmoil by countering with imaginative tales that snarl and bite. How better to stay sane than to upend the madness with satire sprinkled with bits of magic.

A husband, father, and grandfather, and concerned about the future of America, he believes the new generation must come to the rescue. May activists multiply and pursue solutions to our current political malaise.